OLD

Book One of the "Never Too Old" Western Series

J.V. JAMES

Classic Old West Tales

DEDICATION

to the best storyteller I ever knew - my old dad.

CONTENTS

CHAPTER 1
OLD DOG, NEW TRICKS
JULY, 1877. DEADWOOD, DAKOTA TERRITORY

MAYBE I AM GETTIN' old — at least, I surely slipped up, my last night in Deadwood.

Still, I ain't yet so foolish I'd come into Swearengen's saloon completely unarmed — and while I much prefer my old rifle, the little five-shot Remington Rider is enough protection, indoors.

When it happened, it happened *fast*.

The loudest mouth at our table had been getting louder. Aside from his name being Tom, all I knew for sure was, he was the very worst poker player I ever saw.

Almost seemed like he *wanted* to lose.

I figured he was in cahoots with the other two men at our table — just a feeling I had in my bones. And the thing about bones is, their feelings tend to be right.

"Last hand for me, boys," I said as Tom shuffled. "I'm up early tomorrow."

"But you gots to give me a chance to win back my

poke," he said, sounding desperate. "You're into me for five-hundred, you cain't just up and leave with no warning."

"That *was* the warning," I growled, "and you won't get another."

He grumbled something under his breath, but did not look me in the eye.

In the spirit of fairness I said, "You'll *all* get your chance now. We'll ignore the twenty dollar limit on this last hand, if these others agree. No limit at all's my suggestion — but you boys each choose as you wish."

As they nodded agreement, a *look* passed between the other pair and the jaw-flapper Tom, who half-smiled the briefest of moments when he thought I weren't watching.

Me against three, I knew it for sure now — but I had bigger problems than money. They could take back the five-hundred, and I would not care.

"One final hand, boys," I said. "Do your worst."

Thing was, unbeknowed to myself, I was betting much more than I'd chose to. The bet wasn't money or gold — we would gamble our lives.

CHAPTER 2
"WHO KNOWS THIS DEAD MAN HERE THEN...?"

I SHOULDA TWIGGED to it when nothing else changed except for the size of the pot.

Danged if that feller *still* couldn't play poker to save himself.

The other two dropped outta the hand pretty quick, while the jaw-flapper went it alone up against me. I couldn't look every direction at once, so I figured they musta passed cards from one man to the other without me seeing — made sense that my three measly sevens would *not* be enough at the business end of proceedings.

But sudden-like, the hand was all over, and I could scarce believe the result.

"Dammit," the jaw-flapper said, turning over his cards. "I got only two pair."

"I'll leave you ten dollars, Tom," I said, "and hope it changes your luck."

But as I reached out with both hands to pull the

thousand toward me, that no-good jaw-flapper cried out, "Old man took cards from his sleeve, the damnable cheat!"

The first half a moment I wasted, by making two fists as I jumped to my feet — but the second half-moment I seen the light catch his sleeve-gun.

I did not waste no more half-moments, let alone full ones.

As he fired the first shot, I was already jumping backwards and sideways and tipping the table in front as I did so — his first bullet tore through its edge, splintered it some as I drew.

I ain't so quick on the draw as I was in the old days — hell, I doubt I ever *was*. But I know how to get it clear of the holster and aim 'fore I shoot, which was roundabout where he'd went wrong.

Strange how life can slow down and speed up all at once — but that's what happens when life and death gets involved, and argues out a result one way or the other.

The table flew *fast,* same speed as the pretty wag-tails[1] nearby commenced screaming — but how *he* moved was slower than slow. I had plenty of time once I drew to decide either way.

But he did not stop.

I would not have shot him if he hadn't been raising his gun up to fire again. Slow and deliberate I squeezed the little Remington's trigger — and watched the man jerk as the bullet tore through his chest. As he fell I aimed at him again, although already sure he was hit.

Never can be certain a man'll stop shooting, not 'til he's properly done for.

But he stayed where he fell, didn't move — and when I switched my aim onto them, both his two friends had their hands up already, palms showing empty, and eyes showing fear.

The screams and the music and dancing all stopped, and the experts all gathered and spoke what they saw, way they do whenever there's killing. A crush of people pressed in around us, and I pushed my gun up under one feller's chin when he got too close and bumped me.

"I'm sorry, I'm sorry," he yelled. And he backed away, wild-eyed, disappeared in the crowd.

Only moments later Al Swearengen himself appeared halfway down the stairs. Top of his voice, he declared a free round of drinks — then he announced half price on women, the next fifteen minutes. Sure got the men cheering and laughing again, and Swearengen made his way down to the bar, looking pleased with himself.

The Sheriff, Seth Bullock, strode in just a half-minute later. He had not missed much of importance, with one glaring exception — the other two men from the card game had somehow slipped away. Must have been during the ruckus Swearengen caused with his *generous* announcements.

The accusatory jaw-flapping skunk — *Tom, if that really was his name* — stayed alive three more minutes, but answered no questions. He *did* do a whole lotta moaning, but only one short bit of speaking.

"Useless old coot, is he, Newbold? Be easy to kill him, you said. I cain't see you now, dammit Sam, where the hell...?"

He coughed and he spluttered and died then — seemed fitting that *hell* was the word on his lips when he passed. No doubt, that was where he was headed.

Sheriff Seth Bullock stood to his full height, drew his six-gun and fired it once — into a roof beam above him, it relieves me to tell. He was a man who commanded attention, impressive by any standards, and only a fool would have failed to give him his due — but this firing of a gun inside a saloon seemed excessive, even to me. Sure did the job though — even Swearengen stopped his ambulation, halfway back up the stairs.

In the fullness of that quiet moment, Sheriff Bullock looked around at those present and said, "Which of you men is called Newbold?"

Weren't no takers for that, unsurprising.

So then Bullock added, "Who *knows* a Newbold? New in camp maybe, and might be called Sam." When there was no takers still, he turned to face Swearengen, and said, "I'll have you lock the doors if need be, and all drinking and whoring to stop while we sort this thing out."

"You can't—"

"Oh, I can, Mister Swearengen. I can."

"You all heard the good man," Swearengen said, and his smile was about the unhappiest I ever saw. "Anyone here knows Sam Newbold best speak up now, lest the valiant protector of our town starts shootin' the place up again, and puts an end to our fun. Well?" he asked after a pause. "No one here to save all our fun?"

"I met a Newbold back in Kansas City," said a filthy old drunk as he balanced a drink in each hand. "His name weren't Sam though, but Bill. Or maybe Will, now I think on it. No, Wal, that were him, Wally Newbold. Had a outsize fondness for whiskey, a most terrible drunk."

As Swearengen raised up his eyebrows and made a magnanimous gesture with his hands, Sheriff Bullock huffed like a man wounded.

"Who knows this dead man here then? No one moves 'til I know who he is."

Again, there wasn't no takers.

"His own name was Tom," Bullock growled, "and he clearly said the name Sam Newbold. *Someone* must know who he is."

"Perhaps the man was befuddled," said Swearengen, his smile superior, as he looked down on the Sheriff from his place on the stairs. "Him being dying and all, is what I mean, Bullock. Imminent death would surely do that to *me*, weak of mind as I am — unlike yourself of course, Sheriff. You being so sharp, the small act of dying would hardly be seen to affect you."

Seth Bullock waited for the laughter to die off before speaking. "Popular man you are, here in your own place, *Mister* Swearengen. If you're clever you'll stay here. Anyone who witnessed what happened, come speak to me now, I need to take statements."

---

1. WAG-TAILS : prostitute

CHAPTER 3
WHY THE GOOD LORD GAVE US FISTS

A FEW MEN — and one woman — who'd seen it all came and told Sheriff Bullock what happened. And after, he spoke to me. I heard all their accounts as I lingered nearby, and never had cause to argue, for they all spoke the truth, near enough.

Only two extra things I told him about the man's death: firstly, that our two fellow players might or might not been friendly with him, but both had already absconded into thin air; and secondly, that this feller dead at our feet was the worst damn poker player I ever saw — almost seemed like he *wanted* to lose.

Bullock stroked his mustache, thought some on it and finally said, "He spoke no word to indicate he was anything but a drunk who had made a poor choice?"

"Called me a damnable old cheat!"

"Which you ain't, I'd point out, Lyle."

"Well, young Seth," I replied. "There might be an argument for it. I'd say he was maybe *half* right — the

8

damnable half I'd admit to, and the *old* half as well. Though it grates on me some to hear the word *old* spoke so nasty. But a'course, that third half was *all* wrong — just as you said, I'm no cheat."

"So you shot him for saying it?"

"Hell I didn't," I growled. "*Saying* cheat ain't a killing offense — it's only words, they don't hurt. Such situations are why the Good Lord gave us fists, in my estimation — and fists are the weapons I'd have used on that feller, if I'd a'been given a choice."

"It's well known you're an ill-tempered man, Lyle—"

"Hell I am! I never hurt no-one who—"

"Calm down now," he said, placing a hand on my shoulder. "I'm just doing my job. I can't allow you no favors just because you're my friend."

"I know," I replied, unclenching my fists. "Let's sit down a spell, I need a whiskey."

A girl appeared outta nowhere, stepped over the dead man, put down a bottle and two clean glasses. Me and Bullock sat down in the corner — side by side, with our backs to the wall.

"You've had to kill men before, Lyle," he said as he poured. "Could this have been his attempt at revenge?"

"Always possible, Sheriff, but I don't believe so. I've killed eleven men before this one — each one *forced* me to kill him — but I've always tried to *avoid* the employment of lead, death being so final."

"And yet here he lies, shot and unbreathing before us."

"Hell, young Bullock, what's a man meant to do?

When a feller goes for his gun from three feet away, he runs you all outta choices, and you do what you have to."

Bullock took out his pocket watch, looked at it, said, "Almost three. Why can't people kill each other in the daytime? I'm tired of late nights."

"You sure ain't the only one," I said. "I'm getting too old for this now."

Sheriff Seth Bullock nodded agreement, threw his drink down his throat, then he stood. "Listen up, all you no-gooders," he announced good and loud.

The whole place went silent again — except for one man.

"The good Sheriff demands our attention," Al Swearengen said, smirking for all he was worth from behind the bar. "And when the savior of the town—"

"You *will* shut your damn mouth," roared the Sheriff, pointing his gun at him — and although Al Swearengen's eyes blazed with anger, he stayed quiet, and Bullock went on. "All who witnessed the shooting told the same story — that this man here, Lyle Frakes, acted in self defense, and is not guilty of *anything*. But as I'd prefer there to be no more killing, Mister Frakes will leave town right away."

"That ain't hardly fair, Sheriff," I said as I jumped to my feet. There was murmurs of agreement, but none very loud.

"No one here *seems* to know this dead man," Bullock said, casting a hard sort of look at a couple of strangers. "But he's sure to have friends, and they'll most likely work up some courage when they drink to his memory. Well, we all know how *that* sometimes goes. I'd avoid further trouble, so Frakes here will be moving on."

A grimy and gap-toothed young miner — *he looked short on brains, and long on poor choices* — spoke next. "You reckon this dead feller's pals might take revenge on the old man?"

"Not at all what I *said*," answered Bullock, shaking his head slowly, once. "Guess *you* don't know who this gray-beard here is — to make it clear for you, sir, it's not *him* I'm afeared for."

I heard another man murmur, "You don't believe that there ol' goat to be *the* Lyle Frakes?"

Then another said, "No, that sure as hell can't be him, I heard Frakes was killed near the Mexican border a year ago."

A third man looked up from the depths of his beer-glass and said, "I can vouch for the truth of that statement, for I was with my good friend Frakes when he died — and I tell you boys true, Lyle Frakes was a man of great style. Would not be caught dead wearing tasseled buckskin and moccasins, like this old mountain man is."

I had never seen the man in my life — and not only had I kept away from that border five years, I was sure enough breathing.

The young Sheriff raised one eyebrow at me in amusement, then shrugged his shoulders at them fellers' stupidity. "If there was a law against telling tall stories," Bullock said to the feller who spoke last, "I reckon you'd be in such trouble we might have to hang you. Move on and stop spreading untruths, or I'll fill your big mouth with my fist, as preventive enforcement of law."

Bullock was young yet, but did not lack for reputation — so despite the Sheriff casting such disrespect on him, that feller just hid himself under his hat and moved away into the crowd, the way he'd been told to.

In regard to myself though, Sheriff Bullock was completely respectful, not only in his actions, but also his speech — respectful yet *firm,* I would put it — as he motioned for me to move toward the front doors. "After you, Mister Frakes."

As a former lawman myself, I well understood his position. And hell, I had got what I came to Deadwood to get — enough money to head out to California, buy a small place where the weather was kinder and my old horse's bones would not ache so.

"Alright, Seth," I said as I walked out into the clear night, "I'll go fetch my things."

CHAPTER 4
SILVER

I MADE my way across the rutted mud street, accompanied home by the cleverest lawman Deadwood would likely ever get.

Bid unlocked and threw open the door as me and Bullock approached. "Heard shots, but never figured it'd be you," he said as we entered. He took a quick look about, checking we hadn't been followed, before locking the door to our little saloon, and turning around then to face us. "A killing, yes? Anybody we know?"

"Stranger," I said. "Drunk and stupid was all."

"Bad combination," said Bid. "It's why I always close up by ten. Good businessman knows where to draw the line — I draw it halfway above profit, quarter way below risk."

We had all heard this theory of his enough times — but I knew he meant it mostly for himself. Bid was the best human friend a man ever had, but his idea of risk aversion had been to place ME in the path of the danger, more times than not.

Still, it had always been my own choice, protecting him and Georgina.

But it wouldn't happen no more — things would be different now.

I looked into his face, my old friend, and I said the difficult words that would make it all final. "Bid, this is it. Sheriff Bullock's decided I'm leaving."

Bid looked stricken a moment, composed himself quick, turned to Bullock. "No leeway?"

"For the good of the camp," said young Seth.

It struck me as funny then, how a clever man like Seth Bullock still saw this fast-growing town as a camp. But again, I only said, "I'll fetch my things."

I turned away, started to walk, then looked up toward where I was headed.

She was stood at the top of the stairs, the silver hue of her hair all aglow in the lamplight. It was not a dull gray like my own, but a glistening silver — like some precious metal but more so, it being more rare. By the shine of it, I guessed she must have brushed it out for some time before going to bed. It had been years since I seen it untied in such manner, and though it was thinner now than back then, it still fell like a waterfall, its silveriness lovely, all the way down to her waist.

Truth was, it stopped me in my tracks a moment, for with the lamp being behind her, its effect was that of a halo — and she seemed almost like an angel as she watched me walk up, one step at a time, my boots heavy on the boards of the stair treads.

I HAD just killed a man after all. It makes one heavy of

body, of leg and of foot — not only of heart, but that too. And it all weighs together.

Better days, younger days maybe, I'd have *run* up them stairs, or at least took 'em two at a time. As I came to the top I glanced at her, waited for her to move out the way.

She did not move — only stared at me, right in my eyes, with no heed of her husband and Bullock below.

And she looked just how I felt.

"I'll go to the Livery with the Sheriff," said Bid, his voice breaking in through that long moment. I was glad for the intrusion, and gladder still when he kept speaking. "That gray of mine will do fine for a packhorse, and can be ridden if needed. Parting gift to a good friend." As I nodded grim thanks, Bid turned his gaze to his wife beside me and added, "Georgie, get Lyle his money. Amount's written down in the safe."

Strange how little a single man has to show for his years of struggle. Oh, the money was fine, there was plenty of that — but all my worldly possessions were packed in less than a minute.

I dared not go into their room where the safe was.

Never was one for goodbyes.

She came out into the hallway, handed me a thick wad of cash money, the stack tied in some sorta hair ribbon. I stuffed it inside my coat pocket without looking at it — the ribbon had felt soft and smooth, quite unlike the money it held.

I needed to leave, tried to turn, but her eyes held me there. She looked right into me again, as if somewhere inside was an answer to a never asked question.

15

Dammit. That was my only thought. Perhaps I shook, I'm not sure — but I got the sense of that anyway.

Then her words came out, womanly soft — but also as broken and bitter as glass, all surprised when it finds out it breaks. "I just wish ... damn you, Lyle, why did you never...?"

"What?" *I had no idea what she was saying.* At least, that was what I told myself.

In all my life, no one ever looked inside me that way but her — but this time, somehow, it was different. Her hand was a shock, the caress of it, through my beard to the skin of my cheek, and I felt ... I felt like I'd fall. Then she screwed shut her eyes, left me the only one staring. Her thumb moved, ran over my lashes as she sighed, and I knew this was more than all our other goodbyes.

"Go," she growled, clutching my shirt so I couldn't, her eyes screwed tight shut, her breath hot on my face from our closeness, and I wanted ... I wanted...

Then she pushed away — released me. Her sudden tears burst her eyes open, and she said, clear and cold as a froze over lake, "Don't you *ever* come back, Kit. Never ever, no matter what he says. You go to California this time, and you make a life."

Then she spun on her heel, and her silver hair flew behind her, so fast she moved — she fled through her bedroom door, and she slammed it behind her. Georgina was gone.

CHAPTER 5

THE TRAIL TO SPEARFISH

THE NIGHT FELT TOO CRISP, too clear for such an occasion. It should have been raining.

I carried my war bag[1] the hundred yards to the Livery, and they came out as I arrived — just my friends, no liveryman.

My own horse was saddled and ready, his pale eyes shining under the moonlight — high-stepping already he was, and eager for action.

Quite an animal, Horse.

As for the gray, he was already loaded with my soogan[2] and all other supplies I would need for the trip — I could trust Bid for that, and felt no need to discuss it.

"You are headed for Minnesota," Bullock said as I secured my war bag to the gray. This statement surprised me, for he and I had discussed my plans, hopes and dreams only three days ago.

"No, not there," I answered. "I'll go to Cheyenne, and then California."

"Minnesota, far as I know," he said with a slight wink as he mounted his own horse. "Or why else would you ride out of town on the trail toward Spearfish?"

I had just killed a man, and it does strange things to the senses — so, lacking a normal man's docity[3], I was slow catching on to Bullock's game.

"There's a back-trail three miles along, Lyle," said Bid. "It'll only cost you an hour to head that way instead, and it's cheap insurance. Write us when you get where you're going. You know how Georgie is — always likes to know you arrived safe."

Bid walked beside us as we rode slowly up the street. We stopped when we came to our place — *no, not ours. Not mine at all, never was.*

His place.

Theirs.

I was surprised to see her come out. She stood in the doorway, no sign of tears now, her body rugged up against the cold, and the waterfall of her beautiful hair hidden too.

She silently witnessed my departure, yet somehow took no part in it — not a smile, not a word, not a wave.

Bid stepped around behind her and folded his arm across her chest like he owned her — he had always been that way. And yet, this time he did not stay there. Instead, he looked from me to her, back to me, and released her. Stood beside her, way you'd stand beside a good friend.

Me, I looked only at *him*. I nodded a final goodbye, and said, "Forward, Horse."

I didn't look back, then I didn't look back two more times.

I also did not look at such men as were watching me as I rode out. And not one of them spoke a goodbye. I felt Swearengen's eyes upon me as I rode by his place, but I did not look at him.

"I doubt you'll have trouble," Bullock said as we left the town limits, "but I'll sleep easier, folks believing you headed this other direction. I informed Bid Tucker to explain the subterfuge to his wife, so she don't drop hints to anyone on your true whereabouts."

We rode out mostly in silence. Bullock knew me well enough for that.

No one followed, and we had the trail all to ourselves, despite the night being moonlit.

I figured he'd turn back to town when we came to the back-trail, but instead, he said, "I'll ride with you as far as Snake Ridge."

No reason for him to do that, not really — he knew I had no argument with leaving, and indeed, he knew I'd been planning to leave in a week or two anyway.

Guess he figured I needed some company after that killing — and maybe I did.

"You being you, you'll insist on making things difficult," he said after awhile, "and go straight to Cheyenne, rather than Sidney."

"Reckon most likely that's it. Old dogs having trouble with new tricks."

"Figured so. Through Custer City, or—?"

"Not certain on that," I replied. "Gone to hell that place, what I heard, and I dislike the Sheriff. The Chronicle said they auctioned a *woman* there last week —

doubt it's true, but it went to seven-thousand, how they wrote it up."

"The article was sound, Lyle," he said, ducking under a branch. "Seven-thousand, seven-hundred, and seventy-seven dollars. What a thing. They'd best not try it here."

"Reckon not," I said to him.

Made me smile, knowing there was a lawman like him about still. One thing for a man to uphold the *laws* — but Bullock upheld what was *right*, whether lawful or not. He was my sort of lawman.

We rode on awhile longer in silence, each thinking our thoughts. The night was crisp and lovely and quiet, the sounds we heard mostly water, or wind in the trees. I could not have chosen a better companion to escort me that first little way — and decided to take it as a good omen toward the start of my new life.

When we came to the ridge we stopped and stayed silent a minute, just looking at what lay before me — the quiet uncertainty of it.

Then he said, "Good luck, Lyle," and reached over to me, shook my hand. "If you were of a mind to write me from California, I'd be well pleased to read it. Respecting you as I do, and not meaning it as an instruction."

"I'll write," I said. "Respect going both ways, and knowing it weren't an instruction, but something I chose."

For all our mutual respect — and his making it clear I was *not* being run out of town — he made it clear enough too, that I was *not* to return. Not tomorrow; not next month; not if Hell itself ever froze over.

Last year's killing was one thing, and this one another,

but it looks bad when they add up. Deadwood could never be part of my future again — I tipped my hat at Sheriff Seth Bullock and rode away then, knowing he sat and watched.

And I did not look back at *him* neither — leaving almost all my friends behind me, and perhaps only enemies forward.

---

1. WAR BAG: A bag that carries the basics. Extra ammunition, for a first thing. Perhaps a second set of clothes, a harmonica, or precious letters from your mother or sweetheart. And important, a bill of sale for your horse. For a traveling cowboy, this bag contained almost everything he owned. Sometimes called a Yannigan Bag, or a War Sack.
2. SOOGAN: A blanket (usually wool) wrapped inside a waterproof tarp, also called a Bedroll
3. DOCITY: Comprehension, clear understanding

CHAPTER 6
OLD MAN, OLD HORSE, OLD RIFLE

MOONLIT night is useful for travel — but this part of the world, the trees grow thick overhead many places, making it mighty slow going.

Horse was impatient, but we slowed to crawl-pace when we had to. We kept moving through the dark hours, before finally stopping at daybreak to boil some coffee.

Age is a cruel thing one side of the scales, but a real blessing the other. A younger man has all the vigor, but an old —*let's call it 'experienced' instead* — an *experienced* man knows the right place to stop, knows the sort of a gully that's rightly protected, knows when he can build a small fire and when he cannot.

I found myself in a safe time and place, with a trickling stream and fair feed for the horses, and stopped most of an hour to fill up on coffee and food.

There is something about the sound of running water, the crackle and smell and smoke of a fire, the spatter and sizzle of bacon washed down with good coffee, alone on the trail. It cleanses the soul, clears the thoughts, makes room for new hope.

And I realized Bullock was right.

My new plan was to head for Rapid City, and make my way slowly from there down to Sidney — that way being some safer than the trail to Cheyenne, which was sorely infested with road agents, rogue Injuns, and no-gooders of every stripe.

In years past, me and this fine horse would have made Rapid City by nightfall — but by now, I had come to terms with our limitations, and accepted that the forty-five miles was a trip best made over two days, followed by a full day of rest for ol' Horse to recover completely.

Even a year ago on our way north, this had been the rhythm of our travel — twenty-some miles a day for two or three days, followed by two nights of rest before we went on.

After breakfast we hit the trail again, and for such an old — I mean *experienced* — bunch, we were making fair enough progress. But by ten the lost night of sleep caught me up, and I knew it wouldn't be long before I'd need some shuteye.

Tires you terrible too, the taking of a man's life — sorta needles your nerves some and sets them a'jangle, makes you more tuckered out than might should.

Trying to stay out of sight of folks headed to Deadwood, was half of my problem — this at Seth Bullock's request, him having took pains to cover my whereabouts, just in case of revengers.

Keeping an eye out, I branched off from the Custer City trail toward Rapid City, staying out of folks' way when they came along every so often. Kept going awhile, but it was past midday before I spied a suitable place, off a ways to the west. Nice little valley, the bottom of it being completely hid from this main trail — but danged if it didn't lead me back toward Custer City, instead of where I'd decided to go.

Well, I do have a friend there, if he's sober enough to recognize who I am. Even older'n me, Silver Sam — though maybe not so old as that bag a'bones horse a'his. Might be some sorta record, horse living so long. Dammit, I'll go tell the both of them goodbye. At least the horse'll remember, as HE won't be drunk.

So it was decided. I headed west then, made my way down into that valley, unsaddled the horses and ground tied the gray, then had me a proper good sleep.

Having no worries about strangers approaching — Horse would alert me, him liking strange folks even less than I do myself — I enjoyed complete rest for three hours. At that time I grew cold and woke, the sun no longer reaching down into the bottom of the valley.

I had half a mind to stay put, but we still had two usable hours of daylight. And besides, the skies perfectly clear, and would stay that way after nightfall — I never was one to waste moonlight, it seeming to me like a gift that should be made use of.

I saddled up and we headed up out of the valley, picking our way through the trees ever westward — but as we neared the top of the ridge, and the trail that ran from Custer to Deadwood, Horse grew restless and troubled.

He never did that without reason, so it seemed a bad sign.

I kept moving, hoped it was nothing, then wrong noises reached me from a ways off — too far to hear clearly at first, my ears not what they once were.

I stopped, the better to listen — it would not do to run into a bunch of wild drunken men on the trail, and them try to rob me. I had done too much killing already, and it takes a toll on a man — always best to avoid fools like those.

But I listened, listened for certain sounds, just in case I was needed.

I figured the noise was the sound of a stagecoach, its driver urging it on, its wheels all a'rumble along a fast part of the trail, perhaps approaching a station, where the drivers are wont to show off. But the whoops and hollers seemed wrong for that now, and Horse shifted under me, nervous, way he gets before battle.

Gunfire was next; then the cries of road agents; panicking horses; a wagon that traveled too fast along a rough trail.

A *clever* man would have stayed where I was — an *experienced* man, one who'd attained a certain age by his wits, and now old enough to know better. *And yet ... and yet...*

I jumped down off of Horse, untied the gray from him, looped the lead-rope secure around a high branch and checked it. He'd be safe until we returned.

As I climbed up into the saddle, Horse was so keen for action he just about left me behind, and my right foot stayed free of the stirrup that first fifty yards, as he twisted and turned his way through the trees. A half-minute later we left safety behind us, turned left onto the trail, and galloped hard toward those who had thought fit to slaughter the innocent; we rode toward a wrong that must be made right; rode toward screaming and death, and a reason for living.

Old man, old horse, and old rifle — it felt just about like the old days, when we was all young.

CHAPTER 7
GERTRUDE

THERE WAS three men to worry on, I saw, as we turned the corner and sighted the scene that first moment.

It was not a stagecoach they attacked, but a middling-sized private wagon — *too heavy for its single horse,* was a stray thought I had. Its owners had built up the sides with rough timbers, then covered over the top with a canvas to keep their worldly goods dry. But the canvas all flapped in the breeze now, the sides were all broken, and the whole structure tipped on its side at the edge of the trail, cries and shouts coming from its insides.

The heavy-bearded road agents were all down off their horses, and it seemed like they found the destruction a point of amusement — all this I understood in a moment, for their laughing came louder than the screams of the folks in the wreckage.

One road agent casually put a bullet into the travelers' horse, and it went still in death right away, as the second lump of bearded uselessness kicked at a man who was trying to escape from the back of the wagon, fearfully a'crawl on his knees. But the third hard case[1] heard me rounding the bend — and though such a detail was *perhaps* too far off for me with my old eyes to see, I believe the man smiled as he raised up his rifle to point it at *me,* serious, like to cause damage.

As I previous explained you, I am not a man who enjoys killing — but enjoyments is enjoyments, and rifles is rifles, and when a man in the process of murdering innocent folks lifts his rifle toward me, there's only one way that can end, unless it's the *other*.

And the *other* — well, I don't go with that option, or allow such a murderer any chance of it.

My rifle is old by most standards, but strike me down for a fool if Ol' Gertrude ain't somehow sped herself up with age. Her wanting, I guess, to help out by making up for my own lack of speed. That rifle a'mine seemed to snap in place all of herself, then push back her trigger right onto my finger, each action at just the right moment.

Blew a hole through that road agent's face did Ol' Gertrude, which had the effect of him dropping his arms to his sides, and blasting a hole through his boot, before falling faceways into the dirt.

The horse-shooting feller was the next thing Ol' Gertrude aimed up at, and though she was quick, she too is perhaps getting on — for her first bullet failed to kill the man. Took part of an ear though it did, which sure made him squeal.

Age is age, and heart is heart, and too much of the first

seems never to bother the second, if there's plenty to start with. And heart was ever a thing old Horse had in abundance. He flattened his ears and flew 'cross that lovely soft ground ever faster, him being his own master now, ever since me and Gertrude had things of our own to attend to.

As the kicking-out feller raised his rifle and fired — *too soon, it weren't all the way up yet* — Ol' Gertrude upped her game some and put a big bullet right through the heart of the horse-shootin' feller, took him outta the dance.

And it seemed then like things slowed right down — each sound a sound on its own, and each subtle movement so slow I could maybe have stopped and got off of Horse and stood by to watch — and as I slow-squeezed the trigger I studied that kicking-out feller's face. Without doubt, he saw his death coming, and maybe a glimpse of whatever was waiting for him after. And I tell you, he had no liking *at all* for how he foreseen it.

His head didn't like it none either, I guess — for part of it left him, and such bits as stayed found their way to the ground, where they buried themselves in the dirt, perhaps hoping to hide there forever.

Suits me if they did. Damn yellow murdering road agent.

Horse seemed not to believe it all done with, and took more persuading to stop and be calm than expected — but we came to a deal pretty soon, and though he huffed some about it, he carried me back where I wanted, back to the dead men he'd run past while me and Gertrude done our best work.

I stepped down, still some wary — on account of having

trust in my animal, and *him* still acting wary — but there was only the three outlaw horses, so I reckoned things was all fine now.

Maybe Horse had got spooked, seeing that road agent take a gun to the horse who'd been pulling the wagon.

The crawling feller was balding and wispy of beard, and had eyes like some creature that lived mostly in darkness. A most unfortunate feller, looks-wise at least. He had ceased in his crawling, and propped himself up on an elbow to regard me, bleeding from various small wounds where he lay in the dirt.

His eyes were alert, and he cowered some as I approached, my old rifle still at the ready, my finger curled round the trigger. Wasn't pointed at him, not exactly — but Gertrude had ever been a rifle of nervous disposition, and preferred to be pointed at *something*. And what with Horse still acting crotchical[2], I was inclined to stay watchful until certain all danger had passed.

Hearing no signs of movement from the wagon, I regarded the crawling feller and asked, "Sit up straight now if you can, Mister. You all alone?"

Way his eyes darted to the wagon told me he wasn't, but he still didn't speak. He did what I'd told him to though, turned and sat on his rump — but his hand was too near his coat pocket for my comfort, and he had the look of a wrong'un.

Keeping Gertrude pointed his general vicinity, I said, "You been through it, Mister, and no surprise you'd be shocked some. But just keep your hands where I can see, while I check for survivors."

"My wife," he said, "and my daughter." He voiced it okay, but his eyes still had some sneak in 'em, so Gertrude turned more toward him as I stepped across to the wagon.

"Are you alone, sir?" he asked me. "I see your horse carries no pack."

To the trained ear of a former lawman like me, there was a halftone of greed in his voice, and perhaps some plan forming too, in back of his brain.

---

1. HARD CASE: A deadly man, often (but not always) a bad one
2. CROTCHICAL: Cranky, perverse

CHAPTER 8
A CONTEST OF SPEED

KEEPING HALF an eye on the man, I peered inside the wreckage of his wagon. The woman inside had her head at an inhuman angle — no chance she was alive, her neck having been snapped when the wagon turned over. It struck me right off when I seen the little girl, that she was possessed of a radiance of beauty — I glanced back at the dead woman, and could tell right off they was nohow related. This beautiful child was no blood relation of either of those she was traveling with.

The child was small, perhaps as young as seven, and appeared to be quite uninjured. Though sitting mostly upright, she was pushing herself back against the timbers behind her, hard enough she might have broke them if they'd been less sturdy.

She was wide-eyed and pale, and looked up at me fearful — so I didn't move closer, and gentle-soft-voiced as I could, I said, "It'll be alright, little Miss. Are you hurt? You come on out when you're ready, no hurry at all, no one's left here to hurt you."

Her big eyes darted about, from me to the dead woman, then back past me to the man, less than ten yards away. Unsurprising, she looked mighty afeared, every which way she looked.

"I'm sorry, Mister," I said as I turned my full attention back on the feller, and walked halfway back to where he was. "Your wife's journey has ended, but your little girl seems like she's fine. Will be, I guess, when she's over the shock of all this."

"Oh no," he said, just about as insincere as I ever heard a man act, and he scrambled to his feet. Then wiping his dirty hands on his britches he added, "Not my poor wife, not my darling. Oh, whatever shall I do? Come to me now, daughter, let me see you're okay."

I did not hear the little girl move, and did not turn to see if she would.

The man's gaze was on her, then on me, then back on the girl — then sudden as snake-strike, his mouth opened wide and he yelled, "No, don't shoot him!" Then he went for the gun in his pocket, clearly intending to murder me when I turned toward the girl.

Gertrude took unkind to his poor acting and shot the fool in his right thigh as he extracted the Deringer from his pocket. Lucky for him, being shot caused him to fumble the gun to the ground as he fell — making further shooting on my part unnecessary for the time being.

"That was a poorly made trick," I said. "You shoulda

hung about theaters and learned to *act* more realistic, if you wished to inveigle me that way."

He lay there a'panting and a'groaning and a'moaning, and cussed out a stream of bad words that no little girl should have been within three-hundred yards of. His hands was both clutching the leg as he glared up at me, but the Deringer, still loaded, was within what must be tempting distance — not twelve inches away from his hands, and right there between us like a truth we must deal with soon.

Instead of shooting him again like most fellers would have in that situation, I only said, "Take up the gun if you like, and we'll have ourselves a contest of speed. Either that or start speaking some truth, I'm in no mood for falsehoods."

The little girl had not made a sound all this time, but she surely made up for it then. "Kill him, please kill him," she screamed. "He stole me, he stole me, bad man!" And with that she came out a'running from the wreck, as if to run past me and attack him.

Instinctive-like, I scooped her up by the collar with my left hand as she went by me — and he went for the Deringer then.

And Gertrude, she needed just one hand to help her — she snapped into place, threw her trigger against my finger, and drilled that bad man in his chest as he picked up his gun. The fool fired a wild shot into the dirt as he fumbled that forty-one Deringer for the last time.

"Bad man," the little girl cried, struggling to free herself from my grasp, as the bad man gurgled his life away, face sideways down against dirt, eyes looking up fearful as he gasped for each breath, his left lung not inflating as his chest filled up with his blood.

"Shhhh," I said to her. "You'll be alright, Miss, you'll be just fine. Now don't you go nowhere, I'm putting you down on the floor now."

I done just as promised, and she stayed still like I asked, looking at that bad man some and then back to me.

"He stole me," she cried. "A thousand dollars he said I would bring him in Deadwood. Please kill him, please, I don't want to be sold! I don't *want* to kiss a rich man, and live as his pet."

CHAPTER 9
THREADBARE

THERE ARE things we all do — if we live long enough — that we *should* rightly feel ashamed of.

I cannot say what happened next was my finest moment. The full-blooded kicking of a man's face, one that results in smashed bones and broken teeth, is a shameful act to partake of — and perhaps even more so when the victim is already galloping headlong toward the last minute of his life, with no way to change the direction, the matter all settled against him.

But I have ever been ruled by temper, some few situations. And the sale of a child to a rich man — for untoward purposes no less — well, that is one such situation.

I know for sure I ran at him, and kicked him so hard his jaw broke. It made for a sickening sound, that much I remember. I do not recall if I kicked him again — though I could not testify that I didn't, for I was somewhat carried away by base feelings then.

It is also true that the state of his face, when I next looked upon it, was consistent with that of a man who'd been kicked more than once.

More than thrice, if I'm honest.

But please do not misunderstand, when I say that I *should* feel ashamed of what I did to that man in his dying minutes — for I felt no shame then, and indeed, still feel none now.

I take no pride in what I did — but I know for a truth, that given my time over, I would not change my actions.

He earned the pain he received, and likely deserved a lot more than I managed to give.

When I came to my senses, that excuse for a man was still breathing. It was clear he would not last the minute, but one of his eyes was still open — he looked up at me with it, then across at the girl, and squeezed out the words, "Damn you, old man." Then he sorta half-smiled through his damn broken teeth, spat out the words, "Thousand dollar." Then he died with those filthy words on his lips, there in his own blood on that ground.

If the girl hadn't whimpered right then, I'd have kicked that damn snake back to life so I could kill him again.

But whimper she did, and I turned and looked at her. She grasped the collar of her coat, held it up to her throat with both of her hands, and dragged her gaze away from the dead man. Looked at me so surprised, it was like she'd not seen me til then, and was wondering where I appeared from.

It was only right then that I noticed how threadbare her clothes were. At least she had shoes.

I tried to speak but the words got caught in my throat when they started to come. "I'm sorry..." was as far as I got.

She was shaking — not like she was cold, but more the afeared kind of shakes, and I looked away from her to see where Horse had got to. Just a few yards away, he was looking at me too — it had been awhile since my temper had frayed quite so badly, and ol' Horse wore a look of surprise. A horse version of it anyway — it was simple for me to read it, us two having been together so long.

I felt I should maybe apologize to *him* too, but figured it could wait until it was just me and him, private — it seeming to me that the child had seen enough loco behavior for one day. A man saying sorry to a horse might be one thing too far, on top of what already happened.

"Miss," I said, turning to face her square on. "I'm sorry you had to see that. I'm sorely aggrieved that I lost my temper in front of you, and will endeavor to keep it from now on, til we get to our destination."

She looked at me, and I looked at her — and I realized then that I was much better equipped to understand the expressions on the faces of horses, than to comprehend little girls.

"Are you hungry?" I said, then wondered where the hell that had come from, and the use of such a question at such a time. Then I added, "I got plenty of food we can eat."

Not sure why my mouth kept on running, it hardly seemed to make sense to talk about food after all that just happened.

"You won't sell me will you?" she said, her voice tiny and clear as a bird's.

"No, Miss," I said. "I promise I won't sell you. What I *will* do is escort you to safety. Tomorrow we'll ride to Custer City, work out what to do."

"Alright," she said. "Is that bad man dead?"

The tiny girl had not moved anywhere, still stood holding her collar bunched up at her throat as she spoke.

"Yes, Miss. He's dead alright. Dead as dead can be. He won't hurt you no more, and won't sell you to no one who will."

"Alright."

"Miss," I said. And I took off my hat and held it in front of my chest. "That there ... the lady there in the wagon — would she be your mother?"

The child again looked alarmed, and glanced back toward the wreck of the wagon, then shook her head urgently, *No*.

"She was with this man when he stole you? The two were together in this?"

She seemed undecided a moment, started to shake her head, changed her mind and nodded a definite *Yes*.

"It's alright, Miss," I told her then. "We'll get you home to your family soon as we can."

"But I don't..."

"You don't what, Miss?"

She shook her head, shivered again. I took off my coat, took a step toward her and she reeled back a little, looked at me sideways, eyes wide.

This served to remind me that my appearance is that of

a large, rough and dangerous man — and also, the poor girl had just seen strong evidence that appearances ain't always deceiving.

"You're cold, Miss," I said, and held the coat out toward her. "How about you put this on? Then perhaps you can help me by talking to Horse while I clear the trail." The mention of Horse raised her interest, I noted, so I hooked her in with more on the subject. "He's upset with me, you see? I don't misbehave such in front of him, mostly, and he's of a sensitive nature. Likes you too, I can tell."

"He has beautiful eyes," she said. "And he's *such* pretty colors."

CHAPTER 10
WILD CRITTERS NEED TO EAT TOO

TRUTH OF IT WAS, Horse had not been around many children this past year or two, so I watched a moment or three to see how he'd react to the girl.

Need not have worried, of course — he had ever been of a sweet nature with unthreatening types. If it weren't for his battle lust, he'd have been happier to be a child's pet, I suspect, and would have left me long ago.

As for the child, she looked quite a sight in my buckskin coat — it reached all the way to the ground, and probably weighed more than she did.

Considering all she'd just been through, it was a fine and unexpected thing to see that girl smile as she petted ol' Horse. It ain't always easy to warm a man's heart as he ages, but mine felt as toasty as toes by a campfire, watching them two together as I tidied my mess.

No way I was up to burying five bodies — and if them five wanted good Christian burials, they might should have thought some on that, before practicing such unChristian behaviors. I considered burying the woman, but when I asked the child how that woman had treated her, she looked all a'panic, covered her eyes with her hands, and commenced to shiver from fear.

That was enough to decide it.

And besides, wild critters need to eat too.

I dragged the bodies and wreckage off the trail best I could, and let the outlaw horses graze wherever they liked — they were well trained, and harbored no desire to leave. When I was ready to go, I put the outlaws' guns in their scabbards and saddlebags, then lifted the girl up onto Horse. We rode slowly back whence we'd came, leading the string of horses behind us, til we got to where me and Horse had first joined the trail.

We followed the path through the forest a ways, stopping halfway to where my gray pack horse waited. Then I tied the outlaw horses to trees, and had the child wait there awhile.

"Me and Horse'll go cover our tracks," I told her, "so if anyone comes along they won't know which way we went. Then we'll all go have a meal, make camp for the night, and ride to Custer City tomorrow."

Took awhile to cover my tracks, and leave clues that whoever had done this had galloped away toward Deadwood. Clues enough for white men to believe anyway.

Then me and Horse doubled back through the trees. We had no problem finding the child, and burned the last of the daylight getting back down to the bottom of our hidden valley.

The poor little chickabiddy[1] almost fell off of Horse as we stopped, and I had to grab a hold of her as she started to topple. I had not twigged to it, but the child had fallen asleep as we rode, all tuckered out as she was. Unsurprising, now I gave it some thought — that little girl sure had been through it.

She startled a moment when she woke, then remembered who I was I guess — or perhaps it was Horse she remembered, for she smiled up at me and said, "What's his name?"

"Well, it's ... Horse," I said, lifting her down to the ground.

I saw that my answer was unsatisfactory right off, but what was I to do? Given more warning, I could perhaps have concocted a fancy name and even a story to satisfy the child, but I simply didn't have time.

"Hmmm. Don't worry," she said. "I shall think up a *very* fine name, one just right for such a beautiful horse."

"He won't answer to it," I said as I started to tie off the outlaw horses. "He don't even answer to Horse half the time, unless he's in a good mood, and I feed him a biscuit."

"A horse that eats biscuits," she laughed, and the sound of it did something to me. Strangest thing it was. That little laugh reached inside me somewhere — somewhere precious, somewhere that mattered — and again, she reminded me of a small bird, like before.

"Lotsa horses eat biscuits," I told her. "You just can't

give 'em too many. But ol' Horse, he'd eat a hundred a day if you let him, and end up fat as two pigs."

She looked most sternly at me then and asked, "Is his name *really* Horse? You would not *lie* to me would you? Everyone seems to."

And that stern little look, it crumbled away to the saddest look I'd seen since ... well, it was a mighty sad look.

"Well, *I* won't lie to you," I told her. "His name is Horse."

"I suppose you're called *Man* then?"

The way her eyebrows raised up in a question, I figured she'd actually meant it — but she started to laugh.

Clever little shaver[2].

Catchy it was, that laugh, and I chuckled along with her too, a nice moment to share.

"My apologies, Miss," I said as I unsaddled Horse. "Seems I neglected our formal introductions. My name is Lyle Frakes, and I am well pleased to make your acquaintance."

I placed down the saddle and offered her my hand to shake. That big rough hand a'mine looked the same size as her head, and her eyes went wide as she stared at it a few moments. But she solemnly put her tiny paw out, and we shook as she said, "I am Mary Wilson. Thank you for saving me from those bad people, Mister Frakes. Do you think we could eat soon?"

"You can call me Lyle if you want — *Mister Frakes* was my father."

"*Lyle,*" she said, like as if it was from some foreign language. "That *is* a strange name. *Lyle.*"

"Better than Horse though, I reckon."

"Yes," she laughed. "Yes, it is! It would be *rather* impolite to call you by your first name — I learned that from reading, you know. So would *Mister Lyle* be alright with you?"

"That's a fine compromise," I agreed. "Let's go with that then. Don't guess you know how to build a fire, Miss Mary Wilson?"

"No," she said a little sadly. "I'm sorry, Mister Lyle, I never built a fire before. That nasty Mister ... well, if it's alright with you, I'd rather not say his name ever again. But that *bad man* would not allow me to go near the fire, and kept me imprisoned in the wagon almost every minute since we left Cheyenne. And it was the older children who tended the fire at..."

I waited, but she never went on.

Didn't like to push her, but it seemed important, so I gently said, "Tended the fire *at...?*"

She must not have been ready to trust me completely, for she changed tracks and said, "I'm sure I can gather the wood, that seems simple enough. And then you can *teach* me to make a good fire, so I can be helpful the next time. Deal, Mister Lyle?"

"Deal, Miss Mary. Deal."

---

1. CHICKABIDDY: A term of endearment for a child.
2. SHAVER: A child. Usually "a cute little shaver"

CHAPTER 11
SADDLESORE

T HAT POOR WORN-OUT little'un barely kept her eyes open long enough to eat. Kept nodding off even before that, while I built a small fire. I had topsy-turveyed my usual order of doing things — I set up camp and ate first, before tending to the horses only after the girl was asleep.

Horse didn't complain, and his opinion mattered more to me than the rest of the horses anyway. The gray Bid had gifted me was not a bad horse, solid when ridden, and held no malice toward being a pack-horse, way some animals did. But he lacked personality somehow, and intelligence too.

Compared to Horse, that gray was as a small rock is, compared to a mountain — solid and somewhat useful when needed, but lacking excitement and beauty. The gray was a good animal in his own way, but Horse was someone I admired, respected, and aspired to be half as good as, is another way to put it.

As for the three outlaw horses, they were of good quality, but I had no desire to keep them. Still, I could not just turn them loose, they needed looking after.

Not unusual, that outlaws had good horses — but one strange thing, they had no brands.

Well, that suited me, and they would bring a few dollars when I got them to Custer City.

If I did, more to the point.

I took the precaution of taking the outlaw horses a hundred or so yards away from the camp — way I figured, if there was Indians around, they'd have noticed what happened, and knowed too that several dead fellers meant a certainty of some spare horses someplace nearby. My covering of our trail, though good enough to flummox[1] most white men, would not have slowed red men down much.

So if Indians wanted them horses — seemed like logic they would do — I preferred they should take them without having to argue it out. I left the guns too, but no ammunition. No sense inviting extra trouble — and it sent a clear message.

At one point during the night Horse grew some restless and woke me. There was uneasy noises from the outlaw horses as well, but they quieted quicker than they'd started. I reached for Gertrude beside me — but Horse settled within a few minutes, and there was no way I was leaving the child alone.

I stayed wakeful awhile, but heard no sound to alarm me. Horse had gone back to sleep, which only proved I was the foolish one, missing out on some shuteye.

The child woke just on daybreak as I cooked up some

47

bacon — stared at me a moment she did, as if I was a stranger, before wiping the sleep from her eyes, blinking a little and checking again. Most likely didn't think I was real — or perhaps she'd been dreaming.

Before long I found out that little girls don't need to stop talking in order to eat. She talked about the fire and the trees and the camp, and how comfortable her bed was compared to the boards of that wagon. And she talked about Horse.

Tried out some names on him too, she did — names like Blaze Blue-Eyes, and Pale-Eye Champion, and she even tried out Prince Roderick Steamboat the Third.

I managed not to laugh — so did Horse — but it weren't easy.

She sure could talk, which made us a pretty good team, more-or-less.

I listened mostly — and could just about have got by, even if not possessed of a voice — except for once or twice when she asked me a question. But mostly I listened, and that surely suited me fine.

What does one say to a little girl anyway?

I did enquire as to her age — to that, she gave a long explanation, which commenced with her saying she did not *remember* being born, so could not for *certain* say that the circumstances of the event were correct. From there, that journey of words took a meandering trip through the years, sounding for some good while joyful, but later becoming one perfect heartbreak stacked up on top of the next. By the time she got to the bit where the bad folks — those pair so recently deceased — came to the orphanage in

Cheyenne two weeks ago, I had packed up the camp and was ready for us to get going.

At that point she said, "Oh, I'm so sorry! I should have been helping." And she seemed most sincerely aggrieved.

In the lull of her apologetic stance, I finally had a chance to say a few words, which I did. "But what *is* your age, was my question?"

"Oh, yes of course," she said, her little face lighting up corner to corner in a smile to rival the sunrise. "I'm nine, Mister Lyle. *Nine.* Thank you for asking. People never seem interested in me, so it's *very* refreshing that you would ask. And whenever people *do* ask me questions, they never are nice ones, and mostly they don't ask, they *tell*. And not only that, but they seem almost always to *lie*. Why, if I had a dollar for every time somebody lied to me, I'd have a tidy sum indeed, enough to buy a *fine* castle, one with battlements and towers, and ever-so-lovely paintings all over the walls. And — oh dear, I'm talking too much again, aren't I, Mister Lyle? People say I do, sometimes. Or always, really, more like it, then I get in trouble. I'm sorry, I..."

"It's alright, Miss," I interrupted. "I really don't mind at all. And Horse seems to like it just fine. But we best leave right away, or it'll be time for our lunch."

We walked the first little way, as we went along to where I'd staked out the three outlaw horses.

Turned out my thinking on Indians coming had been right — they *had* come for those horses, and good luck to 'em. Took the saddles I left up there too, which seemed a little surprising — but things change, that much I've learned as the years have flew by.

It's likely enough they was Indian horses in the first instance, them having no brands. And the peacefulness of keeping your scalp without battle — to my way of thinking — far outweighs the money three horses would bring. Did me a favor, how I see it, for now I would not be slowed down by trailing three extra horses to Custer City, then having to explain where I got 'em.

Simple life's best, less explaining undertaken the better.

I sat the girl in front of me on Horse while we rode — he seemed not to mind, and she sure didn't weigh much, underfed little nipper she was. I did not even bother to remove her onto the pack horse when we came to the trail. Reason being, she informed me along the way that she had *never* ridden a horse before.

She then described it as, "An experience of unrivaled excitement and wonder," to which I replied that she might change her mind by the end of the ride, which was twenty-some miles away yet.

A strange thing it was, the way I enjoyed all her talk — for as perhaps previously mentioned, I have ever been a man who prefers a quiet life, and I downright dislike idle chatter. Indeed, when forced to travel with men who won't *shut the hell up,* I've been known to get itchy with guns, and threaten to poke the barrels of them right into such men — either one end or the other, depending on just *how* much they'd annoyed me — and firing off enough bullets as would make their talk stop forever or preferably longer.

Well, like I said, it was only a threat. More-or-less.

I tried to figure out my fondness for the child's endless talk. It was most likely because she was possessed of a greater intelligence than most men I'd been on the trail with — though it might have been her turn of phrase, or perhaps her leaning toward positivity.

Whatever it was, she was a joy to be near, taking my mind off my troubles as she did — Horse seemed to like it all too, and made extra good time.

We stopped on the regular, and took longer over our lunch than we might have. But even with all that rest, I could tell the child was saddlesore by the time we neared Custer City in late afternoon.

She was squirming about for a first thing, and talking much less for a second — but she never complained, and so earned my extra respect.

I would probably miss her, I realized, when I left her in Custer City, and went on my way.

---

1. FLUMMOX: Confuse

CHAPTER 12
SCUTTLEBUTT

Custer City felt strange when we got there — less people about than expected, just for one thing. But there was something else too. An electrification of the air, was how it might have been put in a foolish dime novel — *admittedly, the exact kind of foolishness I enjoy reading every so often.*

I made a bee-line for the Golden Brick hotel, lifted the child down onto the boardwalk and tied the horses to the hitch-rail out front. The place had a fancy facade, but its reputation was for lumpy beds and bad food.

But it being the only hotel in town swayed things some in its favor.

We had watered the horses at the creek just outside the town, but it still annoyed me that there was no water in the trough outside the hotel. But as I stomped up onto the boardwalk, little Mary Wilson smiled a tired smile at me, and took hold of my rough old hand with her tiny soft fingers.

Warmed my heart some it did — even chased the scowl from my face, I'd admit if pressed on it.

We walked through the door into the hotel foyer. Hadn't gone two steps into the room when a self-important feller looked over the counter, adjusted his spectacles and said, "I'm *very* sorry, sir, but if it's a room you require, I'm unable to assist you today."

I glanced around, took the place in. Paper walls, held together with sweat and spittle and dust.

I growled, way I do when I'm tired, fixed my gaze on that feller and said, "You can't mean a hovel such as this could be full."

"Overly so, I'm afraid, sir," he said. "Bundling boards are already employed in every available bed. Now if you'd been here an hour ago—"

"Alright," I said. "How much?"

"It's not a question of money, sir—"

My right hand shot out, grabbed that feller's scrawny neck and dragged him across his own counter toward me, his eyes all a'bulging and ready to pop.

Never seen eyes of such size — might be it was his thick spectacles making them look so.

I raised my voice slightly so he'd hear it over the strangled sounds of his choking. "How much, is my final question? The little girl's tired, and this being Custer's only hotel, you got me beat. Any price not worth killing you over, would be one to mention."

Little Mary Wilson squeezed my hand hard right then, and I looked down to see she was frowning fit to give me a lacing. "Please let the man go this instant, Mister Lyle," she said.

And I'm not sure why, but I did what she said right away. The feller reeled away from me, back behind his counter, unbunching his shirt from his throat as he made some strange noises.

"What Mister Lyle means is," she said, as she turned to the bespectacled feller and smiled, "please name a fair price for a room. He's more than willing to pay it. He's tired, you see, for we have ridden a *thousand* miles today, and simply *must* have two beds, to rest our tired bones for the night."

"What a cute little Miss," said the feller. "A *thousand* miles, you say. Goodness, that's such a long way, and you such a small one. But alas, Miss, there is nought to be done, for all the beds are taken already, I promise. A simple matter of chronology, as I was attempting to say."

"Dammit, Mister, we need a room for the girl to rest up in, while I go sort out our problem. Don't make me—"

"Mister Lyle, *please!*"

"Sir," he said, lowering his spectacles, before furtively glancing left and then right, as if making ready to impart some valuable secret. "There has been a ... disruption ... in the town. It happened just yesterday, and may prove of use to you now in your hour of need."

"Go on."

"There may be vacant rooms, I believe, at the Golden Nugget Saloon—"

"A cathouse," I growled, and my one unheld hand

closed itself into a fist. "You'd suggest I take a little girl to stay in a cathouse! What the—?"

"I'm sorry, sir, very sorry," he said, pressing his back against the wall behind him so hard I thought he'd go through it. "The facts are not as you believe, sir. The Golden Nugget's proprietor has ... passed away, sir."

"That skunk Brand? Since when?"

"Since yesterday, sir. And not only he." He looked left and right again, then leaned forward conspiratorially. "Also three men who were in his employ, and the Town Sheriff too."

"So Fleet Darrow double-crossed him? Always took him for a straight shooter — though making allowance for how low that slitherer[1] Brand was, I guess Darrow might just changed his mind, it being more-or-less justified, outlaw code notwithstanding."

"I ... erm, no sir, that's not it at all..."

"Well, spit it out, feller, right now, so's I don't have to reach down your throat and drag it out into the light."

The man adjusted his glasses, making quick worried movements, like he wished he'd kept quiet to begin with, before quietly saying, "Mister Darrow was one of those who ... well, you know?"

"No, that can't be right. Surely no one got Darrow?"

"That very thing is the talk of the town today, sir," he said. "But it's not for I to spread scuttlebutt[2], is it? Perhaps you might go speak to someone who better knows all the details. If you cross the street to the restaurant, I'm certain there'll be someone there who knows *far* more than I — and to be perfectly honest, their food is considerably better than ours."

"Guess we'll do that," I replied, nodding a goodbye. "Much obliged, I suppose. You hungry, Mary Wilson?"

She looked up at me, said nothing, only smiled and nodded. I figured her too tired to speak, but she turned instead to that hotel feller and said, "I'm *awfully* sorry if Mister Lyle scared you. His disposition is sweet in the mornings, but he turns to a terror by the end of the day."

"That's alright, Miss," the feller replied. "I'm quite used to being disliked."

"Oh no," she said, "don't think that way. Why, if you saw what he did *yesterday,* I'm certain you'd count yourself lucky, and be quite convinced that he *likes* you. But I'll say sorry for his behavior, as he *quite* forgets his manners sometimes."

The man's smile perfectly beamed at her when he replied. "Why, thank you kindly, young Miss. And between you and me, I'm certain I'd turn snippy too, if I'd ridden a thousand miles between daylight and dusk. Good day to you, Miss. I'm sorry I had no room for you, you have been a delight."

"Good day," she said matter-of-factly, then she made for the door, dragging me along by the fingers.

---

1. SLITHERER: A sneak. Lower than a snake's belly
2. SCUTTLEBUTT: False rumors

CHAPTER 13

"THERE'LL BE CUTTING INVOLVED..."

I GAVE Horse permission to bite anyone who came near, and promised him we wouldn't be gone long.

I mostly never noticed such things, but it occurred to me then that the street was made of mud, blood and dung, and dashed dreams. I sure didn't want that dear child near it, so I scooped her up and carried her across.

As I wiped the mud from my boots and stepped onto the boardwalk, a hard case I've known for years, Curly Brown, came out of the restaurant carrying a box filled with meals. "As I live and breathe," he said in surprise, "Lyle Frakes. News rides a fast horse, I guess. You come here after the Sheriffin' job, I suppose?"

He was mighty wary, and wishing he had his hands full of gun, and not food — and I knew I needed to set his mind at rest, quick.

I tipped my hat as a greeting, and told little Mary Wilson to run along a quick minute. "Go look in the window of that mercantile next door, but do *not* go inside."

I watched her go, then turned to Curly and said, "I got no interest in law work, or in this town either — only coincidental I'm here, and maybe best you never saw me, if anyone asks. Whatever's gone down, or's about to, you can safely ignore me. I'll be outta Custer City so quick, you won't know I arrived yet."

"That's a load off, Lyle," he grinned, and his mighty shoulders relaxed some.

"Only heard there was news not two minutes ago, when I tried to get a room for the night in that hovel there." I indicated the place with a slight lift of my head that direction — uselessly so, I realized, it being the only hotel, and him knowing so. "Curly, I trust you'll give it me straight, me having no dog in this fight. It's rumored Brand and three of his men bit the dust. Clearly, one wasn't you. Big-Nose okay?"

The nod Curly gave me was better'n a written down contract — today, he would tell me the truth. "Funny thing about that, Lyle. There's a two-hundred dollar bounty on Big-Nose right now — but you know that brother a'mine, he could be most anywhere. Quite certain he hasn't been killed though, if you take my meaning."

"Thought I seen Big-Nose pretty recent in Deadwood," I mused. "Short feller, big-muscled alright — and strange enough, the man answered to that very same name, packed the same gun and spoke the same way. Even wore the same hat."

"It's a wonder how much some fellers seem alike," Curly said. "Fact is, there's one down the Golden Nugget right now — Mister Smith — who looks just like him too.

That Smith, he was one a'the men who helped clean up the town yesterday. Why don't you come meet him? Your friend's down there too."

"Silver Sam?"

He chuckled and said, "You got any other friends?"

"No, guess he's about it," I answered in kind. "At least around here anyway. Not counting horses, a'course."

"Goes without saying, Lyle. If only men could be trusted the way horses can. Silver Sam's still got that same ol' gray sack'a'bones, if you can believe it."

I shook my head slowly a second. "I've knowed Sam a good many years, and that horse was old when I met him. Must be some sorta record."

"That's what Silver Sam always says." Curly glanced at Mary Wilson a moment, and looked back at me, sorta flummoxed[1]. "What's with the little girl, Lyle? If it's okay to ask. Though I should be gettin' back with these meals, me bein' reduced to delivery boy, since the shake-up of the town's high society."

"I need to sort something for the child, get her to Cheyenne. Orphaned awhile back, but got recently stolen by a bad bunch who planned to sell her to a client in Deadwood. I spat before going on — *bad taste in my mouth.* "Thousand dollars, the seller reckoned the price was — being his dying breath, I take the story as true. Don't guess you'd know who the buyer mighta been?"

Curly Brown looked at me then and his eyes told the truth so clearly he needn't have spoken — but he put his voice to it anyway, and it came out hard and bitter and mean. "If I knew who he was, the man'd be dead already.

59

I've done worser things than most men — you know that, Lyle. And I know I'm headed for a fiery place when I leave the comfort of this one. But there's *some things*..."

His mouth curled up with hatred as he thought about what type of man would purchase a child that way.

"I had to leave Deadwood," I admitted. "Escorted from town by the Sheriff — circumstances beyond my control, and no going back. But if you ever find the name of the man that child was being delivered to..."

"Result of it'll make *all* the newspapers if I do, you can trust me on that," he said. "There'll be cutting involved, and such manhood as the man had will be whittled down slow, one slice at a time, and him made to eat it for his last meal."

A slight shiver went through me, but I nodded my thanks and said, "No man would judge you harsh on it. Sometimes legal severities ain't all they should be."

"Get some food and come down to the Nugget, Lyle. We're tryin' to nut out what to do — even Silver Sam's more-or-less sober. Soberest I seen him anyways."

"But I have to watch over the—"

"Bring the little girl, it's alright. There's trustworthy whores to look after her while we talk."

"Place closed for business?"

"For now. There's good quiet rooms empty too. There's Fleet's..." He paused a moment there, and I seen how it hurt him, just saying the name. Even winced before he went on. "There's four newly vacated rooms, and only three taken. And if you're too good to stay with us, that filthy damn Sheriff Grimes has no further use for his quarters — he sleeps in the boneyard, now on, right next to Brand."

"I'm sorry about Fleet," I said. "Relieved too, that I never had to come up against him. My plan being, for now, to stay outta trouble, keep breathing."

"Plan seems like a new one for you," Curly said, then nodded a goodbye and went on his way.

I called Mary Wilson back over, but she seemed not to hear me, so I wandered along to see what had took her attention — more attention than getting to the hot meal we'd been anticipating the final five miles of our journey.

Turned out she was looking at a stitched together pile of rags — or a *dolly,* way she saw it.

Didn't look much to me.

In truth, I found the thing overly garish. Looked like a soiled dove[2] who'd gone overboard when she painted her face before heading downstairs to seek business.

Well, maybe that's just what dolls look like — Mary Wilson sure seemed to like it.

Going by the sign on the door, the mercantile would be open another hour, so I took the tack of waiting to see if Mary's interest would wane while we ate.

Well, it surely did not.

By the time we got through some elk steak and fresh beans and roasted potatoes, she'd invented a dozen adventures for that doll, each one some great episode from its past — and it seemed to me like that piece of stuffed and embroidered rags was a heroine for the ages.

Gave it five different names she did too, each better than the last, beginning with Cordelia and making her way through Winifred and Gwendoline, settling awhile on Regina, but finally ending up at Princess Mayblossom.

It was lucky Horse weren't there to hear it, he mighta got jealous.

---

1. FLUMMOXED: Confused
2. DOVE: Prostitute

CHAPTER 14
SILVER SAM

WE FINISHED the meal off with a fine apple pie — Mary Wilson declared it was "Scrumptious beyond belief, and without doubt created by angels."

I didn't know about that, being, as usual, just generally hopeful the cook or the waiter hadn't spit on my food before they brung it.

Be nice to whoever's preparing your food, and remember to tip well, my Pa always reckoned. That advice served me well down the years, and I recommend it.

I had no walk-around money in my coat, so in order to pay for our meal, I had to take out the money Georgina handed me back in Deadwood.

Guess I musta been struck sorta dumb — found myself somehow lost to the moment, as I sat there running my fingers over the hair-ribbon Georgina had wrapped the big roll of cash in.

Blue. Tiny red stripes, bits of white. It's the one she wore when I met her. Forty years since I seen it.

I'll never see her again. Not ever, long as I live.

"Goodness me," Mary said, breaking into my thoughts then. "Is all of that *real money?*"

I raised a finger to my lips to tell her to be quieter, then extracted some notes, and handed the waitress twenty dollars, in addition to the two that our meals had cost.

"Much appreciated," I said, and climbed to my feet. "Buy yourself something you need, Miss."

That waitress had looked a bit like Georgina, back when she was young. Maybe I felt guilty somehow, over how I behaved way back then. The few extra dollars made the young waitress happy anyway, and I'm sure she don't get such treatment from most that come in — guess it averaged things out some, for her.

When we walked out the restaurant I opened the door for little Mary and followed behind. She could not help but steal a glance to her right, but she quickly set herself straight so as not to let on she was thinking of the doll.

She took hold of my fingers, as was becoming her custom, and we commenced to walk down the boardwalk — opposite direction to the mercantile.

I stopped after just a few moments, looked down at her and said, "I just remembered, I made a deal with Horse to buy him a carrot if he got us here by dark. Best we get one 'fore that mercantile closes, or he'll dig his feet in about it tomorrow when I try to ride out."

"And Swayback Lightning too," she said brightly. "He has worked hard and is also deserving."

"I guess you mean the pack horse — I always thought his name was Gray. And though it weren't part of the deal, I guess you might be right. We'll go purchase *two* carrots, then head down to visit my old friend. Unless *you* want a carrot as well?"

She shook her head No, and we turned and headed back to the mercantile. I watched her as we approached, and noticed she completely ignored the doll in the window, just as good as if she'd forgotten it ever existed.

As we walked to the counter, we had to go right by a shelf with toys on it, right below Mary's eye height — but she seemed like she never even noticed, not even with there being three other dolls front and center, set up like they was having a tea party.

"Give me the two plumpest, juiciest carrots you got," I said to the feller who came out to serve us.

"They're for the two finest horses this side of Australia," said Mary, "so please choose them with care and attention."

A smile came across the man's face and he said, "That a fact, little Miss? I'll choose carefully then."

He went away a few moments and came back with the goods, winking at me before placing the carrots on his counter. "Anything else today, Miss?"

"No, thank you," she said. "Perhaps some other time."

"Well, there was *one* other thing," I said, scratching at my chin, thoughtful-like. "Now whatever was it? Oh yes, now I remember. I see you got a wide range of dolls. We're in the market for one, if you'd care to show them all to us."

I thought that child might faint away then, for the grip

she had on my fingers went deathly tight and then loosened. Her hand dropped away as her face turned toward me, like as if she thought she'd not heard right.

Funny thing then. The feller — natural enough — tried to sell her on the fancier dolls. Or at least he did so, once I told him I held no objection to spending up big on the best of the dolls.

But Mary had eyes only for one — that bundle of rags in the window — and would not be persuaded or bribed to take any other.

"Oh, dear Princess Mayblossom Gwendoline Winifred Regina Cordelia," she said. "We shall be best friends, always."

When the feller extracted it from the window display and handed it to her she sniffled and snuffled and wiped tears from both her eyes — one eye at a time so as not to get the doll's dress wet — and looked up at me and said, "Thank you."

"We all need a friend," I replied. Felt like I had to say something, but it sounded sorta foolish when I heard myself say it — it being only a doll, and not a living thing like a horse.

Mary didn't seem to mind though — neither my words *or* the doll's inanimate nature.

She just sniff-snuffled some again and wiped her nose on her sleeve, so I said to the feller, "We'll take a few handkerchiefs too."

It was a wonder, that doll, like a magic trick it was — for it had the effect of stopping young Mary Wilson from speaking awhile.

I paid the storekeeper and we went and fed the horses their carrots. Then I led the horses along the street, while Mary walked the boardwalk, carrying that doll as if it was some precious baby. And still she said nothing else — only beamed at the doll, and sometimes at me.

When we came to the Golden Nugget, it was quiet as a boneyard, and not even any horses out front. The town's only action was further along, where the Strike It Lucky Saloon was — but even that seemed subdued, compared to the normal.

A few killings'll do that, especially of prominent citizens — even if some of 'em were snakes.

Horse and Gray had the rail out front to themselves, and by the time I tied them to it, the front doors opened up and there — no less gray or old than last time I seen him — was my friend.

"Sam," I said, shaking the hand he thrust out as I stepped toward him. "You're still an ugly bucket a'mud — but I weren't so sure it was you, way you're standing up straight on your legs and ain't fallen down yet."

"Lyle Frakes," he said, sniffing at the air as if he'd noticed something distasteful. "Three hours ago Curly Brown reckoned it smelled as if something had crawled up under the floor here and died — but I told him dead things don't smell *that* bad, it must be Lyle Frakes on his way down the trail from Deadwood."

"Think I liked you better when you were always too drunk to talk, Sam. This here little lady is Mary Wilson — Mary, this ain't really an ugly bucket a'mud. Despite its awful appearance, that pile of scrawn is in fact a real human man, even older'n me. He goes by Silver Sam, but I expect you'll have a better name for him soon — so just call him whatever you like, he's too old and deaf to hear what you say anyway."

"Hello, Mister Silver," she said, shyly offering him her left hand to shake while she clung to the doll with her right.

"And howdy to you, Miss Mary Wilson," he said with a big friendly smile. "I ain't seen too many young'uns in awhile, and I never saw such a lovely polite one in all my born days."

"And that's a whole lotta days," I said, as Sam stepped back inside and motioned for us to follow.

I held the door open and waited for Mary to go first. And as soon as she walked through the door, she excitedly said, "Oh my, Mister Silver — your horse lives inside the saloon!"

CHAPTER 15
"A PROSPEROUS HORSE…"

I T WAS TRUE. That ancient horse was right there, standing up by the bar like as if he was waiting for a whiskey.

I swear he nodded a greeting at me and winked. Maybe not — it had been a long day.

One thing for certain, that skunk Joe Brand would be turning in his grave already, and him only just got there. Didn't mind having men murdered, but he was a stickler for cleanliness in his saloon. Serves the skunk right, I hope the horse never moves out.

Aside from the horse, there was only five of us in that huge room — to be clear, that was five including the child.

"Howdy, Lyle," said Big-Nose Brown, older brother to Curly, as I shut the door behind me. "Smatterin' of trouble in Deadwood I heard."

"A little," I said. "And some since. Been a lengthy two days. But it's rumored I had the easy end of it, compared to a few fellers here."

Big-Nose scratched his bearded chin and let out a sigh 'fore he answered. "We buried Fleet today. And four who deserved it. The two men involved left already — no names, though it was self defense, all three of us here being witnesses to it. It was Brand they were after, for reasons I won't speak of in front of your charge there."

Mary was holding my hand, I noticed now — I'd gotten used to it, I guess.

I motioned toward each man as I quickly introduced her, my plan being to set her mind at ease. The Browns looked like rough men, I noticed now — perhaps even rougher than myself.

"Mary Wilson," I said, "that's Curly Brown, who I spoke to outside the restaurant before. This other one's Big-Nose ... I mean, not ... that is to say ... I'll just start again, shall I? That handsomely big-nosed man there is called Mister Smith."

"And the *horse?*" she cried. "What's *he* called, that beautiful old horse? Does he *really* live inside, Mister Silver? Does he *really?* Please say he does!"

"He does for now, Miss," said Sam, and she squealed with the glee of it, then he went on. "He's a prosperous old horse, Miss Mary, and has made wise investments. Bought this place just yesterday, he did."

"He did *not*," she said, clapping one hand over her mouth in disbelief.

"Well, not by himself, a'course," said old Sam. "He's somewhat well-off, but not rich. Did well a few years back, being halves in a silver mine, but that's a whole 'nother story. Fact is though, he squandered half of his fortune.

Used to be a nefarious gambler — on horse races mostly, a'course — but he don't do that of late. As for *this* place, Mister Smith and Mister Brown and myself all went in on it with him — but only after he convinced us it was a wise investment."

"No!"

"Yes, Miss, for a certainty. It was the warmth of the place sold him on it. Fred's the sociable sort you see — Fred bein' the animal's name, if that was unclear. See, as he gets older, the nights shake the padding from his bones, you understand? And this place is so well built and solid, and has that big fireplace too — so ol' Fred agreed to go quarter partners, on the condition he gets to come inside whenever he likes."

As if to lay claim to the truth of the story, the old gray lay himself down by the bar, then looked across at us, blinking, as if we was keeping him awake.

"That old sack a'bones better not die there," said Curly. "If he does, I ain't helpin' remove him."

"Ha," said ol' Sam. "He'll outlive us all, I've no doubt. Except for this fine young lady, of course."

Mary's laugh was stifled halfway in by a yawn. She looked up at me, sleepy but happy.

"About these vacant room's then," I said. "Also, who else is staying here? I assume all the whores..." I stopped speaking then like I'd been shot, and looked down at Mary, who stared at me, eyes wide, mouth open.

"You *assume* it just right, Lyle," said ol' Sam, real quick. "All the *horses* sleep outside in the barn, except this one here." He winked at me then — it wasn't the first time he'd saved me. Though usually, bullets and bad men were what I'd been saved from, not corrupting the innocent thoughts of nice little girls.

"That's a relief then," I said, happy to stay on the new subject. "And there's room for *my* two horses out there?"

"More than enough," Sam replied. "As for human folk sleeping upstairs tonight, I've taken up temporary residence in the former proprietor's rooms, and my associates here have a room each. There are several nice ladies who live here, each has her own private room. So there's one vacant room that you two can sleep in."

"Two beds?" I enquired.

"Hmmm, easiest we just swap rooms," said Sam. "Mine has two big rooms together, you see. One with a good horsehair lounge, just right for the comfort of a child."

Sam showed us upstairs to the room. It was at the farthest end of the hallway, and had its own private bathroom, including a quincy[1]. While the child cleaned herself up in private, me and Sam made up a bed for her.

"The whores' room are all down the other end," he said.

"Thought I heard one sobbing when we came to the top of the stairs. What's that all about?"

"Poor girl was in love with Fleet Darrow," he said. "Had to drag her up outta the grave when we planted him. The others are looking out for her, and the Doc gave her laudanum so she'll sleep. The Browns ain't no angels, but ain't the types to worry a child, as you well know. I know all the whores, they're all decent. Wouldn't matter anyway, there's a lock on the door, and only you'll have the key."

"Thanks, Sam. It's nice seein' you more-or-less sober. Maybe you'll even outlive the horse. You really taking this place on?"

"Young feller who killed Brand — it was some neat trick by the way, wait til you hear the story[2] — he made the suggestion of turning this place into a dance hall."

"Heard there's money in that too, and maybe less trouble."

"Well, we'll just see," said Sam. "Locals'll pull the place down if we don't open back up soon. So we'll give the whores a week off then open back up if they want to. They've got money enough for awhile, Fleet Darrow saw to that 'fore he died. Richest part of all this, Big-Nose might become Sheriff."

"He won't turn bad on you, will he?"

"I consider he won't, strange enough, Lyle. Something changed in him lately. Brand had put him and Curly off the payroll. So, not under contract, they helped the two fellers who come here, or it would not have worked."

"You had a hand in it too, Sam," I said. "I can tell. There's a death in your eyes."

"Sheriff damn Grimes. Insulted Wild Bill just for one thing." Old Silver Sam shook his head in disgust before adding, "What's your plan for the child? This is no place for her, of course — and neither is Deadwood."

"Figured to leave her with you, Sam. You'll get her on the stage for Cheyenne, back to the orphanage there where she come from. That be alright?"

Seemed like old Silver Sam aged ten years in a moment right then. Rubbed his temples hard with both his palms, before rubbing at his forehead and saying, "No."

"No?"

"No, Lyle, that's no good at all, you clearly ain't thought it through."

---

1. QUINCY: An indoor toilet
2. I previously wrote a whole book about that story if you wanna read it. It's called The Derringer, and it's one of my favorites.

CHAPTER 16

BEST HORSEMAN I EVER SAW

W<small>E HEARD</small> the bathroom door open, and Silver Sam cut the conversation right there.

"Get her off to sleep, then we'll talk."

He told the sleepy Mary goodnight and started to leave — not before telling her the old horse insisted on being told a bedtime story every night.

"Goodnight, Mister Silver," she said as he got to the door. "And please bid Fred goodnight too, from Princess Mayblossom and myself."

"I'll do that, Miss, I promise. And a very good night to you."

I showed her to her bed and she climbed up and in, propped the doll against the pillow and drew the blanket up to its neck. Then she smiled a sleepy one at me before laying her own head down beside it.

"Might I have a story too, Mister Lyle? Please? I'm certain Princess Mayblossom would like it, this being her first night ever out in the big world."

"Well, Mary, I don't really know any—"

"Oh, please, Mister Lyle. Or perhaps we could go back downstairs, and listen in on the story as Mister Silver puts Fred to bed for the night?"

I rubbed at my beard some and said, "Well, let me see."

One thing for sure, no recent stories I've lived would be fit for telling to children. Perhaps instead, one from a storybook. Then again, the storybooks I read, most people end up being shot. Best not tell the child one of those.

Come on now, Lyle, think!

I tried my best to remember the stories I'd been told in my childhood, but struggled to recall even one. Despite my lack of concise memories, I felt then encompassed by a feeling of warmth, and the presence of my dear mother as she read aloud to me in my bed, all that long time ago.

Perhaps I smiled then, or some look of softness came over me, for the patient Mary Wilson put her tiny hand on mine and said, "You look so very young at this moment, Mister Lyle. A wistful happiness, I would call it, if asked." Her eyes fluttered a moment or two, but they opened again and she added, "Goodnight, Mister Lyle. And thank you ... thank you so much ... for..."

She drifted off into sleep then, a smile on her little face as she turned ever so slightly toward Princess Rosethorn, or whatever her name was.

I watched Mary a minute or so, making certain she slept, then quietly went out, locking the heavy door behind me. Made a quick stop at the bathroom, where I washed my face clean.

Didn't help the look of me much, but I felt a little better.

Tomorrow, I'll take a hot bath. I could soak for two days, I reckon, and still feel tired.

I clomped down the stairs, good and loud so they'd hear me coming — some men dislike surprises.

Curly and Big-Nose had gone off upstairs — not to their own rooms, but other rooms more entertaining, I guessed — so me and Sam and his horse had the place to ourselves.

Many fellers I've knowed, finding themselves in a fully stocked saloon like we were, would have took advantage right off, and forgot all about their poor horses tied up out front.

And Silver Sam, he was known around Custer City as the town drunk. And yet, soon as I came down them stairs, he did not even pour me a drink, but instead just walked to the front door and opened it for me.

We went out together, took the horse around to the barn. And while we attended to Horse and Gray properly, we talked some.

He was right too, I had to admit — it would not be safe to let Mary travel to Cheyenne on the stagecoach alone.

"Could end up anywhere," said Sam, and I'd hate to think of anything happening to that sweet child."

"Must be someone we can trust. Thought Curly rode shotgun on the run to Cheyenne sometimes, he'd see she went unharmed."

"He can't do it, Lyle. We got our hands fuller'n a young feller has, his first time in a cathouse."

"It'd only take a few—"

"No, Lyle, you're not thinkin' straight, it just ain't like you, what's happened?"

"Just tired, I guess."

"Alright," he said. "Well, I'll spell it out. What do *you* think's gonna happen when all the hard cases find out this town's open? No, we'll need Big-Nose and Curly both to keep hold of the place. I'd ask you to stay too, if it weren't for the little girl needin' safe passage."

"Well, what then? Must be someone can take her."

"There is. There's you, Lyle Frakes, you slow fool. Why ain't you seen that yet?"

"I can't ride all the way to Cheyenne with a child up on Horse too. Went fine for a day, but what if something goes wrong? I need to keep all my hands free, case they need to get filled up with rifle."

"How is Gertrude anyway?"

"She's been just fine," I answered as I closed Horse's stall. "Old girl's gotten faster to make up for my own lack of speed as I age."

We went inside, poured ourselves a drink and set ourselves down to think some.

After maybe ten minutes of solitude — mighta been thirty, for time goes by different when you're with a good friend — Sam said, "I got the perfect horse for the girl. Quieter than most, and she's tiny, but she'll go wherever Horse leads her. She's been broke to follow along, you see, and don't take no ridin' at all. Just sit little Mary in the saddle, let her hold onto the horn while she figures out balance, and you'll make it to Cheyenne just fine."

"But what if I need her to ride for her life?"

"That little horse'll do as it's asked, got speed and stamina too."

"Sounds a magical sorta horse, Sam. Forgive me if I don't believe in magicians and—"

"Got her off Wally Davis."

"Oh," I said.

Sam raised his brows up a little and tried not to smile *too* superior. "You know young Wally then, do you, Lyle?"

"Wally Davis is the best horseman I ever saw. Not so much the riding, though he's a dab hand at that too — but for breaking and equine care in particular, I never seen another man come close. You ever see Wally break a horse?"

"Not personal seen it myself," said Silver Sam, as he finished his drink. He put down the glass, eyed the bottle a moment before leaving it sit where it was.

"He just speaks to 'em," I said. "Not even that to begin with. Goes in the yard with 'em, then ignores 'em completely. Reads a book, combs what's left of his hair, watches the sky, or just sits about thinking. Waits for the horse to come to him. Days maybe before he *really* begins. Then he lays 'em down, picture *that* if you can — lays right on top of the dang horse, uses it like a pillow awhile. Sings to 'em too, when the mood strikes. Seems loco to any man who sees it."

"Can't argue with his results, Lyle. This little pony's too small for a man, but Wally rescued it from bein' turned into meat, and decided to break it to give it a life with a child. But the child's parents moved back East, so he kept the horse awhile, waitin' for the right owner. He was headin' up to Montana, asked me if I'd take it, find it a right home."

"Montana," I said, rubbing my beard some as I considered what that might be like. "No, too cold for Horse there. It's California for us."

"That filly must be four by now I guess, and be needin' some practice — but she's of a sweet nature, and won't give the young'un a problem."

I looked at that old horse of Sam's, lying there sleeping on the floor now. Wasn't dead — I could see his ribs go up and down. I watched him breathe in and out awhile as I gave some loose rein to Sam's wild suggestions.

"Guess I *could* make sure she gets to Cheyenne safe," I said after maybe ten minutes.

"That's it then," he replied, and he poured us a drink, like to seal the deal. "All decided. We'll introduce 'em tomorrow, give Mary some lessons, and you'll leave the following day."

CHAPTER 17
DEWDROP

I T WAS Mary Wilson who woke me next morning — but I didn't know that at first.

Ripped me from a frightful dream, she did, and I woke in a right flusteration[1] in that strange bed, not a clue where I was.

"Mister Lyle," came her little voice from a few yards away. "Mister Lyle, it's only a dream."

I was still in that place half between, where the dream still seemed like the thing that was real — *the men I'd been fighting had all disappeared, but the battle lust was still upon me.*

I looked at the little girl who'd replaced them and blinked as if that might fix things — *the trees had disappeared too, and the horses and gunsmoke* — the little girl was cowering a little, and had the morning sunlight behind her. Made her hard to recognize, just for a first thing. For a second thing, as my wits came halfway back to me, I realized the sunlight meant I must have slept in.

Never happened before, except once or twice when I'd been sick. *And when I'd been shot.*

For a brief moment, I figured that child must be an angel. They seemed to be everywhere lately, though I wasn't sure where I'd last seen one. "So I'm finally dead then?"

"It's Mary," she said. "Mary Wilson, remember? It's only me, Mister Lyle, don't be afraid."

Her words shook the fog from my brain. "Mary! Did I scare you? I'm sorry, child, I was dreaming, I guess."

"Oh yes, Mister Lyle," she said, staying back where she was. "You were crying out in your sleep, a most *terrible* noise. I do believe you were fighting, or perhaps being murdered. Are you alright now? You were having some sort of conniption fit, I believe, and might do yourself harm if I left you, all thrashing and threshing that way."

"I'm fine now, Mary. Thank you. You're a good girl."

"Mister Lyle," she said, inching closer. "Who is Georgina? I bet she's pretty. I wish I was pretty — all I *really* have is my hair. Who is she? Georgina?"

The dream jumped back into my mind and I huffed out a breath, shook my head. "She's ... she's no one, Mary," I said. "It was only a dream, you know dreams don't make no sense."

I had been protecting Georgina from road agents and thieves and throat-cutters — and Bid was already killed, and there were too many.

"It's *such* a pretty name. Why, I'd wager a thousand beautiful dresses, and a hundred gold necklaces, and all the tea in China that she's pretty. Is Georgina pretty, Mister Lyle? Oh, I just *know* she is."

"We should rustle up some breakfast," I said, sounding meaner than I'd meant to. "You must be hungry by now, Mary Wilson."

"I hear people downstairs," she said brightly. "Ladies, perhaps as many as six, I'd judge from the sound of the voices. May we go and meet the ladies we're sharing this house with? I mean, I know it's not really a house, but a sort of hotel atop a saloon, but I think we should meet them, and besides, they *might* even invite us to breakfast with them, would that not be lovely? But I'm talking too much, and you still are disheveled, and perhaps too, not ready to get up and make your bed and start this day anew, looking forward to ... oh dear, I'm *still* speaking, aren't I?"

"Yes, Mary, you are. But that's alright, I quite like it. Just don't tell nobody I said so, they'd never believe you. You keep watch at the street out that window while I get dressed, then we'll go downstairs."

The Browns had spoken to the calico queens[2] about there being a child upstairs, so when we went down to breakfast they were all dressed like regular ladies, more or less, and on their best behavior. If I hadn't known they worked here, I might have suspected they were just a bunch of storekeepers' wives, having a breakfast meeting together as they planned a church social.

They all made a big fuss of Mary, which sure made her smile. After we ate, I left her with them while I went with Sam to retrieve the little pony from his own place.

By the time we returned, those doves had braided Mary

Wilson's hair, and I had to agree, she looked pretty as a picture.

The heartbroken dove who had loved Fleet Darrow was there, and she even cracked a smile when Mary told her she had "the most beautiful eyes on the entire continent, including all of Canada as well, except perhaps for Mister Lyle's horse, whose name is now Pale-Eye Champion Blaze, though he doesn't answer to it just yet."

That dove's name was Eula, and she was dressed all in black. Seemed like whenever she looked at the child she rubbed her own belly a moment — well, I knew what that meant, but I didn't say nothing, not even to Sam.

Up to her to say, in her own time. Wonder if it's Fleet Darrow's child, that would surely be something.

I asked Eula if she wouldn't mind escorting little Mary up the street to buy some clothes she'd need for our trip, whatever she needed — why, the look on that Eula girl's pretty little face would have been worth putting in bottles.

It occurred to me then that painted doves had it maybe even worse than I'd previously figured. Simply being trusted to take the child shopping seemed to lift the woman's spirits no end — they must have been treated extra bad maybe here, under Brand.

I was even more glad he was dead when I thought about that — and after Eula and Mary and a couple of the other wag-tails left for the mercantile, I told Sam he should do the Dance Hall thing, at least if the doves liked the idea.

He agreed with the thinking, and said he'd discuss it with the Browns before moving on it.

We did a little warmup work with the pony, and she

was a fine little mover. Stood quiet for the saddle — the small saddle had come with the horse, Sam explained, child-sized — and even when I leaned my weight on it, that horse didn't skitter or budge.

"Thank the Lord for such men as Wally Davis," I said.

To which Sam replied, "I already thanked Him, and thanked Wally as well. Might ride that old horse a'mine to Montana someday, so's I can thank Wally again."

Can't beat a feller with unrealistic enthusiasm. Guess such improbable expectations are how the impossible gets done, and records get broken, and mankind keeps on improving. Guess we could all take a lesson from ol' Silver Sam.

When the ladies came back from their shopping, Eula looked proud as a new mother hen as she showed Mary off to us, all dressed up in a good shirt and britches and strong leather boots she could ride in. Looked a different child she did, as she came to the horse and we taught her correctly to mount it.

Well, horses is horses, and naturals is naturals — and them two just got on from the start, like a bee and a flower. Sam led them around in a circle five minutes, then he let go, kept walking beside, and they seemed not to notice he wasn't attached any more.

It wasn't until he stopped walking at all, and was stood next to me a good minute or so, that Mary understood she was riding the horse by herself.

Got so excited right then she almost went for a tumble, but the horse seemed to save her. At least it looked that way to me.

We didn't let Mary ride the pony too long — no sense wearing either of 'em out. The child would learn on the trail on the long days ahead.

We made certain to show her how to rub the horse down and care for it after the ride though. What I *don't* know about children would fill the whole world and a spare one — but I *do* know one thing. There ain't no sense at all in allowing a child to think she can just do the fun parts of life, and not have to do the looking after of the animal too.

We all of us got that responsibility. If an animal gives us its friendship or helps us some way — hell, even if it's wild and just needs assistance — the least we can do is get it back to tiptop condition. "You ride, you also brush feed and water," I told her.

Not that she seemed to mind — indeed, she looked chuffed to do it, and threw herself into the work.

Only strange part was how she never tried to change that pony's name — reckoned Dewdrop was "simply perfect already, as there could be nothing prettier than a dewdrop, for they are put there by angels while no one is watching."

All I knew was, she had finally let someone's name be, and not tried to change it, which at least proved one thing.

There ain't no cessation of wonders, under the sun.

---

1. FLUSTERATION: Confusion
2. CALICO QUEENS: Prostitutes

CHAPTER 18
UNWELCOME VISITORS

I F Mary and I had left Custer City right then, things might well have gone calmer and quieter — for us anyway — not just that night, but over the next week or two, on our trip to Cheyenne.

But wishes is wishes, and fates is fates, and no matter what I wished, my fate was to kill another man before I left town.

Becoming a habit just lately — but a man can scarcely be blamed if fools keep insisting on trying to kill him, and throwing themselves at his bullets.

It was a damn pity too, for I was feeling glad to have changed my course and gone by way of Custer City. Not only because I'd been able to rescue little Mary Wilson on my journey, but also because it was so good to see Silver Sam — and that old horse a'his — one last time.

Did my heart good somehow too, to see such hard cases as Big-Nose and Curly switching to a straight path — they had done many bad things in their time, but I knew from experience they could be relied upon when the chips were down. And even as outlaws, they had always lived by the code.

"Give me a bad man who lives by a code, rather than an average man who has none" — I can't remember what wise feller said that, my memory failing some lately, but I'm mostly inclined to agree.

Seemed like every one of the doves had took a strong liking to Mary. By the time the sun set they had worn her right out, dressing her up and brushing her hair, trying it out in every hairstyle they could think of. They finally settled on a single long braid with ribbons all through it, coiled on top of her head, painstakingly pinned and fixed in some special manner — then they hid it all under a bonnet.

Never will understand women — all that work to pretty something up, then they go and hide it away.

Funny thing too, little Mary kept saying she wished she was as pretty as they were, and how her "one beauty" was her long hair. They tried to persuade her otherwise a'course, but she seemed mighty set on her thinking — seemed to think she was ugly, for some strange reason no one understood.

Eula came with me to put Mary to bed, and for the second night in a row, the child fell into deep sleep before getting to hear the bedtime story she'd just requested. Pity — the dove had one prepared, and seemed eager to tell it.

"You'd better buy a book of fairy tales," Eula said as we went out of the room and I locked the door behind. "They have a few to choose from at the mercantile."

"I'll pick one out for her tomorrow," I answered. Then I made a note of it in my mind, where I hoped it would not get lost, way such notes seemed to these days.

"Thought you woulda took ol' Fred home," I told Silver Sam as I came down the stairs.

The horse *definitely* nodded a greeting at me when I spoke his name.

Then Sam said, "I told him to go — but you know Fred, he's a sociable sort, and I think he's got used to the warm."

"Damn old sack a'bones," Curly growled.

But his brother only laughed and replied, "Don't talk about our business partner that way."

A half-hour later, I was sitting downstairs listening to Curly and Big-Nose and Sam planning out the town's future, when someone rapped hard on the front doors of the saloon.

"We're closed for renovations," called out one of the four doves who were downstairs with us at the time. "We open again in a week. Please come back then."

"Curly Brown," came the whiskey-soaked voice of a hard case from outside the door. "It's Ike Prewitt, come for a talk."

All us men looked at each other — we all knew who he was. *What* he was.

Way Big-Nose pointed his finger brooked no argument, and the women all hightailed it upstairs without a word.

Silver Sam's hand went inside his coat pocket and stayed there — which meant the same thing as what Curly and Big-Nose did, which was take out their six-guns. Only difference being, Sam's gun was small, a genuine

Philadelphia Deringer, forty-one caliber, almost as old as Ike Prewitt.

Curly looked through the curtain a moment, turned to us and held up four fingers.

"You all know the deal," Big-Nose whispered to me and Sam. "Take whoever's closest."

As for me, I didn't have to do much. Though my rifle, Gertrude, was upstairs in my room, her little friend — Wilma, I call her — was willing as ever. The little Remington Rider jumped into my hand, way she does, such indoor situations. I moved to a front corner of the room — it was mostly in shadow — quiet and quick on my moccasins.

"We *will* have our talk, Curly," called Ike Prewitt then. "Up to you how and when, but here and now would be friendly."

"Hold your horses, Ike," Curly said as he stepped to the door. "I was just waitin' for the whores to get clear, you bein' so good-lookin' and all, and me figurin' to keep a few for myself."

"Damn right," Ike said as Curly opened the door. Despite his confidence, Ike hadn't got any less ugly since I last saw him in Deadwood a week ago. Head on him like a mauled badger, when a bear's about done with his playing and decides to start eating. Ike's gun was not in his hand, but it weren't tied down neither.

Just as expected.

Curly waved him in with his six-gun, which made things clear enough — and all three of Ike's brothers followed. The three, anyway, who had not found the end of a rope yet. They stayed several paces apart, no surprise they done that. Their guns weren't tied down neither, and the youngest looked already twitchy. I'd heard tell he was the quick one — and dammit, he was closest to *me*.

"Not the friendly welcome I expected," said Ike, when he noticed that Big-Nose too had his gun drawn. As Ike walked further into the room, he didn't comment on the fact there was a horse lying down by the bar.

"I hope you ain't here to dance," Big-Nose said, moving off to one side, and slowly waving his gun as if *it* was a dancer.

Ike's voice came out unhurried and even. "Let's get straight to business, shall we? This town being open now, you'll need help to run it, and I figure that's where..."

His words trailed off when I took a step forward, and his hand drifted closer to his holster, but did not yet touch it.

Then slow, almost disrespectful, he said, "Lyle Frakes, I might have known. Although now I think it through ... you killed that feller in Deadwood roundabout the same time things went down in here. Related somehow then, yes?"

"Both self defense," I said, slowly shaking my head. "State your business, young Prewitt, you're annoying my friends."

Ike Prewitt laughed, scratched his bulbous nose as he said, "I reckon these Browns has more in common with us Prewitts, than with law-lovin' types like yourself. Ain't that right, Curly? We figure to help you take over — I'll go Sheriff if you like, and—"

"I'll be the Sheriff here now, Ike," said Big-Nose. "And this town'll be run according to fair-enough law — not to benefit owners, way it was under Grimes."

"No," said Ike, casually taking his hat off and running his free hand through his hair, as he watched his reflection in the big mirror up behind the bar. "No, you Browns are like us. But if you think you don't need our help, you're sorely mistaken."

I noticed his brothers had spread out another half-step apart while he'd spoken. I slowed my breathing.

Ready.

Focused.

Aware of each tiny movement anywhere in the room.

And the time all slowed down.

"Let's have a drink and a parley," said Ike, as he turned away from the mirror, twirling his hat in his hand as he smiled. He *seemed* completely relaxed, but each of his brothers steadied themselves on their feet now. If they'd noticed Silver Sam in the shadows at all, they had given no indication.

"Take a bottle with you if you like," said Big-Nose, who was closest to Ike then. "Hell, take a bottle each of the good stuff. Compliments of the house, and no hard feelings — us bein' *friends.*" And right then, Big-Nose's voice turned from friendly to stone — same sorta stone they use for the fancy grave-markers, *important* men in big cities. "Take your whiskey and ride out of town, boys," he growled, "and don't none of you ever come back."

Ike Prewitt laughed so loud then, it was more a guffaw,

almost like a braying mule — his body half-doubled over like he'd lost control of it in his amusement.

And he threw his damn hat at Big-Nose and went for his gun.

CHAPTER 19
ALL HELL BROKE LOOSE

IN ALL THEM dime novels I've read, this is the bit where they mostly say, *'All hell broke loose.'*

And while that makes it sound sorta fun, it is anything *but*.

In the dime novels, the good guy always shoots the hard case, with a single clean shot through his heart or his brain — or if he don't wish to kill him right then, he shoots the gun out of his fingers before saying some pithy line, something quite entertaining.

Well, life ain't really that way — more's the pity, it'd save a whole lotta cleaning up later, once the shooting's all done.

Way it goes mostly, with eight fellers in one room like this — four against four — the grim reality would be a horrible ruckus of carnage, shots fired every which way, glasses and mirrors and windows all broken, men darting for cover, a man maybe shot here and there, and everyone crying out as the room fills so bad with gunsmoke you can't see nor breathe.

Seems too, like every bullet you hear, must be coming right for your head. After awhile, there's men doing frantic reloading, hands shaking so bad they can't manage it, for they're all outta bullets from shootin' at nothin' at all, shootin' every sound, and most every shadow.

No mistake though, most times *someone* gets shot, but not in a way you might reckon. Men get shot in their legs or their arms or their bellies, and sometimes even their privates, which causes a man to make a peculiar sound — you know when you hear it — and when it's all done, there's a stink of excrement too, as well as the piss smell, all a'that mixed in together with the burn of black powder, enough to separate a usually hale sorta man from his breakfast.

But this time, this time was different — every man in this room knew how to shoot, and had plenty experience of it.

Because of that, this time was *quick*. Only twelve shots were fired — *and only two bullets missed.*

They had reputations, them Prewitts. Reputations they'd earned.

They were quick, but not usually sneaky, far as anyone knew. So when Ike threw his hat, I guess he fairly figured he'd won the advantage. Musta practiced that trick in private, and saved it for a special occasion.

Well, it went not so much how he'd hoped — but it worked a little.

Them Prewitts musta been loco, thinking they could

walk in there and throw down on *us* four, and walk out that place still alive. As it turned out, they thought they had *reasons* they just about might get away with it.

Ike's trick was a good one, and Big-Nose fell for it, a little. He was slow on the trigger, and his first bullet only dragged through Ike Prewitt's bicep — same moment as Ike's bullet hit Big-Nose's shoulder, and both those tough men cried out.

Me and Silver Sam are old men — old enough not to die waiting. Sam's only bullet smashed through Tom Prewitt's skull just as Tom's gun cleared the holster.

Reckon I fired a tenth-second later — the youngest Prewitt, name Billy, took my first bullet in his left lung and my second in his right arm, his own shot coming between my two, time-wise. Missed me by not much at all, as it tore up the floor a few inches left of me — and then he was down, his gun clattering from his hand to the floor and away, as he started to wheeze in his dying.

Curly, just like his brother, was distracted by the trick with the hat — he knew he drew slow and he panicked, his first bullet missing Joe Prewitt completely. Joe missed him too, both hitting log walls, one each end of the room. Joe Prewitt wasn't known for missing, he was a dead shot — and he squeezed his trigger faster than Curly for his next shot.

Dead to rights, Curly Brown was then — if Joe's gun hadn't misfired. That misfire musta been a bewilderment for Joe, and it was the last thing he ever knew. Curly never missed twice in his life — his second shot punched a hole through the front of Joe's skull, took half his brain with it, sprayed it over the floor as he dropped to the ground, his soul already halfway to Hell.

Now back to how all this got started, Ike throwing the hat, him and Big-Nose shooting each other and both crying out — if you'd ever been shot, you'd not judge them for squealing that way— well, the thing is, it takes more than a bullet to stop them big stubborn types who are more brawn than brains, and that's what Big-Nose and Ike was.

As they aimed up again, they must both seen their futures and not liked how they looked, with big bullets right close up in 'em.

So both men dived as they fired — Big-Nose shot Ike in the belly this time, and Ike got Big-Nose in the same damn shoulder as the first one, almost the same hole. Difference was, with Ike being gutshot, he doubled up in pain — while Big-Nose, as previous mentioned, being not quite clever enough to know bullets should stop him, took careful aim at Ike's head and put one in his brainpan.

That was the last of the noise, except for some gasping and wheezing, a strange sound or two from a horse, then a few hurried footsteps.

Footsteps was Sam, who was checking his horse — turned out that ol' Fred was only complaining about all the noise — while the rest of us checked to make sure our men were all dead.

Well, it was plain to anyone with two ears that my man was still breathing — if that's what you'd call it. Still alive anyway he was, which maybe showed I was slipping. *Guess I am getting old,* was the thought crossed my mind.

I sure hadn't missed him completely though. Young

Billy Prewitt was sat half-up against the leg of a table, so I held my shooting iron on him, making sure he didn't have another gun on his person somewhere. He weren't going anywhere though, not in this lifetime, for that young man was wheezing fit to use as a bellows.

"Everyone alright?" Big-Nose called from somewhere in the gunsmoke. "My man dead."

"Me and Fred's fine," called Sam. "My man buzzard food too."

"All good, me," Curly said through gritted teeth, but he sounded roundabout the opposite. Then he growled a pained one and added, "My man's gone up the flume also," and sat heavily down in a chair.

"I'm fit as a fiddler's fiddle," I called. "My man shot through a lung, and nought to be done by the sounds."

I knelt down beside young Billy Prewitt, kept my gun pointed at him and said, "What the *hell* was you boys imagining, coming in here, guns still in your holsters, up against *us*? What did you *think* would happen? You wasted your life, son."

He looked up at me, making some terrible sounds as fresh blood mixed with bile bubbled up out of his mouth. He spat hard as he could to clear it, but it only dribbled down his chin and onto his shirt. "Old men," he managed to say, hoarse as death, then coughed up a little more blood. "Two of you's old ... old'n'useless ... Ike said..."

His eyes flickered then and went blank — and without ceremony, his head fell back and he died, having wasted his life, just like I told him.

"Useless are we?" I said, and I kicked his unfeeling

body. *Well, sort of.* That kick would not have knocked the skin off a pudding, for my heart wasn't in it, not really. "Old we might be," I said, "but more useful than you, Billy Prewitt, seeing's how we're still breathing. Useful for worms, 'bout all you are. Disrespectful damn kid."

CHAPTER 20

"A TRAIL WE ALL GOTTA RIDE…"

U NDERSTANDABLE IT WAS, that the doves got emotional — second gunfight in here in two days.

Too close for comfort, if indeed any comfort doves have.

Eula was beside herself, you could hear the hysterics before the smoke started to clear — but once a couple of the other wagtails came down to ascertain none of *us* was killed, they managed to settle her some.

Sam went and fetched the Doc, who was not even drunk yet, it being still early. While we waited for them, Curly and me dragged the bodies all onto a tarp — there was mess enough to be cleaned already — while Big-Nose took a few slugs of whiskey to help with his pain.

"Should not do that, Big-Nose," I suggested. "Makes the blood run too freely. Better you pour it onto the wound as a cleansing."

"Waste good whiskey? You always was a strange duck, Lyle." He grimaced and took another slug.

I was well acquainted with Doc Long, and knew him for a good man — though like many others, he'd been ruined by the War Between States. Him never having being one to tolerate violence, I expected some strong disapproval when he came in, but none was forthcoming.

Instead, he said, "Good thing you were here, Lyle," and went right to work on Big-Nose's shot shoulder. Both bullets had passed right on through, but the wound still needed a level of cleaning that made for a whole lotta pain. Doc gave him strong laudanum first — and after that, I didn't watch, having become increasingly squeamish of such fiddlings and gropings of wounds as I enter my dotage.

After checking on Mary — she appeared not to even have woken — I busied myself scrubbing blood and brains from the floorboards. Well, I had one drink beforehand to settle my nerves.

"The second bullet followed almost the same path as the first," Doc Long said to Big-Nose. "Close as any two I've ever seen, and it's only flesh that's been torn away. "You were exceedingly lucky."

"Yeah, I get all the luck don't I? Bullets bein' so lucky, and me catchin' two in one night. Damn filthy trickster, wish I coulda killed him slower!"

"You always were the lucky one," said Curly, looking out at the street through the curtains. Then he turned around and added, "Lucky you weren't drowned at birth, with that uglified[1] head a'yours, just for a first thing."

"He's gotcha there, Big-Nose," said Sam. "Truth's always a hard thing to beat."

"Don't," said Doc Long, spinning around to face Sam.

"Don't *ever* call him Big-Nose again. If he's to be Sheriff — and that *is* my sincere hope — we must quell any rumors right off, that he's Big-Nose Brown. This town might become a decent place now, if you men can keep the control of it. Don't say that name anymore."

"Tonight should go some ways to keeping our mitts on the place," said Sam with a nod. "And I hear you, Doc. If we could push through an election, make Big-No... make *Mister Smith* the Town Sheriff right away, and get the news out that he defended the town from the Prewitts, it might make other troublemakin' types think things through before tryin' their luck here."

"You're right," said the Doc, as he finished binding up Mister *Smith's* shoulder. "I'll go straight from here to see that new slang-whanger[2], see if he got his press running yet. Plans to call it the Custer City Daily Truth. Seems a right-thinking man. I believe he will help us."

"Send that gravedigger feller to pick up these bodies will you, Doc?" said Sam, as the Doc picked up his doctoring bag to leave.

By the time we had scrubbed clean the floor, the gravedigger arrived. Me and Curly helped him load the dead men onto his buckboard, then Curly said, "I'm off upstairs. Just hope that nice whore I been gettin' close to feels like givin' what I need."

Big-Nose — Mister *William* Smith, Doc Long had decided his name was — had gone upstairs already, but there wouldn't be no *needs* of his being met. Rest and quiet for him, was the Doc's main prescription, and laudanum every two hours.

That left me and Sam all alone, like the previous night — and though we opened a bottle of brandy, we barely touched it to start with.

Sam looked ten years older right then, ten years his looks could ill afford, and his voice was half sad and half tuckered. "Ever wonder about all this killing? Hell, Lyle, where's the sense in it all? Throwin' their lives away in search of money — what amount could be worth dying for?"

"Seems worse up this way than anywhere else," I replied. "Might be some sorta Indian curse on us all, comin' in here and takin' what's theirs."

"Might be," he said, and he stroked his old horse's ears some, as we sat in silence awhile.

"It's different up here, the trees even, you ever notice? Not just in Deadwood neither, where the name picked itself."

"I noticed it too," he said, thoughtful-like. "All that dead wood, entire valleys of it, I never seen such before, how about you?"

"True enough, Sam, I only seen that up this way."

"It ain't just the death of the trees," he said, "but the twistical nature of those still a'growin' that puzzles me."

"Bit like us maybe, Sam?" I poured us a small one.

"I wonder sometimes," he said after taking a sip, "if that twisting comes from its struggles in its dying. I'm twisted up in my body like you alluded, but not *only* there. It's my mind too, it seems, as I age. Though really, ain't it more like it's our struggles of living that cause us to twist in such manner?"

We thought our own thoughts awhile, but the subject stayed on our minds.

"Might just be the whole thing's down to age," I eventually said, looking at Sam's ancient horse. "It's how them top book-learned Doctor fellers figure it anyway. I consulted such a feller in Cheyenne a year back you know — on my way up to Deadwood, it was — and that was how he described it. I had visited him and paid a high tariff, on account of my horse having troubles."

"Horse is worth it," Sam said, a simple statement of truth that could never be argued against. He nodded respectfully, poured us a snifter, and we drank to Horse before I went on with the story.

"That learned Doc being too hoity-toity to trouble himself with mere horseflesh — no matter about its high quality — he consented to consult *only* with me."

"Refused to visit with Horse?"

"Didn't matter, I figured, my own symptoms and that of the horse being largely the same."

"Me and Fred here could have gone quarters in it too, I don't reckon. Aging ain't for the faint-hearted. What was the verdict?"

"Do not travel to Deadwood, was his main prescription, but instead, go south where it's warmer — or better still, California, and take the sea air. Shoulda heard the fancy feller, how he spoke. *'It'll do immense good for the lungs, and relieve the vast majority of your aches and pains — the roo-ma-tizz, as you call it.'* That was just how he said it."

"You punch his impudent nose?"

"Aw, Sam, you know I'm a calm type when I got any

excuse to be. I knew he was speaking down to me some, but I figured him rightfully justified with all his book-learning. So I took no offense at his words or his tone, way I might with an ordinary man."

"His lucky day," said Sam, and he poured us another.

"Way I figure things, that fine book-learned Sawbones[3] woulda give *me* that self-same respect, had I shoved a gun under his nose and explained him how *that* works — one professional man to another."

"Splits fair I guess."

We stayed quiet again awhile — maybe ten minutes, maybe an hour — while we chewed on our thoughts. Then sudden-like, I couldn't just about keep mine in.

"Old," I growled.

"Me, you mean?"

"That's what he called me. That feller tonight, Billy Prewitt, it was his last words. Also, the feller who kidnapped the little girl — *and* the one back in Deadwood. Three men's last words, and each man unknowed to the others."

"Well, who cares?" said Sam with a chuckle. "Ain't like they'll say it again."

"Something about a man's final words though, even when he weren't much of a man. Not always, a'course — but you know it, Sam, well as I do. When a man's dying, he finds himself strongly compelled toward speaking the truth. Even fellers mostly unacquainted, historically, with it, will spend their final moments trying to make truth a friend."

"Well," Sam said as he got up, and he lurched just a little, then leaned on the table for support. "We best get used to it, Lyle. Age only goes one direction, and that's a trail we all gotta ride. Wonder if one a'them ladies might still be awake — I could do with some comfort."

---

1. UGLIFIED: Someone who weren't always ugly, but has been made so by the years or some other factor
2. SLANG-WHANGER: Any sort of writer, but most often a newspaperman. Bret Harte is a good one, and this new feller Mark Twain seems sound on the goose.
3. SAWBONES: Doctor

CHAPTER 21
FRONT PAGE NEWS

ALL THIS KILLING had done some hurt to my spirit. And I knew, once I left, I would never see Silver Sam or his old horse again. I decided one extra day here in town couldn't hurt.

Turned out that new slang-whanger *did* have his printing press ready, and we'd made the front page. Well, I know front page *sounds* mighty fancy — but in a single sheet newspaper, there's only the front and the back page to choose from.

We was all eating breakfast downstairs — free breakfast, mind, delivered to us by the restaurant, without any of us having asked. "In appreciation," said the man who had brought it, "for protecting the town, way you have."

Never one to look a gift horse in his mouth, Curly only thanked the restaurant feller and his wife, then sent one of the doves upstairs to tell all the others. If you'd stacked all that food up, you'd have needed a real top horse to jump over the pile.

We all sat down to lashings of bacon and eggs and corn fritters and flapjacks and biscuits, not to mention much better coffee than we'd been drinking the previous day.

By the time we'd all ate our fill — including the old horse, who seemed to have hollowed out legs — the newspaperman and the Doc knocked at the open front door, then just walked on in, each of them carrying papers.

Doc Long introduced the man to us all — Nate Pendleton, he was called, recently come out from Pittsburgh. He was a small dapper feller in a fancy brown suit with wide stripes, his torso the shape of a pear, his fingers all covered in ink-stains, and he looked mighty tired. But he held himself well, spoke kindly to the doves and the child, and made of himself a good mixture of confidence and respect. I liked him right off, strange enough — despite my being historically distrustful of men who push pens for a living.

I seen that Nate Pendleton feller grow nervous, right about when the Doc commenced to explain how they'd swung a little loose with their quoting of things in his paper — them both deeming it important to get the news out, and not wishing to bother us after the violent events of the previous night.

"The essential thing is to instill in the townsfolk a sense that you all are good men, and doing what's right," Pendleton explained us. "And that all your actions were, and will always be, taken in the *citizens'* interest — and indeed, with the aim of growing a civilized town, where people feel safe in their homes, and also in public places."

Fine upstanding speech it was, even for a professional.

As he and Doc Long handed out the newspapers — one to each person in attendance, including the child — Nate Pendleton said, "These are gratis today."

Big-Nose — I mean *Mister Smith* — shifted uncomfortably in his seat and said, "That mean they're good?"

"No," Silver Sam said, "gratis means they're *on the dead*[1]."

"Ah, no, sir, I'm very sorry to correct you," said Pendleton, "but needs must, and no offense meant. Although the main article written therein is indeed, partly *on,* or *about,* the dead, the word *gratis* actually only means the newspapers are — on this auspicious occasion, it being our first issue — free of charge."

Big-Nose looked at the feller, shook his head slowly and frowned as he said, "That's what Sam just explained — you gave 'em out to us all *on the dead.*"

"Ah," Pendleton said, catching on quickly. "Western vernacular, how wonderful! Thank you for explaining, Mister Smith — or as you'll soon be, I hope, *Sheriff* Smith. I'm keen to learn more such words, if any of you are of a mind to teach me, for vernacular makes our rich language only ever the richer."

No one asked what *vernacular* meant, but you could hear people thinking it. Me, I already knew it — having had it explained to me once by a real nice muleskinner feller.

We all stuck our heads down then and went about reading — even those who could not read pretended to — while Nate Pendleton read the story to us out loud, at Doc Long's request.

And we found that, not only did that slang-whanger know how to wap[2] words, he perhaps had aspirations to perform in the theater — whole lotta fine timbre to his voice at high moments, and done damage to the air too, way he punched it so hard with his fists. Almost like he had plans to maim a few outlaws himself, if some ever came back.

Faithfully reproduced below is that article, from the very first issue of the Custer City Daily Truth.

City's Protectors Triumphant!

Under Attack!

Good citizens of Custer City! Yesterday evening, our fine peaceful City came under attack by men of evil intent. The brothers Prewitt, known in Southern States to be murderers most foul, rode upon our fair City intending to steal its bounties and riches; to murder and massacre ALL of our townsmen; to commit despoilment and depredations upon our innocent women.

Believing themselves unseen, these unwanted visitors, filthy and fetid, gained access to the Golden Nugget Saloon, and attempted to murder its honest new proprietors in their beds! But said proprietors are made of stern stuff — and sent a clear message that they, and this glittering City, are not to be trifled with.

After sneaking into the building with murderous intentions, these filthy blackguards evilly shot the honorable Mr. William Smith, who, although grievously wounded, returned fire, killing the Gang's villainous leader with a single shot through the dead center of his forehead.

The Prewitt Gang

Mr. Smith's business partners rushed from their beds to lend assistance, the result being the swift despatch to Hades of the other three members of the Prewitt Gang. The names of the visiting vermin were Isaac, Joseph, Thomas and William Prewitt — better known as Ike, Joe, Tom and Billy. All four bodies will be displayed today outside the Sheriff's Office, as a warning to any wrongdoer who harbors evil thoughts, and considers this town a suitable venue to put them to action.

—— No! ——

Custer City is home to men of strength and decency, men who will NOT tolerate such behaviors!

Doctor Nesbit Long treated Mr. Smith's wounds, and stated that this staunch defender of us all would make a full and timely recovery, and, in all other ways, displays robust good health.

The other heroes who gave their all to defend our fair City will be hereby named:

THE HEROES

Firstly, the esteemed *Mr. Samuel Silver* – an heroic veteran of multiple wars, and recipient of numerous medals in honor of his bravery.

Secondly, the well-respected *Mr. Curlicue Brown* – best known locally as a respected stagecoach guard, and believed to have killed more than thirty desperate men in defense of his passengers and cargo.

And thirdly, the widely famed and revered *Mr. Lyle Frakes* – one of the finest Lawmen ever to pin on a badge, and feared by outlaws of every stripe in all four States and Territories, he has worked to enforce and uphold the law for the good of the people.

When asked by this humble reporter whether he might consider offering his services as Sheriff to Custer City, the highly respected Mr. Frakes stated, "My days as a lawman are officially over, but I highly recommend this fair City offers that position to Mr. William Smith. I have been acquainted with him a good many years. His honesty and integrity are beyond reproach, while his bravery and shooting abilities far exceed those of ordinary men."

This humble reporter then asked Mr. Frakes just HOW we might improve our City, for the good of ALL residents.

The following thoughts were provided by the honorable Mr. Frakes: "I believe this City should vote in a Mayor when they vote for a Sheriff, the sort of man who will steer this City to greatness. If my own humble suggestion might be considered, I do hereby nominate my dear friend, Mr. Samuel Silver, for Mayor. A better man never drew a rifle from a scabbard, or a pen from an inkwell — and Sam loves this town almost as much as he does his horse."

Citizens of Custer City!

I beseech thee ... nay, I IMPLORE thee: Get behind these good men, and make our City the very best it can become — for ALL honest citizens!

---

1. ON THE DEAD: Free of charge
2. WAP: To throw (something) quickly and well

CHAPTER 22
"YOU WANNA DIE SLOW OR QUICK...?"

WELL, like I said before, that slang-whanger sure did know how to wap words.

By the time he got done with reading to us, I just about *believed* me and Big-Nose and Curly and Sam was upstanding fellers — not just that, but I woulda run right out to vote, if only there was a booth somewhere nearby to do so.

Big-Nose groaned — on account of his painful shot shoulder — and said, "Who or *what* the hell is a Curlicue? If you wanna know Curly's real name, you only got to—"

"You tell anyone my birth-given name," Curly said, "and I'll fire six more bullets through that same hole you already got open, *Mister* damn Smith."

"A curlicue," Pendleton proudly announced, "is an ornamental twist, a flourish, a decorative curl if you will. An example can be seen at each corner of this *quality* newspaper's pages." And he stabbed an ink-stained finger at one person's newspaper after another, making certain we all understood.

"There you go, Curly," I said. "I always heard you was twisted, but now you been officially declared ornamental."

"There's a first time for everything," said Sam, and most of us laughed, even Curly. Then Sam added, "This is all very well, telling the townsfolk we need a Mayor, but I ain't the man for the job, what the hell were you thinking?"

"You *are* the right man," said Doc Long. "And Mister Smith is the right man for Sheriff, I've thought on it deeply. Oh, I know Mister Smith's done some questionable things in the past — and you, Sam, you're the only man in town who's a worse drunk than me."

"High praise indeed," Curly said, then slurped down his coffee.

"When this newspaper gets around, and hard cases realize there's men in this town who will capably, willingly, stand up against them, they will go elsewhere to make trouble."

"Except them that don't," Big-Nose said. "Them ones'll come here and shoot first, then field questions after."

"I believe in this town," said Doc Long. "And I believe in *you*. Will you do this? Please."

Big-Nose shrugged his shoulders, then grimaced like he wished he hadn't. "Guess *Mister Smith* needs a job. I'll do it if ol' Silver Sam does. Is Silver really your last name?"

"A'course it ain't," said Sam. "But we got ourselves a newspaper feller who knows a good story beats facts, so who am I to argue?" Then he turned to Doc Long and said, "You do know Lyle ain't stayin' after today?"

"We've not sent these papers out yet," said the Doc. "But Nate has already typeset an announcement of an election, that we'll give out too, if you'll agree. Allow anyone to nominate for Sheriff or Mayor by tomorrow morning at eight, when we'll have the election. And if Lyle will stay just til then, I'm certain the town's future will be set."

"Up to you, Sam," I said. "I like the idea, and would pay real money just to see you dressed up like a citified[1] feller for the day."

"Oh, *please* do it, Mister Silver," little Mary Wilson piped up, and we all of us just about jumped at the sound of her high-pitched voice.

Sam grabbed at his chest with both hands, theatrical-like, and said, "I forgot you was here, little Mary. My heart just about stopped at the sound of your voice, I'm too old to be Mayor, don't you reckon?"

"I believe you would make the *finest* of possible Mayors, for I read somewhere that age begets wisdom. And Fred could become the town mascot — all good towns must have one, you know, and he is such a *handsome* old fellow."

"Handsome compared to his owner," said Curly, under his breath.

"Well, you all heard the little lady," said Sam, raising his coffee cup high. "Let's all drink to the new Custer City town mascot, the oldest horse in the Black Hills, and maybe the world. Must be *some* sorta record."

"And as for becoming the Mayor?" asked Pendleton hopefully.

"I'll do it, you four-eyed two-fisted do-goodin' slang-whanger — but only if you'll be my right hand, and help me behind the scenes."

"Whatever you need, Mister Silver," the newspaperman said, and his smile seemed ready to escape off his face, and stretch all the way to the walls. "Ah, together we shall make of this town a fine and upstanding place."

We drank a toast to it all — coffee or tea, and milk for Mary — then everyone went about their own tasks for the day.

The newspapers went out with the notice for Town Elections — a couple of town loafers were enlisted to help with delivering them.

"We must keep Mary away from the Sheriff's Office," Eula said once the others had left. "I wouldn't wish her to see such a terrible sight as those four dead Prewitts."

Considerate of her, it was. Even from within her own grief, she'd considered the child. I liked her a lot.

Right then came a knock on the front door. Too quiet, that knock, too uncertain.

Here we go again, was my first thought.

"Upstairs now," Curly barked, but Eula was already scurrying away 'fore he said it.

I pulled back the curtain an inch and looked out the window, expecting to see a whole gang of hard cases with guns drawn. Well, if they *was* hard cases, they was masters of disguise too.

It was two youngish fellers, each looking more like the other than he looked like himself. They was dressed up all fancy, with their hair all slicked back, and instead of guns, each carried a posy of *flowers* in their damn fool hands — they looked like a pair of identical and over-nervous *Bride-Grooms*.

I nodded an *okay* at Curly, and he strode to the door heavy footed and threw it wide open.

"Waddayouwant?" he snarled, wild-eyed, his huge hands curling up into fists.

By the looks on their over-clean faces, them two poor young fellers identically messed in their britches when Curly appeared.

One of 'em turned like to leave, but the other one grabbed him and stammered, "We ... we brought these flowers for you ... you—"

Curly unshucked his revolver and growled, "Flowers for *ME?* You wanna die slow or quick, you dang pair a'fools?"

"No," the other one shouted, throwing his hands in the air and dropping his flowers. "No, sir, Mister Curly, we're *Roy's* friends, don't you remember? The Kid, you called him The Kid. We only ... we only..."

"They're for *Eula*," the first one finally managed to say. "Not *you,* as in *you Mister Curly,* but *Eu-la.* Eula. And Alcie too. *Eula and Alcie,* is what I was *trying* to say. Aw, she's so pretty, Alcie, I reckon, and ... would it be alright if we—?"

"You best fix that stammer, son," Curly as he holstered his gun. "Or maybe go after a girl with a simpler name. I was fixin' to fill you with lead."

"Yessir," that feller said. "I don't usually stammer, I'm just nervy as a cat in a roomful of rockers, I'm sorry."

"Well," Curly said, waving them inside, "I remember you now. So, on account of you bein' good friends of The Kid, and me owing him for his help, I'll allow it this once. But if you think you're gonna wiggle your beans today, you got another think comin', you hear me? We're closed for business, and the whores all got the week off."

"Yessir, Mister Curly," said one as he came in and looked at the stairs, mighty fearful and shaky. "We ain't here for a poke, only to deliver these flowers, and say how sorry we are about Mister Darrow. The ladies looked mighty upset at the funeral. But maybe *you* could just give 'em the flowers instead, and we'll just be on our way and—"

"You do your own dirty work, son," Curly told him. "You sure you wish to court whores? You be honest now with me, or you know what'll happen."

"Yessir, we do," they both said together as a chorus.

Curly called the two women down, and though Eula looked shocked about it, she seemed to like it a little. But that Alcie, I'd bet a horse against a nail she weren't surprised even one bit. Played right up to *her* feller she did, even kissed him on the cheek 'fore he left — which was five minutes later, right after Curly growled something about not havin' time to play nursemaid to whores and foolish flower-fetchin' fellers.

That night I entrusted Eula to put Mary to bed by herself, and thusly escaped having to tell a bedtime story again. But with more than a week's travel ahead of us, I knew I'd best remember to buy a book from the mercantile before leaving Custer City tomorrow.

If I forgot, little Mary would be sore disappointed —

and having grown to like her, I did not want that. She had lived through unhappiness enough, and I would make certain her trip home to the orphanage was more-or-less pleasant — at least insofar as such hard travel can be.

---

1. CITIFIED: Someone affected by living in the city. (Usually in a negative way)

CHAPTER 23
LEAVING CUSTER CITY

THE ELECTION itself took on the air of a carnival — though just about the shortest carnival you ever saw. It threatened to rain early on, but before long the sun broke on through, and a crisp wind blew the clouds away somewhere else. Weren't nothing left in the air then but anticipation — and a'course the ever present smell of unwashed men, horses and whiskey.

Even though the Golden Nugget was officially closed for the week, that newspaper feller reckoned it the best place to hold an election — and none of us ordinary folk felt clever enough to argue.

His reasons seemed sound anyway. With it being the location of us *"protecting the town"* the previous night — and also where Joe Brand and Sheriff Grimes was got rid of a few days ago — the place seemed like a reminder that Brown, Smith, and Silver were the right men to take the town forward.

Guess it didn't hurt neither, that every man who voted was to be given two free drinks right after — courtesy of the new owners of the saloon, as a sign of good faith.

And too, there seemed much curiosity in regard to the *exact* place in the room where the famous Fleet Darrow had died. Not so surprising, I guess, him seeming like one a'them fellers who might live forever, on account of his speed — but also, there was *something* about him, made him seem somehow *more* than most ordinary men.

Wish I'd known him better, I guess — but our work took us different places. And at least I never butted heads against him. Truth is, if Fleet Darrow's guns had ever asked me the question, I'd have lacked for a satisfactory answer.

In fact, they had set up the booth right on the exact spot Fleet Darrow died. Sign of respect, just for one thing.

Right beside the voting booth, Ol' Silver Sam sure looked a sight. He was dressed up fit to be President, having borrowed Nate Pendleton's spare suit, a snappy brown number with thinner stripes than his main one — pin-stripes, he said they was called. Problem with that suit was, the slang-whanging profession mostly involves a whole lot too much sitting down, so the newspaperman's rear end and belly was a lot more generous-sized than ol' Sam's.

First time Sam put on those duds, they fell right on down to his ankles — the doves all laughed fit to bust, and reckoned Fleet Darrow woulda called it a *"fine entertainment."*

I suggested Sam borrow some gallowses[1], but was roundly shouted down and accused of crimes against fashion — well, if *fashion* means dressing with no regard for plain common sense, I'm happy to go through life in my comfortable duds, and keep up my ignorant ways.

Sam had to explain to Nate Pendleton that gallowses was just a much better word for suspenders. The newspaperman wrote the word down with a pencil, and asked Sam if he knew some more good ones.

While Sam taught Pendleton some other fine words, the wag-tail called Alcie took up a needle and thread to sew some tucks in the trousers so they wouldn't fall down.

Well, it turned out that *she* was no tailor.

She accidentally stuck Sam with a needle, in a place I shall only describe as *unfortunate* — at which point the town's soon-to-be-Mayor let out a curse word that seemed pretty fitting, considering what Alcie's usual work was.

Pendleton wrote *that* word down too, and twice underlined it, I noticed. Guess there's more than one type of education, and he was getting a type they never did teach at his big-city University.

Once the election got going, Big-Nose — *I gotta stop calling him that, as I mean Mister Smith* — made for a fine sight. His shoulder was all bandaged, a little blood showed through the dressings, and over the top he wore only an oversized vest, and that wasn't buttoned. He never was much for height, but his muscles showed off to advantage in only that vest — and what with him being so hairy, he looked more akin to a bear than an ordinary man.

Had the rightful appearance of a Sheriff he did, much more so than the two stretched-out cowhands who put themselves forward to run for the position against him.

As for myself, I had only the smallest of miseries to

contend with, so I guess I should not complain. Still, man is a complaining sorta animal, so I might's well spread it out here now so's I can forget it.

Oh, they allowed me to wear my usual clothing — not like they coulda made me wear different if they tried anyway — then proceeded to show me off like a prize bull at a fair, right between Sam and Big-Nose, next to the voting booth.

Doc Long reckoned it useful for folks to see me in attendance, what with my reputation for doing what's right. He said it'd help sway folks to vote for 'Mister Smith' and 'Samuel Silver' — even though the first was rumored to be a Wanted outlaw, and the other well known to be the best consumer of whiskey in the entire Territory.

Worst part was what they made me say. "A vote for *Smith and Silver is a vote for the future of us all. I, Lyle Frakes, strongly endorse both these men.*"

It was not that I didn't believe it — I did. And the words weren't actually stupid — they had sounded just fine from Nate Pendleton's jaws. Problem was that the words didn't fit with my regular speaking — sounded like a damn fool when I said 'em, which musta been near to two-hundred times.

My grandpa once told me, 'Any man worth his salt will sound like a fool a hundred times, if he lives long enough. Best men, a thousand times maybe. You just be truthful, young Lyle, and never mind what other fools think, we all gets our turn.'

I miss Grandpa, and I hope he'd be proud. I still do my best to please him, even though he's long gone.

Two local storekeepers ran against Sam for Mayor —
but the vote was a foregone conclusion, Doc Long
reckoned, and he got it correct.

Voting went from 8am to 10am, then they tallied the
votes while the nominees all watched on. Some folk went
home right after they voted, but most hung about in the
street to hear the result — and at 10.15am, Nate Pendleton
made the announcement.

"I humbly present your new Mayor, the esteemed
Samuel Silver," he announced good and loud from the
boardwalk, and lifted Sam's hand in the air with his own.
Then he tried to do the same with Big-Nose's hand as he
said, "And Sheriff William Smith!"

Poor Nate Pendleton had forgot about Big-Nose's
wounds, and when he tried to lift up his arm — it having a
powerfully painful effect on Big-Nose's shot shoulder — I
thought the new Sheriff's first official act might be to shoot
the town's newspaperman.

Well, it was lucky he didn't — turned out Nate *"Pear-
Shape"* Pendleton was a real good feller, and would do
more good deeds for the town in the years up ahead.

Me and Mary Wilson slipped away a short little while
after that. We had said our goodbyes over breakfast, and
they never was my favorite thing. Well, friends is friends
and goodbyes is goodbyes, and I'd had some that tore me a
little already in Deadwood.

Friends is easy enough, and so is goodbyes — it's the
mixing of 'em together that makes for the difficulty of
feelings.

Last thing, as we rode out, it was just Silver Sam and Eula who waved us away.

"Your hair looks so pretty," Eula said as we started to leave. I could not see Mary's hair, it being under her hat, but I figured Eula hadn't been talking to me.

"Thank you for the lovely ribbons," Mary replied, her face beaming.

Sam and Eula looked half-happy, half-sad, and half like they might jump on ol' Fred and come along with us.

Fred wouldn't have stood for it though, and was anyways not in attendance — he had sneaked back inside the saloon, having worked out how to unlatch the back door by himself.

"I'll come visit when I grow up," Mary Wilson called to them from atop her neat-stepping pony. She sure looked the part too, with her riding boots and new clothes, and the best white hat you ever saw, the right size for her head and all of that hair, with a chin-strap to keep it from blowing away in high winds.

The wind was gusting by then, making it difficult for my old ears to hear what Eula called out. But I guess Mary's hearing must be better than mine, for she answered, "It's alright, Miss Eula, he'll improve once he gets some practice."

Then my old friend, *'Mayor Silver Sam Silver,'* put his arm around the dove's shoulders in a fatherly manner — and they waved til we went out of sight. And that's how we recommenced our journey, the richer for friends and experience.

1. GALLOWSES: Suspenders or braces. The sort that stop your pants falling down!

CHAPTER 24
"BEST MAGGOTS 'TWEEN CHEYENNE AND DEADWOOD..."

THE FIRST DAY'S travel was sure to be easy — all downhill, and most of that gently sloped. Perfect terrain for old men and old horses, and good for training young girls to ride better too.

It was a wonder, that little horse Mary rode — if I ever saw Wally Davis again, I would shake his hand in congratulations.

Hell, maybe I'll even write him, just to tell him what he already knows — that he is a Master of Horsemen. Should be an award for that, given out by the President maybe. Problem is, they might then decide to put it to a vote, and force some fellers to say things that make 'em sound foolish. Might keep that idea under my hat, just in case it goes wrong.

The traveling was quiet, just how I mostly prefer it. I wondered if a cat mighta got Mary's tongue, but I realized then she was concentrating hard on learning to ride the horse better.

To my surprise, I found myself missing her usual yammering. *First time for everything, maybe.*

She didn't even speak to Princess Rosebottom, or whatever that rag doll was called. It was tied to the saddlehorn on Mary's insistence — looking forward, so it could *see the sights* as we rode along — instead of traveling inside a bag on the packhorse where it shoulda been.

Me and Mary spoke now and then, but only a very few words. And even those only when I gave her tips or encouragement on riding technique — or to warn her to keep away from the edge of the trail some places, and how to spot such dangers for herself.

There was considerable more perils and pitfalls about than I realized — I guess, when you've been around long as I have, you tend to take such dangerments[1] for granted, and I trust Horse to steer us right too.

After a solid hour's travel — during which we'd got in a good average of trotting, walking and loping along nice and easy — we came to a particular pretty part of the journey. It was a spot where a girl with good eyes could see many miles off to the east and the south — and each of those miles a dazzlement in its own right.

"Oh, my," she said as we rode round the bend in the trail and that place just appeared, like a gift from the Heavens. "Oh, Mister Lyle, it's beautiful. *Look,* Dewdrop! *Look,* Princess Mayblossom! Oh, Pale-Eye Champion Blaze and dear Swayback Lightning, do you *see* it?"

As I came to a halt and stepped down off of Horse, I said, "Mary. You might wanna cut short a few a'them names. If you don't, you're gonna run outta breath before we get far as Robbers Roost Station."

We stopped about every hour and took a good rest, stretched our legs some and kept water up to ourselves. Came to S & G Ranch well before dark, where we ate a good meal and slept in proper warm beds.

If I'd had any worries on Mary's ability to stay atop that horse at a gallop, I'd have stayed an extra day in Custer City to make certain of it — the second day's trip from S & G Ranch to Robbers Roost was a notorious stretch for road agents and wayward Injuns, and we might have to ride at a gallop some point in that trip.

But with Mary being a natural born-and-bred little horsewoman, I had no such worries at all — still, I adjusted my thinking overnight anyway, and we waited at S & G for two hours after daylight, for the south-bound stage to arrive.

Turned out there was four vacant seats — so while they swapped out their horses for fresh ones we loaded our gear and saddles atop, tied *our* three horses to the back of the stage, paid our fare to Robbers Roost, and traveled in what the stagecoach company calls "comfort."

Well, I reckon their meaning of *comfort* is different to mine — but at least it got us there quick, and with less effort. And best of all, there was none of the usual strife with folks meaning to rob us or kill us or worse.

The twenty-five miles to Robbers Roost at that pace, woulda been impossible hard on our animals if they'd had our weight on them, and the packhorse too would have struggled. Lotta mud and wide creeks through that section makes it hard work for horses carrying loads — same things as what make it a prime spot for men with evil intent to get *their* work done.

But the mud weren't too bad on the day, and even old Horse done it easy, arriving at the Roost fresh as a daisy unpicked.

I knew the hostler there to be good at his job, and sought his opinion on whether to risk further travel or stay there the night. I figured Mary would be bored by our talk, but her ears was just about pricked up with listening, and it seemed like if it was about horses, she wanted to learn.

Hostler proclaimed all three horses still hearty as bucks. "With a good feed of my special mix in their bellies, you can leave in two hours and make the next swing station in plenty of time before dark, even at walking pace. Problem then is, that feller might try to feed you."

"Ah," I replied. "Forgot about him. The feller with the fornent[2] sign?"

"Fornent is the word alright," he said, running a hand down Gray's shoulder, as he double-checked him for soundness, absentminded-like. "That sign a'Skinny Simpson's is about the most opposite sign to the truth between here and Mexico."

I pictured the sign in my mind and said, "Best Grub Between Cheyenne and Deadwood."

"That's it for a word," said the hostler, then chuckled at a stray thought he'd had.

"Could use a good laugh myself," I said, brushing a fly away from my shoulder. "Long as it's repeatable in front of the child?"

"The little lady might enjoy it too — and she's lucky enough not to have ate there, I hope. You heard about that feller done the world a solid, killed Joe Brand up in Custer?"

"Heard all about it," I said, and Mary just nodded.

"On the way up to Custer, the stage made a stop there for food. That young feller — Roy he went by — he walked in, sniffed the food, called it muck."

"Got that right," I said.

"Well, Skinny starts to say it's the best grub around, and that Roy feller says it must be, on account of how there's real grubs in it, and most of 'em maggots. Then he looks in the stew and says, *'Didn't know maggots could swim, but these ones is champions at it, just look at 'em go.'* Well, ol' Skinny ain't lived it down, folks is all callin' him Maggot now, and someone painted his sign so it says *Best Maggots 'tween Cheyenne and Deadwood.'*"

We had a good chuckle about it, then I asked Mary if she'd like maggots for her meal tonight. She screwed her nose up and said maggots sounded just about opposite to scrumptious. Then the hostler told us his wife had prepared some bear soup, and it being second day since the cooking, it was all-fired good.

"Could send you along with some a'that, and you heat it yourself, and stay right off Skinny's food. His beds is bad too. Bedbugs again, so they reckon. But sleep in his barn with your own soogans, and you won't go too far wrong."

He asked me then to verify the truth about what went down in Custer this past two days — turned out, for a change, the rumors were mostly the truth. I did have to set

him straight on how many Prewitts we'd killed though —
they had somehow doubled in number, the story having
grown to include their six Prewitt cousins, who, far as I
knew, were down in Texas somewhere.

But facts is facts, and scuttlebutt's scuttlebutt, and it's
just in the nature of stories that they grow in the telling.

---

1. DANGERMENTS: Things that are dangerous
2. FORNENT: Opposite to

CHAPTER 25
BEAR STEW

FTER WE ATE, I took a quick early afternoon snooze, then we went on our way, leaving Robbers Roost and its inhabitants behind us.

The weather was mild, and we took it slow and easy, the dozen or so miles to the swing station. I knew of a good little spot just off the trail, only a mile or so before the swing station itself — we stopped there awhile, made ourselves about a hatful of fire, and used it to warm the bear stew. I put a portion in a bowl for the child, and started in on my own, direct from the pan.

Mary only prodded at it with her spoon to begin with, and sent it for a trip from one side of the bowl to the other. Then she swapped her spoon to her other hand, and sent it on another journey, right back to the side where it started. Put me off my own stew for about half a moment, almost.

"Mighty fine food, bear stew," I told her. "Grow up big strong and brave if you eat enough of it."

"Its *aroma* is scrumptious," she conceded. "But I've

never eaten bear before, and it seems ... I don't know ... uncivilized somehow."

"Reckon the bear would agree," I said. "But Mary, you'll need to give new things a try on this journey, or you're gonna go hungry. And we sure don't want that."

"But *bear,* Mister Lyle!"

"Well," I said, putting mine down and extending my hands toward her, "give yours to me, and you can take your chances with the maggot stew when we get where we're going, alright?"

Funny how quick a nine-year-old changes its mind at the mention of maggots.

We cleaned our plates pretty quick after that, with not much actual talk, only sounds of *"gastronomic appreciation."*

At least that's what *she* said they were.

When I asked her how she knew so many ten-dollar words, she looked entirely stricken for a moment, but she covered it up so quick you'd a'missed it if you blinked.

Then she said, "My parents were determined that I should have every advantage in life they'd missed out on. We had little money, but our home contained many books. But when they were murdered..."

She seemed disinclined to speak no more on it, jumping up then and setting about packing up. I didn't push the subject no further.

We got ourselves back on the trail and, riding in silence, quickly made it to Skinny Simpson's swing station.

To little Mary's delight, the one sign out the front read

just what we'd been told it did — *Best Maggots Between Cheyenne and Deadwood.*

I thought she might *never* stop laughing, and that got me laughing too. She only laughed it up all the more when Skinny himself came outside to see what the ruckus was about.

I never noticed before — to the full extent anyways — what a comical sight Skinny made for. He was half a foot more than six, with lank hair and a buzzard-like beak — when you coupled that with how he walked, he seemed more like a oversized insect than a real human feller.

Thought Mary might fall from her pony, way she threw herself this way and that. But the joy of her childish laughter was a treat for the ears, as I stepped down from Horse.

Skinny weren't none too happy, I could tell by the face he pulled looking even more squinty and pinched out than normal — but he knew who I was, and only said, "Some fool painted my sign with that slander — one a'them filthy Celestials[1] I wouldn't reckon — and I ain't yet had time to fix it."

Ain't yet had time to fix *most* things, by the look of the place, was my first thought — and Chinese seemed unlikely culprits, the changed word being spelled out in perfect English, was the next thought I had.

Always blaming someone else for his problems — most usually Chinese or Injuns or negroes — but from what I can see, he brings most of his troubles on himself.

Riled me some, was the truth. But Skinny had troubles enough with just being Skinny, so I only said, "We already ate, and we're tired from our journey. We'll go direct to the barn, care for our own horses and sleep there with them."

"But I gots to make a living," he whined, "and who the hell are *you* to deprive a man of...?"

His voice trailed off then and he sorta looked at the ground, kicked at a rock that weren't there. Mary stopped laughing then, perhaps sensing danger, the way Skinny had.

But I'm a reasonable man, and I saw his point. "That's fine, Skinny, don't worry. I'll pay you just the same money as if you fed us and we slept inside."

"Oh, thank you, Mister Frakes, sir," he said. "That's real white of you, you just go round back, and you have a real nice night, sir, a *real* nice night."

I have never liked that expression, and it didn't sound no better coming out of the mouth of a man who most likely *did* have bugs in his beds and grubs in his stew.

"Simpson," I said, my voice all a'growl —perhaps 'cause I'd just eaten bear — "I've met men of all colors and stripes in my time, and there's bad ones of *every* color, white fellers included."

"Yessir," he said, his fear run so rampant it pinched up his face, as he nodded fifteen to the dozen.

I let go Horse's reins and walked over to Skinny, then looked hard in his eyes for every long moment I spoke.

"Men mostly start out okay, then some run to bad, and that's just how it is, Skinny — but it always seemed to me like us *whites* turned bad with least excuse. It was mostly all white men I had trouble with as a Sheriff. And this past few days, I've had nine *different* white men tryin' to kill me with guns, and now they's all *dead,* every one. You see how all that gives me a problem, don't you now, Skinny?"

He shrunk away from my gaze as he managed to say, "Yessir, Mister Frakes, yes I do."

"So when you call me *white* in such manner, I could easy take that like an insult, if you see what I'm saying."

"Yessir, Mister Frakes, sir. I mean nosir, I didn't mean—"

"Skinny," I said, brushing some dirt off his collar and smiling the most unfriendly smile I knew. "Just for me, you're gonna stop using that damnable expression, and any other ones like it."

"Yessir."

"And you're gonna treat all men equal, until they give you good reason to do any different. And if I hear you done otherwise, I'm gonna come back for a visit, and you and me gonna discuss it. First with fists, then with guns. You got that straight now?"

"Yessir, Mister Frakes, sir, I do."

"I'll see you in the morning for coffee then, Skinny. And make sure to use the Arbuckles, not that swill you served last I was here. And wash your damn hands 'fore you make it — I'll be checkin' your fingernails too."

---

1. CELESTIALS: A common 19th Century term for Chinese folk

CHAPTER 26
A STORY HALF-TOLD

ONE THING I will say for Skinny — he never skimped on providing the proper feeding, care and attention for horses. That barn was home to everything a horseman might need to keep his equine companions in tiptop condition.

We took full advantage of the feed and equipment, and by the time we bedded our three horses down on soft straw, they all looked happy as bankers with their snouts in another man's trough.

We laid out our soogans and set up our saddles for pillows, just about the same time the rain started to pelt on the roof. Not only had we put a smart sprinkle of miles behind us today, but we had beat the weather all ends up.

"I'm glad we're sleeping out here," Mary said. "It's nice to be near the horses. Nicer than with those bitey old bedbugs inside. We had those at the orphanage once — nobody could sleep for a week, and they had to *burn* all the blankets!"

"Mmmm," was all the noise I made. Having to speak harsh to Skinny had frazzled my senses, and I hoped to avoid further talk and get off to sleep.

I blew out the lamp, closed my eyes, listened to the nice sound of the rain — nicer for having a good roof between us and it.

We was cozy in our own-made warm beds, in a perfect dry barn with no leaks, a tasty bear stew in our bellies, the healthy smell of horses and good feed all around us, and I reckon there never was a moment I'd felt so content.

Such moments of contentment have a habit of not lasting long — and this one now proved no different.

"Mister Lyle," said Mary, her voice not quite so sleepy as you'd expect, after all a'that travel. "Could you tell me a bedtime story now? Please?"

"Aw, dammit," I growled at myself — *still growling, I noticed, definitely from eating that bear* — before adding, "I meant to buy a book of tales 'fore we left Custer City, but I just kept forgetting. Must be gettin' old quicker'n I thought."

From two yards away to my left, she laughed the sleepy laugh of a child and said, "Your hearing's not the best either, I fancy."

For a moment I wondered what she'd heard, and thought maybe some sound had warned her of danger — my hand went to Gertrude beside me in the dark — but there had been nothing urgent in Mary's voice. So I let the old gun get its rest, laid back and answered in kind. "Did I mishear something, Mary?"

"When we left Custer City, and our friend Miss Eula

called out, you did not hear what she said, did you, Mister Lyle?"

"Something about a horse, weren't it?"

"She remembered as we were leaving, that you'd forgotten to buy us a storybook for our journey. She was calling us back to go get one."

"Double-dammit," I growled — *gotta stop eating bear* — then apologized on both counts, the cussing *and* the forgetting.

"Just make up a story," she said. "I'm certain you can, you're *ever* so clever."

"Mary," I said. "Clever ain't a thing I've been much accused of — and I been accused of a great many things in my time. I'm sorry, but I can't remember no stories fit for a young girl to hear."

"What about that lady you dreamed of, Lady Georgina? Or is she a Princess?" She sighed then, a deep one, contented, then added, "Yes, Princess Georgina. Oh, what a beautiful name."

I don't admit to much, feelings-wise — but if I did, I'd admit them words hurt me, punched me in my already sore heart some.

"Aw, Mary," I said, my voice thinner'n normal. "That was all just a dream, I can't think up stories from no-place like some—"

"Please, Mister Lyle, I can't get to sleep without hearing a story, and Eula's not here, and my mother..." I heard her choke on her voice then, but just as I went to say something she started speaking again. "It's not for me really, it's for dear Princess Mayblossom, you see?"

"For the doll?"

"Yes, but you must use her name, it upsets her when people don't."

"Alright, I'll use her name, but I can't tell a—"

"When she was a *little* doll, her mother *always* told her a story. And she misses her mother *terribly*, you see, Mister Lyle? Do *you* have a mother somewhere? I just bet she's pretty."

It was dark as pitch in that barn, and yet somehow, I knew the exact hopeful look on her kind little face, and the sadness and heartbreak behind it just about broke me. A fond memory came to me then — my own mother of course, by the dim light of a candle, reading a story to me from a book.

I swallowed the damn lump in my throat and said, "Well, don't expect too much, Mary, I'll have to invent it — and I always did lack imagination, along with all the other sorts of brains mostly granted to men."

"Oh, thank you," she said. "Can it be about Princess Georgina? Please? I just *know* she's special, and worth telling stories about."

I had spent half the quieter minutes of my life trying NOT to think of Georgina — in the early days, I had often liked to think of her. But after a year she got married to Bid, and that was the end of the hopeful dreams and thoughts I'd built up in my mind. It was different since then — but thoughts is thoughts, and...

"Mister Lyle? Did you fall asleep?"

"No, Mary. I was just trying to think up a story."

The image of Georgina filled up my whole mind, every

bit of it, corner to corner — not Georgina back then, but how
she looked now. Her long silver hair, like a waterfall under
the moonlight.

I heard Mary grow restless again, and I said, "Alright,
I'll do my best then — but it ain't about no princess called
Georgina, it's about—"

"But it *is* about a princess, *isn't* it?"

"Alright, yes. The Silver Princess," I heard myself say,
and that beautiful damn silver hair was all I could think of.
But thinkin' is thinkin', and stories is stories, and I guess
stories sometimes run free, take on a life of their own,
getting started without no one's help — at least that's how
this one seemed to go.

"There once was a silver-haired princess, the most
beautiful princess in all the states and the territories and
countries in the world. So beautiful she was, that birds sung
her praises in the mornings, and even horses couldn't barely
stand to look at her, knowing she was even more
beautifuller than they were."

"She must have been *very* beautiful, if Pale-Eye
Champion Blaze thought that way about her."

"He did," I said. "Or rather, he would have if he ever
met her, a'course."

"Of course. But *can't* he have met her? Just for the sake
of the story?"

"Yes, alright then, he did. Now Pale-Eye Blaze was
young then—"

"Pale-Eye *Champion* Blaze, don't you mean?"

"Yes, yes that's who it was, Pale-Eye Champion Blaze.
He was young, Horse was then, but even back then he was

clever enough to see *she* was the most wonderful, perfect princess he ever would meet. This was before *I* knew him, you understand — but he told me the story one lonely night on the trail, down New Mexico way."

"I just *knew* he could talk. But what *happened?* In the story, I mean?"

"Well, weren't much to tell, Mary. There was an awful lotta fellers who carried a torch for the princess. But she reckoned some a'them fellers too old, some too foolish — one she ruled out on account of him being a terrible drunk with a price on his head, even though he was almost as handsome as Pale-Eye Blaze."

"Pale-Eye *Champion* Blaze."

"Him too. Both of 'em. But there was two fellers she liked the best, and they was the best friends anyone ever saw. One was a happified[1] feller who everyone liked — handsome as well, I suppose, but not nearly so handsome as a horse. Prosperous feller he was, had all sorts of ideas and schemes, and folks liked to help him achieve them. Brought a three-by-nine smile[2] to your face, when he allowed you to help him with things, he was that nice a'feller."

"What was *his* name?"

"His name was Bid..." *What the hell are you doin', Lyle?,* I thought, and quickly coughed a fake one before going on. "His name was Biddaboo Bedbug."

"Oh, it *wasn't!*"

"Oh yes it was," I said, pleased to hear Mary laugh so. "Now young Biddaboo Bedbug was a real fine one for the ladies. Knew just how to sweet-talk 'em, see? And while he was fond of the princess—"

"The *Silver* Princess — you have to say it right every time, or it's not a proper story, Mister Lyle."

"Alright, the Silver Princess then. So young Biddaboo Bedbug was fond of the princess, but hell, he was fond of maybe ten other two-legged fillies as well, and didn't treat the princess none special. And Biddaboo, he had a friend—"

"A *best friend,* you said so before. I wish *I* could have a best friend."

"You will one day soon, Mary, I'm certain of it. So Biddaboo Bedbug had a *best* friend, and while he was a good faithful friend, he had little else to recommend him — at least to the ladies, would be my main meaning. He was shy around them, you see? Most especially he was *frightful* shy when the Silver Princess was nearby. It seemed to him like that princess quite liked him, but he never could figure out why. And the more she seemed to like him, the more tied up his tongue got when he was around her."

"Oh, that's *ever* so romantic," Mary said, her voice more running to sleep now than it was before. "And did the shy boy ... what was his name though, you left that part out?"

"Kit," I said without thinking, then covered it up with a cough again, before saying, "Kitten Fluff-Hair."

She giggled softly at the name, and said, "Did Kitten Fluff-Hair get over his shyness and *marry* the Silver Princess?"

Then she yawned fit to wake all the horses, and I said, "Tell you what, Miss Mary Wilson. We got more than a week left of travel to Cheyenne. How's about we leave some hay in the feedbag, and finish this story tomorrow, when we ain't quite so tired?"

"That will be lovely, Mister Lyle," she said. "And Princess Mayblossom agrees. And we *do* hope dear Kitten Fluff-Hair will marry the lovely Silver Princess. But not right away of course. First, they must have adventures, and *then* he must save her!"

"You sleep tight now, Mary. We might even snooze the morning away if the rain don't ease up — first hour or two of it, anyways. Pale-Eye Blaze don't much like the wet now he's old."

A half-minute later I added, "Goodnight, girl." But she was already dreaming.

---

1. HAPPIFIED: to be made happy, of course (JVJ has been uglified by the years, but happified by having survived them)
2. THREE-BY-NINE SMILE: A mighty big smile (named for the big piece of lumber that size, used in many fine Old West buildings)

CHAPTER 27
SOAP

THERE ALWAYS WAS something about rain on the roof helped me sleep, and this time was no different. You'd reckon folks would sleep easier as they get older, but it seems to go mostly opposite to the logic of that. But that rain musta fell through most of the night, for I even slept right through my dreams if I had some, and did not stir until daybreak.

I opened up the barn, looked out and liked what I saw. The rain had recently stopped, a dim light broke through the clouds, and I heard the birds singing a perfect day into existence.

"Good weather for travel, Horse," I said. "Nice soft ground, just how you like it, and no rain to dampen our spirits."

Mary too was in high spirits, she informed me, and so was Princess Mayblossom. We decided to risk the lowering of them, and ventured inside to check the cleanliness of Skinny's hands, and maybe partake of his coffee.

It was pleasing to notice the Arbuckles aroma right off — Arbuckles is Arbuckles, and muck is muck, and Skinny was ever a feller who'd serve up the latter if he thought he'd get away with it.

But strangely, the smell of good coffee was just the beginning.

Suffice to say ol' Skinny seemed like a new man. Not only was his fingernails mostly empty of grime, it seemed he had taken my comments to heart, and turned over a whole new leaf.

Funny damn saying that. New leaf. Way Skinny changed, he maybe turned over the whole tree.

His skin was rubbed just about raw, his usually lank hair was shining, and I do believe he had even brushed clean his tombstones[1], which he regularly displayed with an almost permanent smile.

Ordinarily, I would rather have trod on a snake than go near Skinny's food. But what with him being so clean — and his usually greasy plates sparkling up at us from a freshly scrubbed table — we accepted his offer of bacon, and it weren't too bad.

Not good.

But not bad.

"I was up all night cleaning, Mister Frakes," he announced. "And you know, it feels *good* to take pride in the place. Just look how them forks and spoons gleam, and the plates and the tables and everything else, good as new ones. When I ran outta things to wash, I was havin' me such a fine time, I started in on *myself* — and you know what I found?"

"That water don't pain a man quite like you figured? And that it can be heated for purposes other than coffee?"

"Well, yes, I suppose, Mister Frakes," he said, looking some sheepish. "But also, that I quite *liked* the smell of the soap, if you can believe it. Reckon I might bathe on the regular, twice a week, maybe more."

"Folks are happy to pay for a bath, Skinny. And if you had a steaming tub ready, you could charge a premium too. And if the water went unused, why, you might treat yourself to a bath every day, just about. I heard it never killed a man yet, a hot bath."

His eyes widened as his mind boggled some at the thought — so we left him with it and went for a stroll to settle our breakfast.

We departed the place an hour after daylight, waving goodbye to Skinny, who waved back at us with his paintbrush. He had already painted over his *Best Maggots* sign, and was now applying the words *Clean Food and Beds* to it instead. No *Hot Baths* sign yet, but a start's a beginning, more-or-less.

Mary Wilson turned back around. "Do you think he'll keep up his newfound clean habits, Mister Lyle?"

"I've seen men change now and again," I replied. "But mostly they wake up a day or a week or a month maybe later, and find they turned back into themselves while they slept. Let's hope he makes parts of it stick. If he don't, some feller less tolerant than me's gonna put poor Skinny in the ground one a'these days — and maybe just over bad coffee."

We made good time on the better-drained parts of the trail, and took things easy where it was heavy with mud.

The problem we faced for today, was how far we should travel. I mulled it over this way and that, and in the end figured to let time decide for itself.

Not the sharpest choice I ever made.

From Skinny's place to Old Woman Station was close enough thirty-five miles — just me and Horse, years gone by, coulda walked that far backwards in a day, and got there in time to cook dinner before it got dark. These days, not so easy — and less so with a young girl to care for.

We rode without incident the first sixteen miles to the next swing station, and I considered calling it a day. But we were all feeling good, and I knew there was comfortable beds and good food at Old Woman Station. The soft ground went easy on Horse, the skies were mostly clear, and Mary was game — eager even — to ride twenty more miles.

The next seven miles went easy. Then as we rode over a crest I looked skyward, and it seemed like every cloud had been chased away somewhere else, leaving nothing above us but blue.

"I don't like the look a'that sky," I said.

Mary took off her hat, looked up above her and said, "But it's perfectly clear, Mister Lyle."

"Weather-breeder maybe," I said. "Sometimes up this way, the sky going so sudden clear means heavy rain soon to come. Nothing much we can do but keep on and hope it ain't so. Can't speed up to beat it though, the horses are nearing their limits. My fault — we should not have slept in."

Within the hour, my suspicions had proved out correct. Rainclouds commenced to blow in, and it looked a bad one. Reckoned we'd have only twenty-some minutes before it would hit, and hit hard. And with Old Woman Station still eight miles off, we needed to hunker down right away.

A couple more minutes onward, I found a place that would do us. Not just through a storm, but for the whole night if need be. There was a small creek just a few yards away, but no chance of it flooding too deep, way the lay of the land was. The little cave above it was no palace — only a few feet deep — but it was well hidden, and would be enough to keep both ourselves and all our gear dry.

The roof had seen plenty of smoke through hundreds of years, but none of it recent. Important point in its favor, that was — last thing we needed was to be in some Injun's spot when he got there to shelter.

"Look, Mister Lyle," she said brightly. "It's a little stack of wood, enough for a fire, so we won't have to gather any more."

"Enough wood for tonight," I agreed, kicking the edge of the years-old pile. "But if you want more than jerky for breakfast, you might think ahead, and gather some now. I'll leave the decidin' to you."

I quickly unsaddled the horses and packs, set up a makeshift camp while Mary gathered wood for the next morning's fire.

Tonight it would only be bacon and beans, but at least it'd be good and hot — and too, there would be Arbuckles to drink.

J.V. JAMES

Sometimes, on the trail, you just gotta be happy with whatever small mercies you got. And a bellyful of warm food can be sort of a comfort, 'fore the next thing goes wrong.

———————————————

1. TOMBSTONES: Teeth. (Just look at 'em!)

CHAPTER 28

MY SORTA RAIN

THAT STORM that blew in was more of a huffer and puffer, rather than actually brutal. Still, it weren't exactly *gentle* by nature — as storms go I'd rate it maybe somewhere 'bout middlin' to mean. Woulda been no fit place for man, beast or child, to be out in it unsheltered.

Mary had done herself proud, got the fire crackling along all alone, while I took care of the horses. It was a fine fire too — quick learner she was, and a willing little worker when she didn't waste all her time gabbing[1].

She already had the bacon in the pan by the time the rain started to pelt, and we were mightily grateful for our little shelter — all the more for how it smelled as our meal started to sizzle.

I tried to take over the cooking, but the child waved me away, while trying to make herself heard over the fierce melodious sound of the rain. Couldn't quite make out her words, but it was something to the effect that she could cook better than I.

Well, I was happy to let her attempt it. I can burn food good enough so it don't kill me, but that's about near my limit. A man should know his limits I reckon, and as limits go, cooking's one of my most severest.

Happily, it turned out the child was right to back her abilities. She had done a little shopping of her own at the Custer City mercantile, and had brought with her three small tins of different spices. I watched her retrieve them from her pack, pinch a small amount from one tin onto the beans, then sprinkle a picayune[2] of another onto the bacon as it cooked.

She was a brown study[3] of concentration the whole time she cooked. Made for a real sight too in her fancy new clothes — with her long braided hair all hidden away 'neath her hat, she could almost have seemed like a boy, so serious was the set of her face. But then, when the food was almost ready, she looked up from the fire, turned toward me and smiled that great glowing smile that woulda warmed any man's heart.

Made me wish I'd had a child of my own, right in that moment — but that thought dumped its own dark cloud on me, so I jumped up and readied myself to hold out the plates while she served up the food.

Well, whatever them spices were, that child was right — she cooked a dang sight better'n I do, perhaps even as good as Georgina.

Stop thinkin' of her, Lyle, you've left them to it for the very last time. I just hope she and Bid will get by alright without me.

I have always found something lovely about an abundance of rain. To be clear, I mean when it comes down hard for a short while — not when it drizzles incessantly day after day, like some old wastrel who hangs about a saloon, and never stops his complaining.

But this was my sorta rain, singing its tune all around us, filling our ears with its perfectly powerful sound. Has a way of shutting out the world, rain like this — and wrapping you close in its arms, if you see what I mean, and you also feel such comfort.

And the truth was — even though I mostly enjoy Mary's nattering — I was happy for the peaceful quietude enforced upon us by that insistent, inarguable rain.

We ate in silence, and we washed up in silence. And even when the rain slowed to a pretty pit-patter, we sat silently there in our cave, looking out at the wonderful world we found ourselves in, and we breathed it inside us, I guess.

It was the sort of evening to make a man believe that maybe, just maybe, the Lord God *did* care about us folks after all. Then again, it was just the sort of evening some fool pretend Preacher woulda ruined by breaking the silence — but the nine-year-old Mary Wilson had the wisdom not to spoil things with meaningless talk.

We breathed in the sweet fragrant air, watched the glistening rivulets of water run down to join the turbulent creek, and we let our eyes soften along with the light of the day as it faded, gently, gently to dusk.

Our little fire still crackled a little, and by its glow I saw Mary smile contentedly at me.

"Time for sleep," I said. "You're a fine cook, Mary Wilson. A *real* fine cook."

Her face lit up at the compliment, and she tried to thank me for it, but a yawn took her over completely, which set her to giggling. She took off her hat, her long ribboned braid fell down over her face, and she laughed again as she threw it back over her shoulder out of her way.

"Story time, Mister Lyle?"

She sounded mighty hopeful, and no man worth his salt could have denied her, not with that smile she gave.

"Alright, a short one," I answered. "You climb into bed while I put out the fire, and we'll see what we can remember."

"The adventures of Kitten Fluff-Hair and the beautiful Silver Princess," she said as she clambered to her feet. Then she yawned one that woulda woke a bear in mid-winter, and giggled as she wiped her eyes.

"Alright then," I said. "Give me a minute or two, I gotta go see a man about a horse."

"A man? What man? Oh, you mean…"

"Won't be a minute, Mary," I said. "You and Princess Rosebottom get into bed and relax."

"Princess *Mayblossom,*" she said, half-laughing, half-yawning. "You *must* get people's names right if you want them to like you, Mister Lyle."

"Alright, Mary, I'll try. Princess Mayblossom it is."

By the time I got back from relieving myself Mary was already sleeping. Maybe it was the pit-patter of the rain —

for I too was asnooze within less than ten minutes, and slept the whole night like a dead man.

---

1. GABBING: To talk endlessly, often of trivial matters. (Often used by JV's wife when speaking about him)
2. PICAYUNE: Tiny. (Smaller than small, bigger than something invisible)
3. BROWN STUDY: Deep thought; absence of mind

CHAPTER 29
THE BOOK OF HOUSEHOLD MANAGEMENT

BY MORNING the skies were suitably clear, and the sun stuck its head up over the horizon to light up a lovely clean world with its brightness.

Well, most of it would be lovely — excepting the mud and the ruts and the washouts we would surely encounter once we hit the trail.

While that over-bright child busied herself making a fire, I moved the horses to where they could graze.

It was a pretty little spot we were in, and it only got prettier once my belly was full. Turned out that small child's cooking weren't limited to bacon and beans. She had procured a few eggs from Skinny the previous morning, carefully wrapped them and brought them along for just such an occasion.

Not only did the child prepare the best biscuits I've ever had out on the trail, these eggs she brought along were cooked in a way I never saw before in my life.

When I watched her break the first egg into her cup,

and put aside the shell, she sparked my interest. When she swished the simmering water around in a circle, I was somewhat intrigued. But when she tipped the egg into the water, I figured the girl knew nothin' whatsoever of cooking, and the previous night's tasty meal had been only good luck.

Well, that egg didn't just dissipate every which way how I thought it would — the circling action of the water she'd set up, helped to keep the egg all together. She soon put a second egg in, then another, and finally a fourth.

Before long she dished it up onto the bacon, with the biscuit at the side of the plate, and it looked mighty strange to my eyes. Didn't expect much from them fluffy, soggy-looking white lumps, is the truth of it — and she'd not used the spices this morning, I noticed.

Well, you coulda knocked me on my rear with a barn swallow's feather, when I cut that strange soft white orb of egg with my knife — and what ran all over the bacon was the brightest, beautifullest yellow you ever saw come out of an egg.

And the *taste* — no wonder she held back the spices — the taste of that egg made me wonder if I'd died in the night, and someone had made a mistake and sent me to Heaven for breakfast. Only an angel coulda cooked somethin' so good, I decided.

"Mary Wilson," I said, after cleaning my plate within an inch of its life with my tongue. "That is without doubt *the* best breakfast I ever ate. Where'd you learn to take eggs out their shells and boil 'em up in that manner?"

"They're *poached* is all, Mister Lyle," she said, a hint of pride in her voice as she smiled up at me. "I learned that simple recipe from Mrs Isabella Mary Beeton."

"Well, you tell Mrs Beeton a hearty thank you from me when you see her."

"It's a *book,* Mister Lyle," she said, and she sounded surprised. "Surely you've heard of *The Book of Household Management?* It's really quite famous, you know. Mrs Isabella Mary Beeton is its author. She knows *all* about cooking, and many other things besides."

I thanked little Mary again for the wonderful breakfast and left her in charge of packing up the campsite, while I went off to saddle the horses for the trip to Old Woman Station.

I had Horse and Dewdrop all ready to leave, and was loading up the gray packhorse when the trouble began.

When I heard that small *whoof* and *sizzle* a fire makes when you throw water on it, I did not even bother to look up — I prefer to mix dirt through the crumbling ashes myself, but many men use water to extinguish their campfire, especially when there's a creek just a few yards away, as was the case here.

Now, fire is a friend that can quickly turn on you, but mostly is only a help to us — we all know the danger, but long experience teaches us to do the right thing, is my main meaning here — then again, most of us don't have a three-foot long wick made of ribbons and hair that we need to keep clear of the fire.

You would not have thought such a mighty scream of anguish could come out of such a small child. So high-pitched it was, it set my blood to a curdle. For a moment I figured us under attack, and believed her accosted by Injuns, or maybe a bear.

Gertrude leapt into my hand, but I saw right away that a rifle would not be a help. I cannot recall if I let Gertrude fall, I only know that I ran, and I yelled as I did so.

Mary was running about every which way, and slapping at her long braid — but the running served only to fan the flames as the hair trailed mostly behind her.

"The creek, Mary," I heard myself call as I ran. "Jump into the creek."

Even the most sensible of full-growed men and women are known to be panicked by fire, so you can't hardly blame a nine-year-old girl for not listening to me right then.

She kept up her running, and I kept up mine — those ribbons the doves had threaded through her braid was the problem — and it was more good luck than good management that I finally caught her.

I scooped the squealing child up in one arm and ran into the creek, where I dropped her, reached down and dunked her whole head, and the whole burning braid underneath for what seemed several seconds.

When I pulled her up out of the water, she was like a drowned little rat, all eyes and silence as she stood there beside me and shivered. That weren't the worst of it though. Her hands went to the soaked and charred braid — she tried to dry it by squeezing, I think — and it came away in her hands.

I have seen some forlorn sights in my time — but for reasons I do not understand, the heartache of a little girl holding a thick length of still steaming hair in her hands is one of the uppermost mournful.

And my melancholy only doubled and trebled when little Mary's sad eyes looked into my own, and she managed to say, "Oh. My one beauty. Gone."

CHAPTER 30
"YOU CALLIN' ME A LIAR...?"

GRIEF IS A STRANGE THING ALRIGHT — and it comes in all shapes and sizes.

I am a rough man, grizzled and uglified now, to a point where losing my own hair would make little difference. But I still remember the feeling of happiness and pride when I grew my first beard — and knew too, how much *more* important Mary's hair was to her.

And right then, I was stricken by the thought of how little else she had — no parents, no siblings, no family at all. And no friends.

Of course, she must have friends at the orphanage, though she has not yet spoken of them.

I resolved to care for her as well as I could, but to get the child home with all haste, where her life could go back to normal.

As for her own grief, she was struck down by it for only a very few minutes.

We were standing in the creek. The water only came

up to the child's knees, but was flowing quite strongly. I asked her, "Is your skin burned at all?"

She shook her head *No* and whimpered as she tried to hold back her tears.

I gently took what was left of the long braid out of her hands — the rags were almost all burned away, and had been the thing that caused it to catch and flame up so badly — and I lay the braid over my shoulder. Then I picked her up and carried her back to the campfire, which still crackled a little.

She clung tightly to me as I walked, and her little body shivered as she sobbed.

"I'll build up the fire again so you can get dry," I said, and attempted to place her down on the ground.

But she clung to me as if panicked, and let out a small squeal of sorts. So I waited, continued to hold her, unsure what to do.

"It's alright, Mary," I said. "No hurry, we'll get dry in a minute."

We stood there that way, watched by the horses, and I felt like my heart might break for her. But I had no words, no knowledge or wisdom, no way to fix what she had lost.

It was hair. It was gone. Only time can fix some things, and luckily, time *would* fix this one.

"It'll grow back soon enough," I said. "And who needs so much hair anyways? You're still the prettiest child I ever saw. Let me look at you now."

She allowed me to place her down on her feet then, but as her hands felt the burned edges of what was left of her hair, she looked up at me and said, "I'm not pretty,

Mister Lyle. I know that. You don't have to lie, it's alright."

"You callin' me a liar, Miss Mary Wilson? I'm a lotta things, but I ain't no liar. You take that back now, y'hear?" I placed one of my hands on each of her little shoulders, moved her this way and that while inspecting her newly scorched hairdo. "My opinion stands. Short hair can be most becoming, and you have the cute little face that can wear it with pride. Chin up now, girl."

I lifted her chin with two fingers, and she looked right into me then. I reckon she found no trace of untruth in my eyes, for instead of arguing with me, she only said, "Can you cut away the burned parts? I don't like the smell."

With my Bowie knife I cut the hair as gently and well as I could. "We'll get you to a proper barber soon as we can, Mary. He'll make it straighter and a little more stylish, I promise."

Only then did she consent to get dry and change into her spare outfit. Once she had done so she called me back. In silence, we finished loading the packhorse and left that sad place behind us.

The trail was washed out here and there, and there was trees fallen across in two places, but we just rode around them. No sense one man struggling to move a tree off the trail himself, when a wagon will be along soon with multiple men there to help.

Mary stayed quiet the first hour, but as we neared Old Woman Station she seemed suddenly cheerful again — or at least partly so.

"Are you *really* going to move all the way to California,

Mister Lyle? Forever and ever? Even though you don't have any friends there?"

"Reckon so," I said. "I never thought about not having friends there, but it won't matter none. If you *want* a friend, *be* a friend — that's what my Ma always told me, bless her dear heart. And a real fancy Doc told me it'd be the best place for Horse."

"You do have Horse for a friend though, of course," she said, managing a little smile.

"What's this *Horse* business?" I said. "You must mean Paleface Champion Blue-Eyes."

"Yes, Mister Lyle," she answered with a chuckle. "Although no, you *still* got it wrong. It's Pale-Eye Champion *Blaze*."

"I knew that," I said as we rode through a small creek. "I was just testing you, making sure your brain didn't get burned off with your hair."

She frowned and murmured something so quietly I couldn't hear.

"You're still pretty as a picture, Mary," I told her, as we rounded the bend to see Old Woman Station a ways up the hill in the distance. "And your hair'll grow back soon enough, if you want it to."

"Of course I'll *want* it to," she said, looking at me like I'd grown an extra head out my elbow. "My hair *is* my one beauty, after all. Or rather, it *was*. Mister Lyle, I was just wondering. Does an old woman own Old Woman Station? I find I get along better with older folk, rather than people my own age."

"Naw, Sourdough Dick runs the place. He ain't really old though. Maybe sixty I guess."

"Sixty *is* rather old," she said. Then she sighed a deep one and added, "I *suppose* I shall have to rename the place then. Old Woman Station won't do, if there isn't one there."

I laughed and told her, "I never said there weren't one there, Mary. There's an old woman alright. But she don't own the station for one thing, and she ain't exactly the sort of old woman you might be expecting to see. Only comes out at night, but she is a sight to behold. Didn't see her on your way north then?"

"Those people kept me in the wagon," she answered as we approached the station. "But who *is* the old woman then?"

"Oh, you'll see, Mary," I told her. "We'll have to sleep here the night, but Sourdough keeps a clean place, and the old woman's worth staying to see. Just let's hope there's a moon out — only way you'll see her proper. And if she don't make you forget all your troubles, I'll be mighty surprised."

CHAPTER 31
SOURDOUGH DICK

W E WEREN'T EXACTLY best friends, me and Sourdough Dick — but we weren't enemies neither.

One way to describe us would be that we had a shared past, along with a mutual respect for the other's abilities. Another way would be to not dance around it, and just come out with the truth — Sourdough and me used to butt heads and fists on the regular back in the old days, when I was the Law in the same place he was the town drunk.

Indeed, he once got himself so jingled[1] on whiskey he could barely stand on his two feet — yet he somehow managed to fire his Sharps derringer in my direction as I walked past the saloon he was being thrown out of. The result of this being, a little twenty-two bullet that felt a lot bigger being deposited a half-inch into the flesh of my posterior — and me locking him up on a charge of shooting the Town Sheriff, whether by accident or not.

Not only did I refuse to release him until my rump

healed, I fined him what he would have spent on whiskey those ten days, and did not allow him a single drink the whole time.

He was angry at going without for about the first week, but by the time I released him he was no longer a lushington[2], and indeed swore off whiskey altogether. Switched to brandy, way I recall it, though in much smaller quantities — at least for awhile.

Despite the improvement it made to his disposition, finances, and job prospects, he never quite seemed to give up the grudge held against me for putting him through that dry week-or-so with no respite.

All that was long ago now, back between the wars, when I was Sheriff of Snaggle Rock down in Texas.

That whole town is now dead and gone, and I figured ol' Sourdough mighta been too, until I seen him on my way up to Deadwood last year.

After introducing Mary to the old codger — *guess he was nearer sixty-five now I looked at him closer* — we went round back and looked after the horses, while Sourdough made up some lunch.

Soon's we sat down to eat Mary asked our gaptoothed old host about the "nice old lady the Station was named for."

I quickly shook my head for him not to tell her and said, "That lady's a better surprise if no one describes her I reckon."

Mary kept her hat on her head while we ate, then I persuaded her to go have an afternoon nap. There was nothing much else to do, except wait for the night-time, so as we could see the old woman. While Mary and Princess Maybottom napped, me and Sourdough reminisced about the old days.

He even sorta-half more-or-less thanked me for locking him up — though his recollection of it was quite some different to mine.

"Hardest three months of my life, Sheriff," he said as he poured me a cup of his excellent coffee. "I never went so long without drinking before."

"It was only ten days, you old fool," I replied. "And stop callin' me Sheriff. You're not going weak in the head, are you?"

"Not yet that I know of," he said with a gleam in his eye. "But it *felt* like three months, I can tell you. And you'll always be Sheriff to me ... *Sheriff.*"

Further questions — and a few rather costly hands of poker — revealed that ol' Sourdough Dick was not only in full control of his faculties, but was possibly sharper than ever.

Three stagecoaches came through that day, and it was a relief to help my old adversary with the horses, rather than keep being fleeced of my money.

"You need some help here," I told him.

"Didn't used to," he replied. "We're all gettin' older, I guess, Sheriff. And there's more stages comin' all the time. Still, ain't so easy to find the right feller. He'd have to be quiet, not a loudmouth like most are these days."

"And he'd need to be bad at poker," I suggested, "so you could take back his wages all legal-like."

"Maybe that too," he agreed with a wink. "Gotta teach

them young fellers to keep away from gambling somehow. I do it to help them, you see?"

"Selfless man, you," I replied, with a roll of my eyes and a chuckle.

Late afternoon, Mary awoke from her slumber. She emerged bright of eye and bushy of tail, showing no signs of her distress at losing her *"one beauty"* that very morning. Indeed, her spirits seemed high, and she traded recipes with Sourdough in his kitchen — which, judging by their smiles as we ate the resultant delicious meal, was something of a treat for them both.

"It's a terrible sin how more men don't show interest in learning to cook tasty meals," said ol' Sourdough. "Serves 'em right when they're chewing on food with the taste and texture of soggy old boots dipped in horse dung."

By the time we washed up the plates it was just about dark, and we made sure to draw all the blinds. The night was near enough clear, and the moon was up early, and doing her job very nicely. We kept Mary inside, fending off all her questions, until what Sourdough reckoned the best moment to view the old woman. Then outside we went.

I had seen this miraculous sight once before, so I watched Mary's face instead as we went out onto the trail and turned toward the rimrock, where some unexplained trick of the moonlight showed an old woman — and not just a still shape, but one that somehow shimmered and moved.

Why, the look of wonder that came over the face of the child when she beheld it!

"Oh my," little Mary cried out. "Oh my, just look, Mister Lyle, she's dancing! She's an *Indian,* isn't she? Oh goodness, look at her *headdress!* The old woman dances and sways, but how, Mister Lyle? How, Mister Sourdough, sir? Is she *real?* How can she be so huge? So humongous, so colossal, so gargantuan, so—"

"Where in *tumbledown* is all them big words comin' out from?" laughed ol' Sourdough. "They could not all have been stored inside such a small girl."

"Mary Wilson here's a big reader," I told him, as I stared at the fascinating sight, an optical derangement of a sort I have never seen anywhere else.

"They say she's the ghost of an Indian Princess," said Sourdough, and he let out a sigh as he watched the vision dance against the rimrock. "She's the reason I stopped in this place, and never went a step farther. Strange what makes a man happy, I guess."

"Oh, she's wonderful," Mary said wistfully. "And *anyone* can tell she's a Princess, just by how she moves. So exquisitely lovely, so aristocratic, so charmingly, stylishly elegant."

"Here we go again," Sourdough said. "I should write these words down and sell 'em to rich folk that stop by on their way up to Deadwood."

"Thank you both for letting me see her," Mary said then, and she even took off her hat and held it in front of her chest, having clearly forgotten about losing her hair. "I promise you both, I shall never forget you for letting me see this magnificent sight — not even if I live to the grand ripe age of one-hundred-and-seventy-seven."

Me and Sourdough raised our eyebrows at each other then, and it was a race to think up something good. Well, he

always was too quick on the draw for me speaking-wise —
and before I could think up a quip he said, "Funny you
chose that exact number, young Miss, it bein' the very same
age ol' Sheriff Lyle Frakes here was, back on the day I first
met him."

He got me good with that one, and fair play to him too
— but Mary seemed not to hear. And not only did she not
answer, she gave up talk altogether for a good long while, as
we stood there and watched the old Indian Spirit Woman
dance.

The longer I stood there and watched, the more
magical the old woman seemed — and I was happy to be
there, to share it with Mary. And happy too to know, that
even if it *was* only a trick of the light, the child would never
forget it.

And perhaps it was true, that on account of sharing this
moment, she would never forget me and Sourdough either
— and it made me feel like maybe, somehow, I mattered to
somebody else.

At least in a small way.

---

1. JINGLED: Drunk
2. LUSHINGTON: A drunk

CHAPTER 32
ROAD AGENTS, RIFLES, &
RIDICULE

WHEN WE SAID our goodbyes to Sourdough Dick the next morning, it was with a genuine affection on all sides. Perhaps the fondness he and I shared for Mary was what brought us closer — or perhaps we had mellowed some as we aged, and found in each other a feeling of friendship impossible when we were younger, when we had cause to butt heads so often.

I felt proud of Mary as we rode away from Sourdough's place. She was a fast learner alright, and had not only packed her own things up this time, she had tied Princess Rosenbloom to the saddle-horn all by herself. Not the knot I'd have used — but when I mentioned it, the child insisted the doll had complained that my usual knot was too tight, and affected her breathing.

Well, I ain't yet so old and foolish I'd bother to argue with a doll, so I left it alone.

"I heard Mister Sourdough warn you there might be danger on today's journey," Mary said, as we went around the first bend in the trail.

"I won't lie to you, Mary. It's more than a single day's travel for an old horse, and the breaks between here and Hat Creek are favored by road agents. We would have ridden the stage like before, only the drivers press too hard through these breaks — and after that big rain we had, we woulda been risking our horses to trail them through 'hind the stage. But it ain't always dangerous. Let's just hope things stay quiet."

"Do you *really* hope for that, Mister Lyle?" she laughed. "Miss Eula said you're a man with a penchant for trouble."

I turned in the saddle and stared at her a long moment before asking, "Penchant mean a hankering?"

She giggled that sparkly giggle that would have softened even a banker's heart, and said, "Yes, of course. Even Princess Mayblossom knows *that,* Mister Lyle."

"Well, let me see," I said, thinking it through some. "It's a changeable thing, that — maybe I used to like trouble, but not any more. See, Mary, a younger man hopes for *adventure* when he gets on the trail — but an older man just hopes for peace. Less eventful our journey the better, I reckon. Maybe I *am* gettin' old."

"But what if we *do* run into danger?"

"That's why I had you practice how to gallop young Dewdrop there. You're a fine little rider, Mary Wilson, and she's a prime piece of horseflesh, lack of size notwithstanding. If I say *Go,* you just hold on and set her to running, and leave me to deal with the problem. Only a mile, remember, any further could kill her."

"I know. Less than full speed, count to a hundred then hide somewhere off the trail and wait for you. But I'm still a little worried, what if—?"

"We'll be just fine, Mary — I didn't get this old without learning a trick here and there."

We made fair time most the day, the weather was favorable and the conversation pleasant. I wondered what Bid and Georgina would think if they saw me, gabbing away like a barber as I rode along — and I thought then that maybe an old dog just *might* learn new tricks, and some a'them tricks might even make his life more pleasant.

We'd had some good rests, and still had three hours of daylight left, but I figured we best save our horses and make camp for the night.

I knew the sorta campsite I was looking for, and knew too that I'd find it soon.

"I like your new hatband," Mary said then.

"You noticed the change, huh?"

"Of course," she replied, steering her pony around a small puddle. "It's the one you had your money wrapped up in. I like this blue one better. It seems special somehow."

If only she knew.

"I just like a change sometimes is all. Blue or yellow or red, I don't much care. Long as I got a hat to keep the sun and rain off me."

"Uh huh," she said. And she smiled such a knowing one then, she seemed wise beyond her years.

Well, I just said nothing and smiled right back.

It was a pleasant moment alright — then things suddenly changed.

We'd been going along slow and easy, side by side with the afternoon sun on our faces, and Mary was asking one question after another.

"Are you *really* going to live by the ocean, Mister Lyle? It sounds so lovely, I only wish I could go too. Tell me again what it's like."

I had told her three times already that day, but I guessed that the talking was keeping her calm, so I told her about it again. "Well, Mary, they reckon it glistens like diamonds and silver, though the first rays of light in the morning turn it to bronze, on account of its glow in the sunlight. They reckon the fiery appearance a feast for old eyes. I surely do hope so, these eyes a'mine ain't what they—"

"Don't reach for the rifle or we'll shoot the damn child dead," came the whiskey-soaked voice from just ahead of us, behind some trees to the left.

I knew the man was a fool, for this open stretch of trail was entirely the wrong place for a robbery. Still, unable to see him, and as yet unsure if he was alone, I could not risk Mary's life.

"Stop, Mary," I said, and under my breath I added, "Be ready."

As we stopped, the man spoke again. "We don't wish to kill, but we will if we have to. How much money and gold you got with you, old man?"

Old.

I was insulted, but it gave me an idea.

"Mister," I said in a rickety old-man voice. "How 'bout I do you a deal? I'll give you all I got but ten dollars, and you let us ride on unharmed."

"How much you got then, old-timer?"

By now I knew where he was, and knew too that his horse was not with him — Horse would have told me.

"I got sixty-some dollars," I said. "That's fifty for you. I'll reach into my pocket, hand ten to the child, and drop the rest on the—"

"Don't go near that pocket," the man growled. "You got your sidearm in there, I just know it."

It was true that I did, and I did not argue with him, for he could perhaps make it out, and to lie right now would not help. My hands were still holding the reins, and not knowing if he was alone...

"That's some beautiful horses you got there, mister," came a high-pitched, young-sounding voice from somewhere in the trees on the *other* side of the trail.

So, there's two of 'em after all.

Then Whiskey-Voice said, "If fifty's the best you can do, we'll be needin' two a'the horses. Gots to make a living, you see?"

"Alright, you got me," I said, sounding sad as I could. "I got another two-hundred wrapped up in my soogan back there on the packhorse. You're welcome to it, just don't take our horses. My granddaughter and me don't want trouble, we just need to get to Cheyenne, we got money in the bank there."

I sensed Mary's head snap toward me when I said *"granddaughter,"* but I ignored her.

"We can't take their horses, Pa," the high-voiced feller called out. "That just ain't right."

"We'll just take one then, to be fair," Whiskey-Voice chuckled. "Get down off'a that fancy-faced horse, old man, and tie the packhorse to a tree. You'll be leavin' *him* here for us."

"Not Swayback Lightning!" cried Mary.

"Quiet," I said quickly, and thankfully she obeyed.

"That's a mighty fool name for a horse," Whiskey-Voice said, as I gingerly stepped down, still holding Horse's reins.

"I'll need to tie this one up first or he'll run off," I said, although it was a lie. "Good old horse mostly, but he always has liked his freedom. Chased him ten miles once, only found him because he went lame. Near foreleg fails him sometimes."

I led Horse to the side of the trail to tie him. I groaned as I went, moving stiffly, playing the part of an ancient doddering man with a mighty bad leg.

I guess I'm a better actor than I thought, for *Whiskey-Voice* came out from his hiding spot then. He was wearing a bandana over his face, and he laughed it up as he said, "Looks like *you're* the lame one these days, old feller."

"You'll allow us to keep our soogans, of course," I said, lifting my hand up as if to shield my eyes from the sun, as I slowly tied Horse to a tree. "That a gun you got there?"

"A'course it's a gun," he said, slowly shaking his head. "Six-shooter Navy Colt's what it is, and I know how to use it. And my boy's a fine shot as well, so don't you try nothing. So listen up good now, grandpa. We won't hurt you if you give us the money — we ain't greedy like some."

Well, I been around enough liars to know how they sound.

He was only a few yards away now, as I untied the packhorse's lead rope and walked toward another tree — one that put both men's line of fire nowhere near Mary or Horse.

"Aw, you don't need no gun," I said, cackling like an old fool. "It ain't like I can fight back, you got us to rights. Why, I cain't see but five feet in front a'my face. That's why we was walkin' the horses so slow all the way, and got stuck out here so late lookin' for someplace to camp."

"Wondered about that," he said with a gravelly laugh, then the high-voiced younger feller stepped out from behind his tree, his rifle down by his side and not even pointed. He was halfway between hay and grass[1] I guess, no longer a boy but not quite a man neither — which mostly explained the high voice.

"Money's in here," I said, pretending I was half blind. I had my back to the first man, but as he got closer, I never took my eyes off his shadow — and sure enough, he lifted that six-gun to hit me on the back of my skull.

"Go Mary," I shouted as I spun about and punched that fool Whiskey-Voice square on the jaw. As the damn outlaw fell, Dewdrop took off and I rolled, pulling my sidearm from my pocket just as young High-Voice fired.

And now we had started to dance, we would surely find out who was *OLD*.

1. BETWEEN HAY AND GRASS: Old West expression for a child not quite yet become a man. (Usually said only of boys)

CHAPTER 33
A GOOD BOY

THEM TWO SO-CALLED road agents weren't hardly worth the name — not that it's worth much anyway in my estimation, road agents being lower than a rattler's belly.

As Dewdrop and Mary took off at a gallop, High-Voice raised up his rifle and fired at where I had been, not where I was going.

As for the one who I punched on the jaw, well, maybe I *am* gettin' old — he did hit the ground pretty hard, but he was still conscious.

I came up from my roll, fired at young High-Voice, hitting him in the hand. Never heard a feller squeal so bad, and that Winchester fell to the ground. Dang kid weren't clever enough to hold onto it with his good hand — instead he jumped every which way yelling all sorts of cusswords, none of which helped him at all.

While High-Voice squealed and cussed, ol' Whiskey-Voice gathered his wits back and tried to scrabble his way 'cross the ground to his Navy Colt, but I was too quick — at least my *boot* was too quick. Kicked him so hard upside his head it made my dang foot hurt, moccasins not being made for such violent work.

But still, it done the job near enough. My other foot kicked the Navy out of his reach as he groaned then yelled, "Shoot him, Rob, dammit."

I walked around the father so I had them both in my line of sight, and no sun in my eyes. Then I said, "Good idea, that one. You listen to your Pa now and shoot me, young Rob. Oh, wait, you dropped your dang rifle. Well, why don't you go pick it up? And let's find out what happens then, it might be fun."

"He shot me, Pa, right in the hand," cried poor high-voiced young Rob. Seemed he had no intention of trying to pick up that Winchester — he had walked about two horse-lengths past it, and seemed much more intent on nursing his hand than on trying to hurt me.

"You stand still now, Rob," I told him, and he done just what I said.

Whiskey-Voice was sitting on his rump in the middle of the trail now, his hands up in front of his face as if that might protect him. "You gonna kill us, old man?"

"Guess I should," I said. "Seeing's how you was gonna kill me."

"No we wasn't," he cried. "We was broke, that's all, me and my son. You understand that, don't you, mister? Please, please don't hurt us."

"You're a damn liar," I growled, pointing my sidearm at his face.

"Hey," he cried, peering up at me. "What happened to your voice anyway? You ain't so old after all, are you?"

"Older'n you'll ever become, if you keep lying to me."

"I'm sorry, mister," he said, keeping his hands up. "I was only gonna knock you a little senseless, take your money and your packhorse, I promise. Just like I said."

"No," I said, slowly shaking my head. "That weren't your whole plan. Having worked some years as a lawman, I know the sound of lies when I hear 'em."

"But it's true," cried the son, his voice desperate and afraid. "Least the *not killin' you* part is. Please don't shoot my Pa, mister, please. We didn't kill them others, and we weren't—"

"Shut up!" cried the father.

"One more word outta *you* and you're dead," I said, pointing the gun at the father and closing one eye as if to take careful aim. "You scared the little girl and made her ride off, and now she'll be worried about me. That's fair enough grounds for killin' you *right now,* I reckon."

"No, please," called the son, even more desperate now. He stood there still as the dead, supporting his shot-up hand with the other, and his voice cracked sometimes when he spoke, way teenage boys' voices do sometimes when they're troubled. "Please, sir, we never killed no one, we only roughed up *one* man a little when we robbed some people, that's all. And I'm certain he will have woke up, he weren't even bleedin' much when we left."

"Who'd you rob? The truth now, son, or I'll shoot your Pa in the face, I promise I will."

He hesitated a moment, looked across at his father,

then at me. I raised my eyebrows, smiled a wry one, and thumbed back the hammer of my sidearm, theatrical-like.

Ain't nothin' like a wry smile to set a boy's mouth to running — well, MAYBE it was the thumbing back of the hammer that helped.

"Just some folk a day's ride south of here, sir," he cried out, his words tumbling out so quick they just about tripped over each other. "A family of square-heads they were, headed north. Yellow-haired folk, you know the type, speaking gobble-de-gook. Two parents, four children, all nice little girls. Didn't even have guns, the poor fools."

Then the father jumped in and said, "We're good Christian people, mister, we didn't touch them little girls, the way some would, and—"

"Speak again and you're dead," I growled at him. Then I added, "You or your Pa spend some private time with the lady, boy?"

"No, sir, we did *not!*" he fired back, and I could tell it was the truth. "That lady was *awful* pretty too, but we just ain't like that, and ... well, we never touched her, I promise."

"And?"

"Well, we took their wagon and sold it. Pa reckoned we couldn't leave 'em with horses, they—"

"*Rob!*" shouted ol' Whiskey-Voice — but he shut his mouth when I fired a bullet into the dirt, 'bout a foot away from his privates.

"Next one turns *you* into a high-talker," I said.

"Please, mister, don't kill my Pa," the son pleaded.

"There's hope for *you* yet," I said. "How old are you, boy, and why aren't you home with your Ma?"

"I'm almost fifteen, sir. My Ma died a few months back, and my Pa went some loco, it's true. But he ain't a bad man, please don't—"

"Money. The family you robbed had money, of course, so where is it? You give me that money, and I'll let your Pa live, that's the deal. But if you hold back one single dollar, I'll find it, and I promise, I'll kill him."

The boy looked at his now wide-eyed father, then back at me, and he shook. Not just his hands, but his whole young body got up a shake now, and he burst into tears like a girl. "I'm sorry, Pa," he wailed. "Ain't worth you bein' killed for. I'm sorry."

I was careful of the father as the three of us went to their horses to fetch up the money, but the fight was gone from him by then.

Turned out them poor Dutch folk they'd robbed had been on their way up to Deadwood to open a store — turned out they'd had five-hundred dollars on them. Added to that was the two-hundred the skunk had got for the horses and wagon and supplies.

I pocketed the seven-hundred, and left them with twenty-six dollars and change.

"How we gonna survive?" said ol' Whiskey-Voice.

"You might try honest work," I replied, as I mounted Horse to ride on.

"But our horses and guns. We can't survive without those, what are we meant to do?"

"What were them Dutch folk meant to do when you took all *they* had? Well?"

He seemed not to have no answer for that, but his son said, "It was mighty wrong what we done. But please leave us our horses, sir, my Pa ain't so bad, it was only when my Ma died that he—"

"You're a good boy, young Rob," I said. "There's water aplenty through these breaks, so you won't go thirsty. I'll leave your horses and guns for you at Hat Creek Station."

The father seemed not to understand how kind I was being, and growled, "But that's a helluva long way to—"

"Walk?" I said, staring hard at him. "Might give *you* time to think on how you been behaving, and figure out a more honest way to live. You got a good boy here, sir, and make no mistake, he just saved your life. You might use the time to consider how best to raise him, now he earned you one final chance. Enjoy your damn walk."

CHAPTER 34
A SAD LOSS

ME AND HORSE trotted away from them fellers, leaving them with nothing but four cans of beans, that $26, a bottle of cheap whiskey, and some cloth to bandage up the boy's injured hand.

The hand weren't too bad, and it pleased me to know it. He seemed a good boy, and at least he had only lost skin and a bit of meat from it, outer edge of his palm.

It would heal up fine, and he'd have a nice scar to always remind him it makes more sense to be lawful.

I had no trouble finding Mary and Dewdrop — I realized then I should probably teach her how best to cover her trail. But a few days from now I'd be dropping her off at the orphanage in Cheyenne, so it was unlikely she'd need to know such a thing.

Still, you never can tell where such knowledge might come in handy, and she had a long life before her.

She was mighty happy to see me in one piece, and begged me to recount every bit of what happened. Problem was, she was so busy talking fifteen to the dozen, I could not get a word in edgewise.

She breathlessly went on and on, explaining how she had done what I taught her — gallop Dewdrop fast, but not quite full speed; count to a hundred then slow to a soft canter and search for a good place to hide off the trail; go a hundred yards off the trail before tying the horse in a hidden sort of place; find higher ground herself at least a hundred yards from the horse; stay hidden and don't make a sound until she hears me calling her name.

All these things she had done, and by the time she explained all about it, we were back on the trail and making good time toward Hat Creek Station.

If it weren't for them would-be road agents, we'd have been camped by now — but I wished to put a few miles between us and them, just in case. And we needed to concentrate harder than ever, watch the trail up ahead for other no-gooders, for we could not expect Dewdrop to gallop so hard again before she got a good night's rest to recover.

I explained that to Mary once she let me get a few words in, and we rode along steady until almost dark, before finally finding a campsite. It's a quizzical[1] thing, how a man getting old can't hardly remember what he ate for his breakfast, and yet somehow he knows exactly where the good campsites all are — even though I had been this way only once. I guess I had written down notes in my brain, or what's left of my brain anyway.

"In here, Mary," I said, and we left the trail between two large rocks. I hadn't actually *seen* the spot we would stay, but knew there'd be a cave back along the creek a ways, and there sure enough was. Guess a man's brain learns such things without him, for that cave was right where I'd figured it should be.

And although there seemed no chance of rain, it felt good to find a place so well sheltered — and only one direction anyone could sneak up on us from, that was the best part.

I suggested we make ourselves a hatful of fire, heat up some beans, and call good enough perfect.

"Been a long day," I said as I opened the cans with my knife. "Cans of beans were surely made for such days, and we're lucky to have 'em."

Mary must have been tuckered out, as she never argued for cooking a proper meal, way she normally would have, such situations. She got the little fire going — without setting any part of herself alight this time — while I unsaddled the horses and watered them, before tying them up near good feed. No shortage of that along here, what with so much good water about.

I threw down the soogans as she dished up the food, and we ate by the glow of our fire, warm and contented.

Food even tasted good — the child had put at least one of her good spices in it.

"Well cooked, Mary," I said through my tiredness. "Only you could make beans taste so good."

The now short-haired ragamuffin smiled up at me, then yawned before blinking a little. It was easy to forget how young she was sometimes, with her big words and strong capabilities. But she truly was very young, and needed her sleep.

"Bedtime, I reckon," I told her.

"Story?"

"If I stay awake long enough to tell stories, I'll be surprised," I said, "but I'll try."

As I dragged my tired self to my feet once again, my creaking bones reminded me of my age. Seems like all that rolling around in the dirt, and punching and kicking bad men in the face, was the sort of thing best left to younger fellers — *still, it was fun at the time, more-or-less.*

"I'll go check the horses while you ready yourself and climb into bed," I told her. Then I went off to give her some privacy.

I moved the two would-be road agents' horses away from my own, in case of Indians, just as I had done the day I met Mary. It seemed a long time since then, as I thought about all we had been through — and I felt a pang of regret that I would have to leave her once we got to Cheyenne.

I wonder if we might write to each other, I thought. Might be she'd like it. I could leave her some money for paper and stamps and the like.

I had just staked out those two horses when Mary screamed, top of her lungs.

Not again.

I spun around quickly, and could see the little flames of the campfire.

No problem there.

"Princess Mayblossom, Princess Mayblossom," cried Mary, her voice shrill with panic.

"Only lost the damn doll," I said to the horses, then called out, "Quiet, Mary, you'll raise the dead with such yelling, I'll come help you find her."

"She's gone, she's gone, she's gone," the distraught child was muttering when I got back to the fire a half-minute later. She was wringing her hands and pacing every which way, and I saw her tears glisten whenever she turned toward the firelight.

"It's alright, child, Princess Rosycheeks will be here somewhere. You get in bed while I find her."

"You don't understand," she cried, hopping from one foot to the other. "She must have fallen off when we galloped away from those men. She's gone, oh, poor, dear Princess Mayblossom!"

Well, I knew the child was sorely distressed when she didn't correct me on calling the doll the wrong name. But I figured I knew just how to fix things.

I knelt down in front of her and held her firm by the shoulders to calm her, and looked into her eyes as I spoke. "Mary, you listen up now. There's no way of knowing quite where your doll is. We've come more than ten miles since you galloped your horse, and the doll could be anywhere between here and there — including somewhere in the trees where you went to hide."

"But I'm sure we can find her if only—"

"No, Mary, listen. When things get lost on the trail, they tend to stay lost, and we can't go back there, you hear me? Only ever invites trouble, when you go back and cover old ground. There's them two road agents back there for one thing."

"But—"

"Mary, listen to me now," I said, certain my next words would fix things. "I'm gonna buy you a *new* doll, the best doll you ever saw, I promise you that."

"Noooo," she cried, and commenced to strike out at me, pummeling my chest with her two little fists as she sobbed. "No, Mister Lyle, that's *horrible* and *heartless* and *mean*. Don't you *care* about poor Princess Mayblossom?"

"She's a doll," I said softly. "Just a doll, Mary, and not even a good one. Only a bundle of rags, we'll get you a new one, a good one, the best doll you ever saw."

"You don't *care!* I thought you were *different!* Oh, Mister Lyle! I thought you were *loyal* to people. But you *don't care,* do you? You *don't*. Nobody does! *Nobody* cares about me and Princess Mayblossom, nobody ever did really, not since my parents were..."

And with that, the little ragamuffin stopped pounding my chest with her fists, threw herself against me, and clung so tight to me I just about couldn't breathe, as her tears ran all over our faces.

I already knew she was thin, but clinging to me that way I was shocked by how frail she seemed. Nothin' but bone skin and hair she was — and not much left of the latter. And I knew then that what Mary was mostly made up of was *hope — hope and goodness and truth.*

And as even her sobbing gave out, became silent and wretched as if all the hope had drained from her, I said, "Mary, you're wrong on that count. People *do* care. *I* do. I forgot what she meant to you is all. Listen, I'm an old man and you got to forgive about half my stupidities, just on *that* count, to be fair. But Mary, we cannot back in the darkness — so get a good night's sleep, and first thing tomorrow we'll go back and we'll find her. She maybe just went for a walk, dolls do that sometimes."

---

1. QUIZZICAL: Mild or amused puzzlement

CHAPTER 35
"UH OH... YOU CALLED LYLE OLD..."

WELL, I always reckoned women and children to both be strange cattle — and Mary's reaction did nothing to change my opinion.

I figured she would just stop her crying, maybe smile and wipe off her tears, then jump into bed and go off to sleep.

But a'course, she's half-woman half-child, ain't she? So it should not have baffled me none when she only howled worse, drowning us both with her tears, while continuing to cling to my neck and start kissing my hair.

Took the best part of a minute to get her to stop.

And when I asked her what was wrong *now,* she only explained how her tears were from *joy* and *happiness* and *relief* that I really did care.

Well, I won't never understand women *or* children I reckon, so it's lucky I soon won't have much of either in my life.

I mean, I guess that's lucky.

Truth is, as she went off to sleep and I lay there thinking things through, something rose up from the depths of me, something uncomfortable — a melancholy of sorts, you might call it — and once again, I felt sorely aggrieved knowing that the moment of our parting would be one of the saddest things I would ever go through.

But man was made for such sadness, I guess — otherwise, why would such sadnesses happen again and again?

I hoped Bid and Georgina were well, and though I had no real reason to doubt it, a sort of dread feeling clung to me as I slept, and again I dreamed badly.

But at least I woke early next morning, and by the time Mary stirred I was ready to go.

She wanted to cook breakfast, but I refused to allow it.

"Folks on rescue missions ain't got time for cooking," I told her. "Think of poor Princess Mudbottom waiting to be rescued, she might be cold."

"Princess *Mayblossom*," Mary insisted, and her bright smile showed me her hope had returned, and she had forgiven the lack of caring I'd showed.

We kept a sharp eye out as always — not so much for the doll, for it would almost certainly be back where we first had our troubles the previous day. No, our eyes were better employed in looking for humans seeking revenge.

Sure, I had taken the would-be road agents' guns and their horses — and the father did not seem clever enough to have hidden a spare weapon elsewhere. But he would be angry about being bested, and he would be footsore from walking. And in my experience, men who seek easy riches are also the type to hold grudges.

And while the son seemed a good boy, the father had stayed mighty sullen right up til I left them.

"I still think we should have left the road agents' horses tied back where we camped," Mary said to me after an hour.

We had just come up out of yet another shallow creek, and once again, one of those horses had been troublesome, refusing to enter the water when we'd come to it.

"I've had a change of heart, Mary," I said. "I figure the man and his son learned their lesson by now, and I'll allow them to ride along with us, then give their guns back when we come to Hat Creek Station."

"Will we still make it to Hat Creek Station today?"

"If nothin' else tries to kill us."

Right on cue, that's when the shooting started — I gotta learn to stop speaking out loud about killing, it seems almost like it makes it happen.

This time though, for once, the bullets weren't nowhere near us. Up ahead a half-mile it was — and it wasn't just shooting, there was yelling aplenty as well.

I jumped down off of Horse and tied the string of trailing horses to trees as quick as I could.

Then I told Mary, "Get ready to hide, I'll go see what it's about," then rode toward the ruckus. The shooting had stopped, but the shouting had gotten much worse — sounded like several voices, and not only men, but at least one woman as well.

Horse laid back his ears and he galloped headlong

toward it, while Gertrude jumped into my hand, ready as ever for action.

I was there in under a minute, and was not surprised in the slightest to see a stagecoach stopped on the trail, and several men and a woman all spilling out from it. The shouters and screamers went silent and turned round to face me as I rode in.

There was a body sprawled out on the ground — a gangle of limbs he was, clearly dead. No one even looked at him.

It was the Whiskey-Voice man who had tried to rob me the previous day — and at the edge of the trail, a hard case had a rope around the neck of the dead feller's son, making ready to hang him from a tree.

"Please, Mister," cried the boy, but the hard case pulled tight on the rope and choked him into silence.

Gertrude pointed herself at the hard case and I growled, "What the hell's going on here?"

Well, he answered I guess, but I couldn't hear it, on account of everyone else there starting up too. Seemed to me like some of 'em wanted to spare the boy's life, while others supported the hard case in wanting to kill him.

"Quiet," I yelled. "Or I'll shoot the next person who speaks."

"They're killin' me," cried the boy, his voice higher than ever. "I tried to stop Pa, but he thought he could steal the stagecoach. He wouldn't listen to sense, he just..."

Well, he kinda choked up then and couldn't speak no more words. He looked a sad sight, his hand still bandaged up from where I shot him the previous day, and no fight left him in at all. He just sorta pleaded with me in silence, his eyes brimming over with tears.

"You got no legal right to hang him," I said to the hard case. "You let go that rope or so help me, I'll—"

"You'll *what,* old man?" laughed the hard case, lifting the rope so the boy's feet came off the ground and his eyes bulged in fear.

Well, I guess Gertrude didn't like that behavior — or maybe she took offense about the insult regarding my age. Bullet hit the ground about two inches from the toes of the hard case and he let go the rope real quick.

"Next one's through your left eye," I said, as the hard case looked back to the shotgun he'd left on the box seat.

"I'm the official guard of this stagecoach," said the hard case, "and you just made a big mistake, mister. I'll have you arrested for interfering in the duties of a—"

"Aw, shut the hell up, you young fool," cried the driver from under his tight-pulled-down hat — and his hoarse voice was immediately familiar. "Sorry, Lyle," he went on. "I told the damn guard not to hurt the kid. Real hard to get good help these days, least it is since Curly left."

"Morning, Joe," I said, not taking my eyes off the hard case. "You want me to rid you of this upstart, old friend, so's you can find a guard who's less trouble?"

"Naw, it's alright," Joe chuckled. "He means well, he just got ornery when that dead'un down there jumped on him from a tree back a ways. Feller almost rassled[1] his gun off of him, and if I hadn't elbowed the road agent skunk in the face, he'd have done for young Bert here. It's Bert's first time out as a guard, so I guess he figured it made him look bad, which might justa soured his mood."

"That true?" I said to the guard. "Joe here's a trusted friend a'mine, and if he says you're alright, I guess I gotta take him at his word. But I tell you, Bert, you look like a low skunk to me. You the sorta low skunk to hang a child for somethin' his kin done?"

"Who the hell do you—?"

"He's Lyle dang Frakes," said Joe then with a right gleeful laugh. "That's who the hell *he* is, young Bert, so you best shut yer cake-hole, less you want it filled up with his boot. And ... uh oh ... now I think on it, you called Lyle *old*. He don't like *that*. It was real nice knowin' you, Bert."

And just like that, the young hard case guard turned into a respectful, halfway decent young feller.

"I'm sorry, Mister Frakes," he said, his palms out in front of him now in apology. "It's just like Joe told you I guess — I maybe got carried away, and some a'the passengers reckoned it my job to hang him."

"Don't listen to other people, young Bert," I said. "Especially passengers, they don't know nothing, look at 'em — greenhorns every dang one, not worth opening your ears to. You best invest some time in the study of law, or you're gonna get yourself into trouble. You woulda hanged for it yourself if you strung him up — he's a kid for one thing, and he weren't even armed for another."

"I never even thought about that," he said, sheepish-like. "But he *was* helping his father, or why else would he be here?"

"Well, that's mostly my fault," I said. "Kid's name is

Rob, and he ain't a no-gooder like his Pa was — he just got dragged into it, that's all. You take that rope off his neck now, and I'll take responsibility for him, like I shoulda done yesterday."

---

1. RASSLED: Wrestled

CHAPTER 36
TWO ORPHANS TOGETHER
AWHILE

I GOT it all sorted quick enough. Joe was keen to be on his way, and it seemed like young Bert the guard had learned a good lesson.

We tied the dead body atop the coach to be transported, then I handed Joe a few dollars to have the man buried, and some extra for his trouble.

The passengers all quieted down, and Joe made two of the men apologize to the lady — that was for them goading the guard into wanting to hang the boy. Then I told them two fellers I'd have seen them hanged too for their part in it — and that by the letter of law, they'd been part of a lynch mob. Their apologies became mighty fervent after I told 'em that.

While they all climbed back into the coach, I dragged young Rob up onto Horse with me and rode on back to where I'd left Mary.

I could see the path she had taken to hide, but did not call her back right away. The horses were tied right where

I'd left them by the trail, and one of them seemed almost excited when he seen young Rob.

We waited there a minute, watched the coach go by us, and gave Joe and Bert a solemn wave. Although now I think about it, young Rob mighta been waving goodbye to his father's dead body — that'd make sense I guess.

Once they went out of sight Rob turned to me and said, "I'm sorry to be so much trouble, Mister Frakes." There was tears in his eyes when he said it, but he toughed it out best he could.

"Not your fault, Rob," I said. "I gave Joe ten dollars to have your father buried proper. Joe's a fine man, he'll see it gets done right. And there's no shame in shedding some tears, Rob. I cried buckets when my own Pa died, you better believe it."

"I don't know what I'll do now he's gone," he said, wiping his eyes with his sleeve. "Poor Pa. He went loco I think, when my Ma died. He was a good man til then."

"Then *that's* the man you should remember. You got any other family?"

"No, Mister Frakes, it was just us. My five uncles was killed in the war, every last one. I think maybe that's why he took my Ma's death so hard."

I called Mary to come on out then, and introduced her to Rob. She had not yet met him, of course, for the previous day she had ridden away just as he came out from the trees.

"Mary," I said. "This is Rob, whose father tried to rob us yesterday. Rob's an orphan now too."

"Oh no," she said, her face crumbling. "I'm so sorry."

"It's alright," Rob replied. Though his face clearly

showed that it wasn't. "It was only a matter of time, the way he was going. I tried to get him to stop, but since my mother..."

His voice trailed off, then after a few silent moments, Mary said, "I know I'm only young, and a girl ... but if you want to talk, I've had lots of practice at being an orphan."

"No," he said quickly. "But ... thanks. I need to think about what to do."

I explained to Rob why we'd come back, and while he seemed disbelieving that we would come all that way back for a doll, he said nothing about it.

We all rode in silence the rest of the way, and sure enough, we found the doll in the scrub a short way off the trail, nearby where Mary had hidden.

"I told you I'd always protect you, dear Princess Mayblossom," was all Mary said to the doll. And to me she said, "Thank you, Mister Lyle. This means more to me than you know. I *do* understand it was foolish, but I could not see her left behind. I'll never forget what you did for me." Then she wrapped her arms around my torso and hugged me awhile, looking up into my eyes, a blissful smile on her now dirty face.

I shrugged my shoulders and mumbled something that probably weren't even words, then I swallowed a lump that had somehow got in my throat, as I looked all around us at nothing much in particular.

It seemed about time to start making sense again, so I patted her on the back a few times, letting her know to release me. Took awhile 'til she got the message, but she finally let go.

I decided we should eat lunch there, and while Mary made a small fire and cooked up some cakes, I spoke to Rob, private-like, while we watered the horses.

"Thought about what you might do, young feller? I'm headed for the orphanage in Cheyenne to drop Mary home."

He looked at me like I'd told him I was married to a bear. "You'd leave your own granddaughter at an orphanage? I thought you were a better man than ... I'm sorry, sir, it's not my business."

"Oh, that's right, I forgot what I said yesterday." I swatted at a dang pesky fly then, but missed it. "Rob," I went on, "it's not how you think. When I told you and your Pa little Mary was my kin, well, that wasn't true. Me and her ain't related."

"Ah, that explains why she calls you Mister Lyle," he said, nodding. "It seemed odd, her calling you that."

"Observant. Good way to be."

"But she *looks* at you like you're her kin," he said then. "Seems to me like ... I'm sorry, Mister Frakes, my brain overruns me sometimes, and my thoughts all tumble on outta me. I'll mind my own business, now on."

I raised up my eyebrows and gave him a nod as I said, "Another good way to be. The minding your business part, to be clear, not the rest."

"Yessir," he said, "I know it." Then he knelt down by the stream to wash the dust off his face.

Once we was both cleaned up I said, "Yesterday you told me you're almost fifteen. That the truth? It's okay if it ain't. We all lie, some situations."

"Yessir, it's true. That too old for the orphanage to take me?" He looked just about as miserable as you'd expect of a boy who had just lost his Pa. "I can't think what else to do, I don't have any money."

"Oh, I reckon the orphanage'll take you alright. Almost fifteen, you'll soon be a man. It's likely they'd get you adopted out quick, strong young feller like you. I been doing some thinking myself though, young Rob. It'd be all up to you, so don't feel pressured none by what I say now, alright?"

"Yessir. I mean, no sir."

"I got a friend back a ways up the trail here, up at Old Woman Station. It's a swing station for the stagecoach company, and it's getting too much for one man, now there's more stages coming this way. He's called Sourdough Dick, did you meet him at all in your travels?"

"This is as far north as we've been, Mister Frakes, so no. We were on our way to Deadwood, but — well, you know what happened."

"Well, young Rob, think some on this then. Ol' Sourdough could do with a hand, and you could do with a job. You own these two horses and saddles, so I guess you *could* sell one, use that money to go somewhere else. But the truth is, you're still a bit wet 'hind the ears, and you'd soon run into trouble again by yourself — and that's just a fact, not meant as an insult."

"No offense taken, Mister Frakes, I know I got plenty to learn."

"Sourdough Dick's an upstanding feller these days, and

I reckon you could do with his influence. Maybe a year or two anyway, while you do some more growing."

"But when he finds out what me and Pa have been up to..."

I put a hand on his shoulder and squeezed it a little. "Rob, you listen to me now. Ol' Sourdough, he weren't always *exactly* the most innocent feller around. Truth is, I had cause to arrest him more than once in the old days. He won't judge a young'un like you on what your Pa had you doing, would be my main meaning."

Rob cracked a bit of a smile, but that smile fled from his face just about before it arrived. "Even so, why would he trust me? He might even think I'm lying about you sending me to him and—"

"Mary's got a pencil and paper. I could give you a letter to give to Sourdough when you get there. Me and him trust each other, you see? He'll give you a chance — but from there, it'll be up to you what you do with it. You of a mind to give it a go? You can think on it while we go eat."

"I don't need to think," he said, and this time his smile stayed right where it grew, from one side of his face to the other. "I trust your judgement, Mister Frakes, and if you think it's what I should do, I'll be happy to try it. I won't let you down, sir. And I won't let Mister Sourdough Dick down either, I promise."

"You better not, son. Sourdough ain't exactly the forgiving type. Took him thirty years to forgive *me* just recent, and I ain't got thirty left in me to go through it again."

WE PARTOOK of our lunch in relative silence, Mary's cakes being tasty as ever. Tastier maybe, from *cinnamon* — whatever that is.

Our conversation was limited to a few a'them *gastronomic delight* sorta sounds, about all. Before we'd gone back there to eat, I had advised Rob not to mention his plans to Mary. I gave him no reason for this instruction, and he did not ask for one.

Truth of it was, I didn't want Mary to spoil the surprise about the Old Woman. Way I seen things, Rob deserved the enjoyment of that experience same way as Mary had it — as an unexpected miracle of sorts.

I stayed quiet myself, writing the letter of introduction for Rob to give Sourdough Dick.

Mary stayed quiet too, on account of being respectful for Rob's raw feelings, him being freshly orphaned and all.

When we saddled up, still she said nothing — aside from asking *me* to tie Princess Mudblossom to the saddlehorn for her — but when we got back to the trail it was time for goodbyes.

I handed Rob the letter, and said, "Give this to my friend when you get there. And good luck, young Rob. I'll send word of where your father's buried."

"Thank you for all you've done, Mister Frakes," he replied. "I won't let you down. And goodbye to you, Mary. I hope things work out for the best."

He nodded a final farewell to us, and went on his way north. In addition to the $26 in his pocket, he had the guns he and his father had owned, and was trailing a spare horse and saddle. Along with the letter of introduction, it was enough for a young feller to get a good start in the world if he did the right thing.

I sure hoped he would.

We watched in silence till he went out of sight, waving a final one to him as he turned the corner. Soon as he was gone from our sight, Mary spoke up.

"Is he going to Custer City?"

"We best get a move on, Mary," I replied, wheeling Horse about to resume our journey south once again. Then over my shoulder I called, "He's going to stay with ol' Sourdough awhile."

"What?" she squealed, and urged Dewdrop forward so they were quickly beside us. "But why? Why does a robber get to—?"

"You can't blame young Rob for the sins of his father."

"But *why,* Mister Lyle? Why does *he* get to live in such a nice place, while *I* must return to the orphanage? It's simply not fair!"

"What are you on about, Mary? Rob's fifteen, almost a man, while you're just a—"

"A *girl?* I have no rights because I'm a *girl,* that's it, isn't it? Isn't it!"

"I was going to say *child.* But yes, you're a girl, and such places ain't fitting for—"

"But I'm clever, and capable, and I'm a fast learner too. And Mister Sourdough *liked me,* I know he did. Why are you being so unfair?"

Having no idea what had come over the girl — she was shedding actual tears now as we rode along — I did not know what to tell her. Seemed simple enough. Rob was a boy, not far off becoming a man, and would earn his keep there — also, he'd learn things from Sourdough that would stand him in good stead.

"Girls can't do that sorta work, Mary. And even if they could, you're too little yet. You're nine years old, you seem to have forgotten that fact. No, orphanage is the best place for you. They'll find you the right sorta home, with a nice lady there who can teach you all sorts of girl stuff."

"Hmmmppphh."

For the first time since we two had journeyed together, Mary rode off in front, took the lead — but not before giving me a look so dark it woulda stripped flesh off my bones if I weren't so thick-skinned.

Suited me fine anyway. If she wanted to sulk, all the better for me, always having preferred a quiet journey. Funny thing though, within less than an hour I found myself wishing she'd speak to me.

Wasn't about to say so.

She stopped when I told her to, but we watered the horses in silence, and once again resumed our quiet journey. Pretty much went that way thereafter — but what could I do?

And besides, it had ever been my habit, silent travel — if it came down to who would break first, she would find herself in a good contest.

We came to Hat Creek Station an hour after nightfall. The man who ran the place never mentioned Rob or his father, so I knew Joe and Bert had kept all those goings on to themselves.

By the time me and Mary attended to the needs of our animals, we were neither of us ready to be sociable.

We ate the stew that was offered us and retired early to our beds. I blew out the lamp, and for a few minutes, I figured Mary still had nothing to say to me. But finally she spoke up again.

"I'm sorry for my poor behavior today, Mister Lyle. I *do* understand your position. And also, that I could not be of any use to Mister Sourdough either, being so young, and a girl. I was disappointed, is all. And a little jealous of Rob's luck, I'm ashamed to admit. Goodness, the poor boy had just lost his father."

"It's alright, Mary," I replied. "Don't be hard on yourself now. Besides, you got *nothin'* to be sorry for. I been thinkin' some on your circumstances today while we rode along."

"*And...?*"

For some reason that single word came out of her sounding mighty excited — but who knows *what* the reason for *that* was. Could be anything at all, what with her being half-woman half-child, and mighty strange cattle besides.

Being unable to see her in the dark, I had no help there neither. So I kept my voice plain and simple as I said, *"And* nothin' in particular, I guess. Life ain't easy for you, child, and I *do* understand that, would be my main meaning, is all."

"Oh," she said, not hiding her disappointment. "I thought perhaps..."

We lay there in the warm darkness, and it seemed like there was a sort of a question between us. No idea what it was.

She sort of whimpered then, so I figured I was meant to ask her about what she said. Well, maybe — hard to tell really. Then I reckoned I figured things out.

"I think I'm with you now, Mary," I finally said. "But you surely weren't thinkin' I'd send *you* to Sourdough too. Wouldn't be no more right now than it was before."

"It's ... it's alright, Mister Lyle. You know how I am, it was a mere flight of fancy, was all. Being possessed of wild imaginings as I am, I believed for a moment you were planning to adopt me yourself. But of course—"

"What in tarnation!" I heard myself cry out. "Why, if that ain't the most foolish thing I ever heard. That's just plain loco, Mary, and you know it. I ain't even married!"

"I know," she said a few moments later, her voice small and defeated and timid. "It was only a thought. It's just ... you've treated me *so* very well, Mister Lyle. Better than anyone else since my dear parents were killed. And I thought you really did care for..."

Well, her voice sorta broke then, and it done my sore heart no good at all when I heard it. But what could I do?

"I'm sorry, Mary," I said. "But I'd have you know for a truth, I *do* care about you. Why, if I was married, I'd scoop you up for a daughter without no hesitation. You'd be the finest daughter any man ever had, I'm sure of it. And whoever the family is who adopts you, I'm struck certain they'll be the luckiest folks of all time. You're one of a kind, Mary Wilson, and don't you forget it."

"Alright," she squeaked. "Thank you, Mister Lyle. Goodnight."

"No story?"

"I ... I'm ever so tired, Mister Lyle. But thank you. Goodnight."

And though there was nothing else to be done — and I'd made my fondness for her clear as a man ever could — for some reason unknowed to myself, I felt like just about the worst skunk who ever disappointed a child.

CHAPTER 38
THE DUTCHMAN, THE BUTCHER,
& TWO-HATS MAGEE

IN THE MORNING we had a good breakfast, and Mary never mentioned the previous day's disappointments. Indeed, it was as if none of it had happened. Fine girl.

When last I'd been through here, Hat Creek Station had been just one man and a whole lot of horses. Not now. More than a dozen men were working at building new structures.

I'd first met the owner, Pete Samuels, some years back, when I'd had cause to arrest him for smuggling down by the Mexican border. Not a real bad feller, mind, but I weren't about to trust him *too* much. Secretive type, and it's best to let that go both ways. When he brought me a second pot of coffee, I told Mary to go to our room and pack up. Soon as she left I asked Pete about all that building work going on.

"Seems like some towns grow themselves," he said. "They made this place a postal office a month ago. I didn't mind, only having the horses to attend to. And the money split *more* than fair."

"Handy, bit extra," I agreed. "I best call you Postmaster Pete now, I guess."

"Postmaster," he chuckled. "Who'd a'thought it? I've behaved this ten years though, I guess. But when changes commence, they come quick, Lyle — two weeks ago, a pair of fellers traveling together put a proposition to me. A baker and a butcher they are, and they seen the potential." He paused a long moment, looking out through the rear doorway then added, "Well, I guess we'll see..."

"You sound like you maybe don't trust 'em, Pete?"

He shrugged his shoulders and said, "The baker's a nice enough feller."

"But the other?"

"Butcher was fine the first week. But then, these other men came to help him ... well, let's just say he became less polite once they got here. Just hoping he settles down once his building's all done and his rough crew moves on. I'll deal with him if I have to, but for now I'll keep calm."

Pete's tongue had got about as loose as ever was likely, and it was time to ask questions, before he went quiet again. "Any Dutch folk come through just recent?"

Through the open doorway we could see one of the buildings being constructed. Pete nodded that direction and said, "That outsize blond-headed feller there. Sad story. Him and his missus and a whole tribe of daughters, robbed of their wagon, their horse, all their money."

"No personal damage? He sure looks healthy from here."

As we watched, the Dutchman easily lifted a massive log into position all by himself. Despite the early hour he was already shirtless, and the morning sun made the sweat glisten on his powerful frame.

"Looked half-dead when he arrived, if you can believe it," said Pete, slowly shaking his head. "That was only two days ago. He was weaker'n a kitten."

"Strong as a lion now," I replied. I didn't let on that I already knew what had happened — now I'd got Pete talking, I'd find out more by keeping my mouth shut.

"He'd been pistol whipped," Pete went on. "Hit hard too, I reckon. Woulda killed a lesser man. Quick healer though — one day in bed, he was fine. I felt sorry for him, so I let him and his family sleep in the stables, and told him I'd feed 'em for free awhile. I got no work for him myself, but the butcher offered him some paid building work. Not exactly a fair rate of pay, but that ain't my business."

"How low? Not less than a dollar a day, man like that?"

Pete shook his head slow and sad-like. "Let's just say, I'll be watching the butcher close when it comes to money."

"Thanks for your help, Pete," I said as I stood. "I'll go speak to that Dutch feller now. Just might be I can help him."

Pete grabbed my shoulder and looked in my eyes. "Lyle, you watch out for that butcher. He threatened to cut a man's throat just for looking at his building two days ago."

I nodded my thanks and walked out to go speak to the Dutchman. Shielding my face from the low morning sunlight I stopped several yards from him and said, "Mind if I have a quick word?"

He looked me up and down, glanced behind him a moment then said, "One minute only, please, I am working."

There was a stirring among the rest of the work crew, and one mumbled something, causing the others to laugh.

"It's important," I told the Dutch giant, "and will only take a few—"

"He's busy," growled a bull of a man, stepping clear of the others. He was balding, heavy-muscled, red-faced and jowly. He was perhaps thirty-five — and he wielded a twelve-pound sledgehammer like it weighed nothing. "I don't pay you to gab all day, Dutchie, get back to work."

"Please, he asks only one minute—"

"Back to work. Right now, or your family can starve. The old-timer can come back after dark, once you're done for the day."

The Dutch feller's fists curled, causing his forearms to ripple with muscle — but he blew out a breath and did nothing.

"You'd be the butcher I heard of," I said, removing my hat so the rude skunk could see my face proper. And I smiled at him then, in a way he *should* have understood.

He advanced heavy-footed toward me, the big hammer in his right hand. He ignored the Dutchman as he went by him, took several more steps, then stopped just out of hammer's reach from me. Spittle flew from his ugly mouth as he growled, "You deaf, old man? I said *LEAVE!*"

Fearsome weapon, big hammer like that — and though the butcher was shorter than me, he outweighed me by a good forty pounds. He had the hammer raised and out to the side now, ready to strike. If he hit me with that it would kill me — but *an IF ain't worth half a maybe,* as my grandpa would say, time to time — and the butcher had made the mistake of standing right square in front of me, instead of to my right and half-turned. He did not allow for the arc of the hammer, would be main meaning, I guess.

"I got just one question," I said through my smile. "How'd you ever get so fat and stupid?"

He was quick, I'll give him that — he swung that big hammer toward me and bellowed like a bull too. But as previous mentioned, the damn fool was poorly positioned. One step leftways and backways had me safe from the hammer, and my second step was toward him.

While he was unbalanced from swinging the sledge, I drove my right fist hard into his ear, then my left smashed into his jaw as he spun.

He had strong legs alright, and a jaw made of iron, not glass — and if he'd given up on the hammer, he mighta made it a fight. But the slowness of swinging it a second time brung him undone, and I finished him off with punch after punch to his chin and his jaw and his ears and his eyes and his nose. As he fell I drove a knee into his ugly face for good measure. His grip unloosed from the hammer, his eyes rolled back into his head, and two-hundred-forty pounds of garbage crashed backways into the dust with an almighty thump.

"*Look out,*" cried Pete from his doorway, and I looked up to see the rest of the building crew rushing toward me — they hadn't yet got as far as the Dutchman, who turned to regard them at the very same moment as I did.

Them four men was all armed with whatever had come to hand quick — the lead pair had bits of lumber, the next feller had a small axe. And for reasons knowed only to himself, the tall skinny one at the rear carried only two hats, and was waving one in each hand like as if they was swords, and he was a damn storybook musketeer.

Well I read that book too, and enjoyed it — but he looked a damn fool, that feller, and I knew right off he'd be no trouble.

Even so, four against one — *I figured the Dutchman would not join in* — was odds I didn't much fancy.

What these fellers need is some time to rethink their position, or they might get hurt.

Gertrude was back in my room, but her little friend Wilma Remington leaped into my hand — and I woulda fired a warning shot into the ground, but for what happened next.

As the leading pair got almost to him, that huge Dutch feller crouched some, then unwound like a six-foot-six Jack-in-a-box toy. As he sprung up he spun in a circle, his arms and legs moving so quickly you barely could see 'em. First feller went down from a fist to the jaw, second one from a size fourteen boot to his ribs.

By now the axeman had arrived, but he'd had second thoughts by the looks — well, there ain't no use waiting and thinking, once you've already raised up your axe and made people nervous.

The Dutchman crash-tackled that skunk, drove him back maybe ten feet — at which time the hat-waver ran slap bang into the pair of 'em. Well a'course, they all hit the dirt in a big mighty tangle.

I stood where I was and enjoyed the entertainment — Dutchman needed no help, as the axe was long gone, having been loosed from the other man's hand with the impact of the tackle.

Dutch feller didn't even use his fists, he just sat on the chest of the axeman and slapped his cheeks some, one then the other, again and again and again. Made a terrible loud ringing sound, the cheeks being clean-shaven. And while that went on, the other man was hitting the Dutchman with both them two hats.

Funniest thing I ever saw — funnier still when the Dutchman stood up to face him, and the feller threw both the hats at him and started to run. For a man who was last to arrive at the fight, he sure had some speed once he got moving. Them tall skinny fellers usually do, once you give 'em a reason.

Anyway, I don't know *where* he hightailed it to, but one thing for sure, he was hatless — and he never came back.

CHAPTER 39

THE SCATTERGUN WAS BIG, BUT
THE SMILE WAS BIGGER

ASIDE FROM THE HAT-WIELDING FELLER — who's maybe still running now — it was only the rib-kicked man who weren't beaten unconscious. And *he* had no mind to cause trouble, his ribs being broke how they were.

First to stir was the butcher, and he made some unpleasant sounds. He was choking on blood from his nose being smashed, is my best guess.

Me and the Dutchman checked the four men for weapons while Pete walked toward us. The scattergun Pete carried was big, but his smile was bigger.

"Hoowee," he said as he arrived, and he whistled through his teeth. "That sure was something. You *hear* about men who can take on four at a time, but I never seen such a thing with my own eyes. Well done, Joseph, well done! You too, Lyle, I guess — but I've seen *you* in action before. Just glad it wasn't me you were hitting this time. Age ain't slowed you much, has it?"

221

I shrugged my shoulders and turned to the Dutchman. "Thanks for the help," I said, and offered him my paw to shake. "These fellers mighta got 'emselves hurt if you hadn't been here to calm 'em."

The blonde-headed giant raised his eyebrows a little, then smiled a wry one before warmly shaking my hand. "I believe my employer not see things that way. I believe I losing employments."

"Never mind that, Joseph," said Pete. "I got twenty dollars each for you and Lyle, soon as these men all ride out — for helping them make that decision, if that wasn't clear. If they need more persuasion, I'll do it myself with this ten-gauge."

The others had woke, more-or-less. The baker and another feller helped the beaten men to their feet, once I gave the okay.

"You hear all that, butcher?" I said, holding him up by the collar and brushing some dirt off his shoulder with my free hand. "You and your little crew are all leaving right now. And don't call me old-timer again, I got sensitive feelings. Well? You hear me or what, you damn pile of cow-dung?"

He looked at me, then at Pete. Didn't look so brave now without his big hammer. He turned his head to the left, spat out some blood before speaking. "What about the money I put into this place? I'm out more than two-hundred dollars."

Pete looked at me, a little uncertain.

I smiled a real friendly one and said, "Give the skunk fifty, Pete. And if he's still here in an hour, you can take it back off of his corpse. I'm offended by his ugly face — if I see it again I'll make sure to put it under the ground."

Then I pushed the skunk's chest so hard he snorted blood out both nostrils all over his shirt, before landing rump-first in the dirt and groaning with pain.

The baker's building crew — more respectable men by the looks — had stopped work and wandered over by now. One of 'em looked about and said, "Where's Stretch Magee got to, anyways?"

"Hightailing it north on his fast-moving feet," replied Pete, leaning down to pick up the two hats that Stretch had discarded before he took off. "If anyone sees him, best give him these, he might need 'em."

The baker seemed pretty happy the others was leaving. He gave the butcher's building crew twenty dollars each, telling them it was a gift, no hard feelings — but they should *never* come back. And he even bound up that one feller's busted ribs for him.

"Deadwood's better than this mud-hole anyway," mumbled the butcher, then spat out a broken tooth. "Get saddled up, boys, we're leaving."

Said it like it was HIS own idea.

"Quiet word now?" I said to the Dutchman. He retrieved his shirt, put it on. Then we walked away from the others, leaving Pete and his scattergun in charge.

"I believe I better off now," the blonde giant said, as we planted our behinds on the edge of Pete's porch. "Even without job, is better for Joseph. Twenty dollars equal to forty days pay, when work for this terrible butcher man."

"You can have my twenty as well. Worth it just to see you fight. Maybe buy something nice for your wife."

"No," he said, shaking his head, a little distrustful. "No man give away money, no reason. What you want with Joseph? Why you come see me?"

"You got a wife and four little girls, yes?"

He looked at me dangerous-like then, but when I didn't react he only said, "Is true. No boy yet. Next time maybe."

"You get robbed sometime recent? By a man and his son?"

At this, his eyes flared with anger. But he reined himself in, and through gritted teeth he said, "Yes."

I looked around, made sure no one was in earshot, lowered my voice some. "How much did they get, if you don't mind me asking?"

He looked into my eyes, told the truth. "Five-hundred dollars. Also horse, wagon, all clothing, food. Building tools too. Joseph good builder. You know thief? I break this thief neck."

"Too late," I told him. "The man who robbed you is dead."

"Good." He shrugged his shoulders, let out a sigh, made the sign of the cross over his heart. "You kill this man?"

"No, not me. He tried to steal a stagecoach."

The Dutchman's eyes went suddenly sad. So very blue, so very sad. And he said, "The young man dead too?"

"The man's son was an unwilling helper. You understand that? About the son?"

"Yes," he said. "This boy pleading with father to stop. Good boy. Joseph sorry for this boy."

"The boy's alive and unharmed."

"Good," he replied, nodding slowly and smiling now. "Deserving a chance, this good boy."

"I sent him to work with a good friend a'mine," I said. "He'll get his chance to grow straight now." I looked about us again, leaned closer to the giant and whispered, "I got your money back for you. It's in my room."

That big Dutchman stared at me for several long moments, struck dumb. Then he pinched himself hard on his arm. "Joseph having strange dream. We go to room now before Joseph wake. Good dream."

We stood and went off to my room, where I introduced Joseph to Mary. Then I explained him that the road agent feller had sold his horse and wagon — and I gave him the whole seven-hundred.

Danged if that giant man didn't get his big blue eyes all filled up with tears — then he gripped me by both of my shoulders and *kissed* me! Kissed me not once but twice! Planted 'em right on my beard, right cheek first, then the left, before letting me go from his powerful grip.

Might shoulda punched him one on the jaw, if only I weren't so surprised — *would not fancy my chances against him, if it ever come to it* — and the spectacle sure set Mary to laughing, so *someone* enjoyed it at least.

"Thank you," that Dutch feller said in his great booming voice, wiping his eyes before repeatedly nodding his head fit to loosen it off of his neck. "Good man. Good man."

He explained then that he had been planning on going to Deadwood to build houses and shops. But Pete had been so kind, he'd probably stay awhile, help the baker and anyone else with their building.

"I got a feeling you might do well here," I said, and I meant it. "You might end up building a whole town."

He said we must come for dinner with his family tonight, but I told him we had to be on our way, no delays.

Then he told us his wife was a barber — *a woman barber!* — and that we must allow her to cut both our hair 'fore we left.

Well my hair was fine as it was, having been cut just a few months back — well, a year or two maybe — but Mary's eyes lit up at the prospect of having her hair cut some straighter, so we all went to the woman right away.

Sure was some joyful tears and excitement when he showed her they'd got back their money — felt good too it did, to see him and his wife and their happy daughters all dancing about with excitement.

He tried to give me a hundred as a reward, but I promised him I didn't need it, I had more than enough of my own.

Then I warned him not to tell no one else how much money it was — "Just say it was fifty I reckon, or however much seems right to you," I said.

Him and me left his wife to cut Mary's hair, while we went off to watch them other skunks ride away toward Deadwood. Then he helped me to ready the horses for travel.

"Looks plenty stylish now," I told Mary when the lady and her young'uns brung her back to me. I noticed there was no ribbons in it, and it was a good ways too short to catch fire now. "All the rage in the cities, so I heard, shortish fancy-cut hair."

"Oh, it's so much nicer than before," Mary agreed, and thanked the lady for her "wonderful, artistic, magnificent, intricate work."

They all waved us goodbye as we rode away. Mary was so proud of her fancy new hairdo, she even allowed her hat to hang down her back by the drawstring.

As we rode around the first bend leaving new friends behind us, Mary said, "I wish I'd left something behind. Something to prove I had been there, I suppose."

"They'll remember you, Mary. You're still there in them people's hearts, would be my main meaning."

"I know that, but I can't help wishing I'd left something more."

"You did, child," I said, as Horse took a small detour around a fair sized fallen branch. "There's the hair the lady barber cut from you. She'll turn it into the soil, and it'll be there for all time, plants growing from it and such like. You're a part a'that place now, forever."

She smiled at that, satisfied, then the smile fell off her and she said, "I wish I'd thought of that back at Old Woman Station, I'd have snipped off a lock and left it there. Of all the places we've been, I believe *it* to be the most special — and a piece of my heart is there, somehow."

"Well, Mary," I said, my face just about splitting from grinning, "I guess you won't mind what I done then."

"What, Mister Lyle?"

"When your hair braid burned off, I kept it. And I saw how you liked the Old Woman. So when I sent young Rob back to go live with Sourdough, I gave him the braid and asked him to bury it, right by where we stood when we seen the Old Woman. I hope you don't mind."

"Oh, thank you, Mister Lyle, thank you. That means I've left bits of myself in two wonderful places. *No, three!* Because Eula cut a lock from my hair back in Custer too — so that means I'm in all the best places, with the best friends I've made."

"I know what you mean," I said. "You don't make that many new friends in your dotage, but I surely did like that Dutch feller."

"His family were *such* lovely people," said Mary. "I'm so glad we got their money back to them. Most people I've known would have kept all that money for themselves — but not you, Mister Lyle. I'm glad."

"No wonder I never got rich," I said, giving Horse a little extra rein so he could speed up to a trot if he wanted. "But at least I can sleep when I lay my head down at night."

Felt good it did, to make a difference — and I wondered if maybe, just maybe, I might take on some sorta work helping others again, when I made California.

CHAPTER 40
A SAD END TO AN OLD STORY

W E CAME to Rawhide Buttes Station in late afternoon, our pace having been easy but steady.

The horses were all doing fine, and so were us two-legged animals. We could just as easy have gone on awhile and made camp, but this was a place of high winds — whirlwinds no less — that could start up from nothing and just about blow you away.

We decided to stop there the night and enjoy proper shelter again.

Mary was excited to see it when we arrived. "It looks like a fort," she said. "How truly ancient it must be!"

But the telltale signs were all there, that it was built recent. No battlescars from gunfire, the first and most obvious sign. Two years old, all it was, and I well knew it. But not wanting to ruin it for her, I said, "Maybe one-hundred years, maybe more," and that seemed to please her.

I paid the hostler to take extra good care of the horses, and we went inside.

"Oh my," Mary said. "It's so sumptuously elegant. Just like a princess's castle!"

More like a fancy damn big city cathouse, I thought. But I only said, "Best get a room then partake of a meal."

I rented a room in the quietest part of the place — feller gouged me for extra to fetch in a second bed — then we ate a good meal of beef and potatoes and carrots and nice fresh green beans, followed by apple pie.

By then the painted doves had started to appear out in the main room, and I suggested we retire to our beds. "Early night, early morning," I said. "Big day of travel tomorrow."

We both had steaming hot baths before going back to our room. Felt civilized again, more or less.

Once back in our rooms we climbed into our beds, as outside the sun disappeared below the horizon.

"Story?" said Mary. "Please, Mister Lyle, it's been so long since you started to tell me about the Silver Princess, and naughty Biddaboo Bedbug, and dear Kitten Fluff-Hair. I simply *must* hear some more of the story, or I'll faint right away, and be needing a doctor to cure my ills."

"That sounds a powerful ailment," I answered. "Dose of snake oil might cure it better than a fool made-up story."

"*Mister Lyle!*" she scolded me. "There is a truth in *all* stories, but *especially so* in made-up ones. And there is *nothing* in the world so powerfully healing to the spirit as a wonderful story."

"Alright," I said. "But I'll need time to think it all up, how 'bout we aim for tomorrow instead?"

"Oh no, that simply won't do!"

"But I don't know where we were up to. Take pity on an old man, you young ragamuffin!"

"Why it's simple, my dear Mister Lyle," she said — and the sound a'them words together sure warmed my old heart. "We had only just begun, hadn't we? The beautiful Silver Princess was being pursued by *all* the young men of the kingdom. And lovely Kitten Fluff-Hair was too painfully shy to tell her how he felt, and kept muddling his words quite fitfully when she was near."

"Sounds about right," I murmured, not so loud she could hear how it pained me.

"And Biddaboo Bedbug, he was quite handsome — though not nearly so handsome as Pale-Eye Champion Blaze, who was the handsomest horse in the kingdom, in fact the whole world!"

"Sure was."

"But Biddaboo Bedbug was insincere in his affections, being of a frivolous nature, and spent his days and his nights kissing *every* young lady who'd let him."

"I don't believe I said *that*," I retorted.

"It was *implied*, Mister Lyle," she said. "I may be only *nine*, but I've read books that would curl your hair, I assure you. And I know things of this world that would—"

"Alright," I said, "I believe you."

"Well go on, don't think about the story, just speak. It's the best way, you know, for thinking just ruins the surprises, whereas *speaking* what's on your mind—"

231

"Causes all sorts a'trouble," I said.

"Yes, perhaps," Mary laughed, "but it *does* make life fun. So go on. Tell me about how the Silver Princess gets in danger, and dear Kitten Fluff-Hair saves her, and they fall in love and live happily—"

"Who's tellin' this story, you or me, Mary? In fact, that's a better idea, why don't *you* tell the story instead?"

"Oh, that's just silly," she countered. "Do go on, I'll be *ever* so quiet now."

"First time for everything," I muttered, then the words of the story somehow came tumbling from me. "First time the Princess got in trouble—"

"The *Silver* Princess, Mister Lyle, *please* say the names right."

"First time the Silver Princess got in trouble, it was over in Kansas. She was living with her father them days, having both come out from Ireland a few years before."

"Oh, how perfectly wonderful, she's *Irish,* of course."

"Well, not only that," I replied. "It's her father was Irish, and her mother was English, and she was a mix of all sorts I guess, with maybe some Viking throwed in, if you go by her fierceness and bravery — but not by her hair, which was black in them days, back before it went silver."

"Oh, I just *knew* she'd turn out to be brave."

"She was, girl, she was. So what happened back then, these rich men come out from Boston, start throwing their weight around, making low offers for land, and not taking *No* for an answer. So the Princess's father, he tells these fellers they can take a long walk from off a short pier — he had been a man of the sea in his younger days — and they sent some hard cases to kill him."

"Goodness, what happened?"

"Well, ol' Murphy weren't home when they came. But his daughter was there, and they took her. Kidnapped, I guess you'd call it. They left a note, real dramatic, written in blood on his table."

"Oh my," Mary gasped. "Not the Silver Princess's blood? I'm afraid to find out!"

"Well, no one knew *whose* it was. But it was blood alright, and there was plenty about. So when ol' Murphy comes home, young Bid and his over-shy friend—"

"Biddaboo Bedbug, you mean, you *must* say it properly!"

"That's him," I said, making a note in my brain not to use Bid's right name again. "So Biddaboo Bedbug and Kitten Fluffhair goes along with ol' Murphy, and let me tell you, the old man had his dander right up. Only thing more dangerous than an angered Irishman is an angered Irish*woman,* that's the truth."

"So the Silver Princess must have been angry too, Mister Lyle!"

"Dare say she was, judging by later events, and such truths as came to light in the fullness of time. She had took a bite outta more than one a'them fellers, as it turned out — *that's* where they got all the blood for the note. So Biddaboo wants to get help, go get the Town Marshal, you see, but the ransom letter expressly forbid it. And besides, ol' Murphy never much trusted the Law. So the three of 'em go it alone, up into the hills to a tumbledown shack in the middle of a clearing in the forest."

"Where the note said the Princess would be!"

Mary sure sounded breathless by now, and less sleepy than she should, but that weren't no excuse to stop the story, so I plowed on with the telling.

"So when we got up there near the shack—"

"We?"

"We what?"

"You said *we*, Mister Lyle. *We* went to the shack."

"Well, that's stories for you," I replied, glad she couldn't see my face in the dark, for I surely flushed bright with color right then. "I just got carried away with the story, you see? Put myself in the middle of it, I guess, so's I could find out what happened, and continue to tell it."

"Alright," she said, "go on then."

"Well, Biddaboo Bedbug lost his nerve some — not his fault, mind, he was only nineteen after all, and more built for ideas than for fighting. So Murphy tells him to get to high ground and keep watch, while he himself goes to the shack with the deeds to his ranch."

"And Kitten Fluffhair?"

"He was only nineteen as well, and no braver'n Bid was, just less clever was all."

"No, I mean, what did he *do* then?"

"He sneaks round the back way — Murphy's idea — and the plan is that once they get the Princess safely outside, Kit and Murphy'll blast them filthy skunks to Hell'n'back."

"Did they have swords?"

"Why would they? No, Mary, keep track, it's just an everyday story with regular guns."

"Sorry, Mister Lyle. And then what?"

"Well, Biddaboo almost steps on a dang snake and cries out, right when Murphy gets near the door. Real bad timing. And Bid should have expected snakes there, them hills is full of 'em. Why, one time me and him walked right into a nest of 'em, and ... well, that's another story altogether."

"You can tell me that one tomorrow! But go on with this one now, please!"

"So Bid cries out like a girl, and the hard cases all come out shooting when they hear the noise, 'cause I guess they think it's a posse. And ... well, it was bad, Mary, and I'm still sad to this day about it. That good man Murphy gets killed 'fore he gets to the door — shot right through his big Irish heart, and cut down in his prime."

"Oh, no! And Kitten Fluffhair?"

"Well, I seen Murphy killed — Kit seen it, I mean — and he can't think a'nothin' but saving the Princess. Why, a more foolish feller never went runnin' and shootin' at hard cases without so much as a plan. Wonder he weren't killed himself — but somehow he was blessed, and managed to kill the first three before he got shot."

"No!"

"Well, that's what happens, Mary. But lucky for Kit, he only was gutshot — and not proper gutshot, just shot through his side, where it missed all his innards completely. Mighty painful though, when you get shot through there. I sure don't recommend it."

"But what about the man who shot Kitten Fluffhair? Did Kitten manage to kill him and save the Silver Princess?"

"Well no, he did not, as it went. Young Kit woulda been done for, if it weren't for Bid. See, even a feller unsuited to fighting can rise up to the occasion when his best friend's about to be killed. So after Kit got shot the once, that hard case raised up his rifle to finish him off — and Biddaboo shot that hard case right through his eyeball."

"Goodness gracious, he was a *very* good shot then!"

"Well, it was lucky he was, or young Kit woulda been done for. In truth, I suspect Bid was aimed at the chest, and only got lucky anyway. His shooting since then ain't never been *quite* up to scratch."

"I'm glad he shot so well *that* day," said Mary. "And then, did the Silver Princess come running from the cabin? Did she run to Kitten, throw her arms around him and kiss him? And did they get married right away? Did they?"

"Well, not exactly. See, Kit lost his mind to the pain, and passed out right where he was. Happens sometimes, most especially first time you're shot. And by the time the young fool had come to, young Biddaboo damn Bedbug had scooped up the Princess for himself, and painted himself out the hero. Which he sorta was, way I see it."

"No," Mary insisted. "Kitten Fluffhair was the *real* hero. And surely the truth came out later, and *then* she and Kitten got married?"

"Wish I could say that was the true of it, Mary, but sometimes things don't work out how you'd like. Young

Biddaboo realized then what the Princess meant to him — so like I said, he scooped her up."

"But why would she—"

"Well, she was sad from losing her father, I guess — and besides, Bid was an upstanding feller, and said all the right words. And he was, and still *is,* a real good feller. Better than Kit in just about every way. Anyway, them two lovebirds was married two weeks after that, and lived their lives more or less happy."

"And dear Kitten Fluffhair?"

"Well, he was happy enough for the most part, just from seeing how happy them other two was together. Stayed friends with 'em a'course, and was part a'their lives when they needed his help now and then. Don't feel sorry for him, he had a good life, no complaints."

"But surely—"

"Now let's get some shuteye, Mary Wilson. All this telling of stories tires a feller right out, and we got ourselves an early start in the morning."

CHAPTER 41
MULESKINNERS, MONTANA, &
MORALS

T HE NEXT FEW days went by uneventful. We worked our way south, mostly sleeping in warm beds at swing stations. A long and difficult journey for a child, but she never once complained of the hardship.

Only moment of note was when Mary came clean about her being stolen.

"I don't want you thinking I lied, Mister Lyle," she said. "Those bad people didn't just drive in and steal me, it wasn't really like that. They adopted me, and I was so happy. But once we drove away it all changed. They wouldn't let me look out of the wagon, and told me they'd beat me if I spoke to anyone. And they'd seemed so nice at the orphanage. Then one night, when they thought I was sleeping, I heard them discussing how much money they'd make when they delivered me to the rich man in Deadwood. I'm sorry if what I did was lying — but they really *did* steal me, sort of."

Made me want to go back, find that filthy skunk, and kill him all over again.

"You didn't lie, Mary," I said. "I knew it must be something like that. Thank you for telling me."

We had taken to short days of travel, only ten or twelve miles — I made many excuses for this, mostly blaming ol' Horse — but the truth was, I treasured each extra day with the girl, and wished to prolong our time together.

I believe she knew what I was doing, and did not mind at all, for she always played along with it.

She never once mentioned young Rob or Sourdough Dick or Old Woman Station again. At times though, I got a strong feeling she might bring up the subject of me adopting her — but each time, I guess she had the good sense to remember the reasons it could never happen, and left it unvoiced.

By now, I knew her well enough to notice when she was entertaining foolish thoughts. A wistful look in her eye, a sideways glance at me, followed by a half-smile as she dismissed it.

And today — on what must surely be our final day of travel together — she had already looked at me in that way several times.

Painful to me, it was, but what could I do?

This time, as we rode slowly along side by side, she looked embarrassed by me catching her in that look, and she spoke to cover it up.

"How far to go, Mister Lyle?"

"Aw, not too far. Maybe two whoops and a holler — perhaps a coyote's yip longer."

"You don't talk like regular people."

"No?"

"No. You talk kinda funny, Mister Lyle. But I like it."

"I used to be even worse in the old days. But I met this real nice muleskinner feller, and he set me straight on a big word he called *vernacular*. Who ever heard such a strange word? It's a biggun, even by *your* standards, Mary. He explained me how I used too many *local* sorta words — said it made for a problem sometimes, made folks' brains work too hard. Been a real help to me, that, and I thank him for it. I maybe still do it a little, but I do my best not to."

"Goodness me, Mister Lyle, *everyone* knows what vernacular means — but what an awful job that man had, skinning *mules*! Oh, the poor animals, why *ever* would he do such a thing?"

I laughed just about fit to bust, and explained. "A muleskinner's a man who drives a mule team, Mary. Now you mention it though — guess I do still talk kinda funny."

"Well, I like it," she said, and she gave me a ten-dollar smile that lifted my heart. "Indeed, I like it very, *very* much. And you *always* tell me the truth. I like that too."

She was hurting, I knew it — hell, I was too — but she was plucky and brave, even knowing this was our last day together, and I surely admired her for it.

"It'll be alright, Mary," I told her then. "Some fine family's gonna come along soon and scoop you right up, I just know it."

"Sometimes it's the wrong person who scoops someone up," she replied. "Just like Biddaboo Bedbug scooped up the Silver Princess, and dear Kitten Fluffhair missed out. I know he still loves her."

"It was only a story, child," I said. "Let's stop and rest the horses awhile, ol' Pale-Eye Champion Blaze is feeling tired."

"You remembered his name!"

"I'm only old, Mary, not stupid. About some things, anyway."

We climbed down and let the horses go free in the sweet grass by a little creek, while we stretched our legs some.

Then out of the blue she asked, "What will you do with Dewdrop?"

"I ... she's your horse now, Mary. You'll keep her with you at the orphanage, a'course, and ride her and—"

"Mister Lyle," she said, awful matter-of-fact. "We must both be practical now. I think you know, as I do, that I shan't be allowed to keep a horse at the orphanage, even if I *could* afford it."

"But you can, child," I said, afraid to look in her direction, as I watched the creek-water tumble over the rocks. "I'll not leave you without money. You'll have enough to keep the horse, and extra besides. I'll stay in touch, sending money each month for your needs."

"They'll take it, Mister Lyle. The money. And they'll sell the dear horse to the wrong sort of home, I just know it. You *must* take her with you. *Please.*"

"But Mary, I'll make sure they—"

"Promise me, please, Mister Lyle! Promise you'll take her to California with you. Perhaps someday, when I'm a grown up lady, I'll go traveling in a fine coach, come visit you all. Promise me."

For such a fine lovely image her words made, she sure sounded sad.

"I promise," I said. "I'll leave you money for paper and stamps and books and such like. And I'll write you, Mary, every week. You don't have to answer 'less you want to, that'll be up—"

"Of *course* I shall answer. And you will tell me all about the ocean, and if it does truly sparkle like bronze in the sunlight."

"I will."

"I know I won't *really* have a fine carriage," she said, and I looked at her then, and her sadness near did me in. "But perhaps," she went on, "when I am grown up, I can visit? And we can take Dewdrop to visit the man who trained her so well, Wally Davis? Where was he again, in Montana somewhere, did you say?"

"We'll do that, Mary," I said, but I could not look at her, for fear I would break. "Ol' Silver Sam reckons young Wally went to a place called Come-By-Chance[1] — yes that's it, Come-By-Chance, in Montana. I feel cold just thinkin' about it, so Pale-Eye Champion Blaze will have to stay home, but us others can go."

"It sounds a place of rare possibility," Mary said, and the hope in her voice fairly forced me to look at her.

Her smile was perfect, the sun was behind her, and I stored up the moment in my memory.

"Well," I said, "Montana ain't for me, but I hope young

Wally finds happiness there. Yes, we'll go visit him sometime, I'm sure we will."

"And when we do, we shall tell him the truth, tell him how much Dewdrop has meant to us, and thank him for saving her life, and bringing such happiness to us."

"Alright, Mary," I said. "If you say so."

"I *do* say so. Now, Mister Lyle, please tell me — what was the moral of your story?"

"Moral? It was only a story, girl. Not every story must have a moral to it, you know."

"Oh, but they *do* have a moral," she said, her eyes boring through me so hard I could barely stand to meet her gaze. "The storyteller may not yet know what it is. But stories *must* always have one, I know this for an infallible truth."

"What you *know* is some mighty big words, child, *that's* what you know. But that story, it didn't have no morals or lessons, or any other fancified messages to it. It was only a foolish old story, and not even a good one."

"The moral of *your* story, dear Mister Lyle — is that when we care deeply for someone, we should tell them so, and not hide it away. No matter *how* much you insist dear old Kitten is completely happy with his life, there is no doubt he would have been happier if he'd spoken up and told—"

"It ain't always about our own feelings, Mary. It was about *her* happiness too, and she chose who she chose, and that's just how it went. Change the dang story yourself if you—"

"No," Mary said, her head high, her demeanor unforgiving. "No, Mister Lyle, I'm sorry, I shan't change it, and I'm *quite* sure you're wrong. The Silver Princess missed out too, don't you see? She missed out on marrying *her* one true love. And *that* is an inarguable truth, is it not? See, you can't argue it, can you? Because you *know* it's true."

"I ... I guess. But it's only a story."

"But she *knew* — women *know,* Mister Lyle."

"It was only a—"

"I shall never forget you, my dear Mister Lyle," the child said then, looking into my eyes with such heartfelt expression it set my damn face all a'wobble. I gripped my face with my left hand and rubbed at my cheeks the whole time she went on. "You are a dear, wonderful man, have been like a father to me in our short time together — and I shall love you always. Also, I know you to be incapable of saying such tender things, even when you do feel them. And I *know* you care for me too. So you don't need to say so, I already know it, I do."

"I..." I wiped a small wetness away from my eye as I stood there, a useless great lump with no words. I do not know if she saw how my bottom lip wobbled — my beard being useful for covering such weakness of character. But she did see me nodding a yes, the best yes I could manage.

She *knew* how I felt.

"We'd better get moving now, Mister Lyle," she said, and her voice was matter-of-fact once again. "The people in charge at the orphanage don't tolerate late arrivals."

As she walked to her horse and climbed into the saddle, I bit down my feelings and followed. And I felt so heavy of heart — and of boot and of leg and of body — I felt sorry for poor Horse, there being so much of me to carry the rest of the way.

————————————————

1. If Wally Davis interests you, the story of how he gets hitched has its own book. That book is called KATE — and was written by a fine young filly called Juliet James. It's set several years after this story — but if you like smart horses (and smart women too), maybe give it a try.

CHAPTER 42
THE ORPHANAGE (GETTING IT WRONG)

WE RODE the last hour slowly.

A grim prospect, our last hour together. But what could I do?

We did not avoid conversation. Indeed, we filled the space between us with meaningless chatter: observations about birds or cattle we saw; the lay of the land; other travelers.

And soon — *too soon* — we came to the outskirts of Cheyenne.

It being near four o'clock, I suggested we change our plan, get a comfortable room in a good hotel for the night, have a real slap-up breakfast — after which I would finally take her to the orphanage. But she declined.

"Best get it over with," she said, her voice quiet yet clear.

I admired her braveness, but made no attempt to change her mind.

We had a quick argument then, when I tried to give her a hundred dollars so she could buy books and pens and paper and stamps and such like — in the end, she let me give her twenty, which she went to great pains to hide so it wouldn't be stolen as soon as she got there.

Weren't the only thing we was hiding — five minutes later we rode up the drive to the orphanage, our sadnesses hidden away behind our blank eyes.

A slow-moving feller pushed himself up from his rocking chair, took two heavy steps forward, leaned his huge bulk against the porch rail to watch us ride in.

He was ugly as two pigs mating in mud, long of beak and more-or-less baldy. If I had as many chins as that feller did, I'd have growed a big beard so folks didn't have to see 'em — but that's just me I guess, and folks is all different to each other. Anyway, he was clean-shaved, and it sure didn't suit him. Extra to that, the man had growed his belly so fat he was wider than what he was tall. Well, maybe he couldn't help it — but I never did cotton to folks who were lazy, and I just couldn't see how he coulda got so wide if he weren't.

He swallowed the last of his drink — top-dollar imported brandy it was, I could tell by the shape of the bottle on the table beside him. Then he took a deep puff from his cigar, and blew out the smoke all in rings.

As we came to a halt, he looked from me to Mary and back again, his heavy-lidded eyes darting quickly from one to the other like some nervous old rat. "How might I assist you, sir?"

He had one a'them voices that never changed tone much, the sort that gave nothing away — except for him having too much pride in himself for no reason.

I disliked the feller right off, but what could I do?

"I've brought Mary Wilson here back to you. The folks who adopted her run into trouble, and both of 'em died on the trail. No great loss, I reckon. Turned out the sneaky rotten skunks planned to sell her in Deadwood."

I watched him real close when I said it, and he did sorta stiffen. But when he spoke he sorta bristled a bit, his voice not quite so flat as before.

"They *seemed* decent people when they came here. If you are insinuating I'm not careful who I adopt to, please make yourself clear, sir. Well?"

Hard to be certain, but I guessed he was telling the truth. Maybe I'm too suspicious, what with my background in Law work.

"Keep your hair on, mister," I said. "I was just letting you know, so you don't make the same mistake next time. And with Mary being an orphan again, I guess you'll be wanting her back."

He relaxed then, just a little, I noticed — which coulda meant many things, and not all of them bad. And I knew I should not judge him harshly, for how *could* he have known what sorta skunks he let adopt her? That other man had been tricky, and may have pulled the wool over this feller's eyes with his talk.

"I assure you, sir, I'll be extra careful. But as I said, the man and his wife seemed quite decent."

"Well, I'll be checking up on whoever she goes to, I can promise you that."

He looked taken aback when I said it, but he quickly turned his attention to the child. "What a terrible thing for you, Mary, but you're safe home again, that's the main thing." Then a little too sternly he added, "Remove your hat this instant, child, have you *completely* forgotten your manners in such a short time? We must keep up our standards!"

She pushed back the hat so it hung down her back by the chin-strap. Looked a little defiantly at him she did, and I thought, *Good girl, you'll be fine.*

The man regarded her with disdain, turned to me and said, "Fine clothing for such a small child. Was it *you* who dressed her that way, sir?"

"What are you tryin' to—?"

"Apologies, sir, I did not mean to imply anything untoward, if that's how you mistakenly took it. I only wondered if *you* had bought her the clothing?"

"Her other clothes weren't fit for rags."

He stubbed out the cigar on the porch rail, straightened himself to his full five-foot-three, and stared at me as if insulted. "I assure you, sir, when the child left here she was sensibly and adequately dressed. Clothing aside though, sir, I fear I must ask you — *whatever* have you done to this poor child's hair?"

I figured she might answer for herself, but Mary did not say a word. She only climbed down from Dewdrop, stood beside the little mare, and her little face was quite blank now.

"Fire," I told him. "Happens sometimes on the trail. My fault it was, so don't you go blaming Mary. Her locks'll grow back soon enough, but it suits her shorter I reckon. Modern somehow, way it's styled. Female barber y'know, what'll they think of next?"

"Kind sir," he said, shaking his head very slowly as he rubbed away at the lowermost of his chins. "I simply *cannot* take the child — not looking like *that*. Not a soul would ever adopt her. I'm very sorry, but you must understand my position?"

"Oh, did you hear that?" cried Mary, and she rushed toward me, grabbed my leg and went on. "It means you *must* take me, it's what's meant to be, I'll be such a *good* daughter, please!"

"How dare you interrupt your elders, you wicked child," the orphanage feller shouted. "This is none of your concern, and if you say one more word—"

"You best shut your mouth right now, mister," I told him. "Or I'll shut it for you, you hear me? And I promise, you won't enjoy it."

Seemed like his anger was telling him to growl some harsh words, but his good sense argued against it. Didn't take long for him to decide. He clamped shut his mouth.

"Please," Mary said, looking up into my eyes. "I know it's what you really want too. It's why you slowed our trip so much these past several days, I know it, I know it, it's true!"

"Mary, you're a dear child, and I ... well, you know how I feel. But you know that can't happen. I can barely look after myself, let alone—"

"Then why slow our trip how you did? I *know* why, and so do you!"

"No, Mary, I'm sorry, you're mistaken. It was a long journey, and me and Horse was both tired by halfway, that's all. I'm sorry, child, let me speak to the man now, try to work something out."

I felt a most terrible skunk, lying to her that way — but what could I do?

She wiped her eyes, nodded a meek one, said, "I'm sorry," and let go of my leg. Took two steps forward so I couldn't see her sad face.

"What's the problem, mister?" I growled. "And how do we fix it?"

"I don't believe it *can* be fixed," he said smugly. "You see, if she was a *male,* her looks would not matter — but female children are chosen for their handsomeness. At least to a certain extent."

"That can't be true," I growled, stepping down from Horse, who nickered a little, sensing my mood.

The feller raised his hands in front of him, defensive-like, and said, "I'm sorry, sir, it's simply how things *are.* And as you can see, *this* child has little else to recommend her. Why, we couldn't believe our luck someone took her at all!"

I looked at Mary then, but she held her head high, as if she'd not noticed the insults. As for myself, I was ready to do him a well-deserved mischief — he at least had the good sense to notice, for he backed away now toward his door, his heavy-lidded eyes growing as wide as they were capable of.

"You wait right on that spot and don't move," I

commanded. "If you go through that door I'll knock it right down and come after you. And I'll give you this one for free — it'll go even worse when I catch you."

"Sir, please," he said, but he stopped short of going inside. He looked at Mary another long moment, then let his gaze settle on me. Then, cunning as a sewer-rat who'd worked as a banker *and* lawyer, he said, "Perhaps we could ... come to an *arrangement?*"

Way that skunk said *arrangement* made it sound sorta sinister.

"What sort of ... *arrangement?*"

"It's extremely expensive to care for these children, kind sir. And we *do* provide excellent care here — far superior to that given at most institutions. Why, we're well known for it, quite famous throughout the industry."

"Thought you got some sorta funding to take care a'that?"

"A pittance, sir, an absolute pittance. Why, it barely covers their food! And we *care* for these children, you see? Give them *all* that they need, so as they might be happy, the poor little unwanted wretches."

"Go on then."

"The sad truth of it is, Mary may be here several years — certainly, it'll take a whole year for her hair to grow back to a passable length. And no one will take her before that happens, believe me, I've years of experience. But if you, kind sir, were to make a ... *contribution.* To the orphanage, I mean. Pay for the child's upkeep awhile, is all I would ask? Not too much, only what's fair."

"How much?"

Them darting eyes a'his summed up my wealth now as near as he could — I seen his brain ticking over, numbers up, numbers down, as he waggled his finger at the air like as if he was writing. First thing he took in was how well dressed the child was, then he added a good tidy sum for the quality of my horses and saddles. Pretty sure he took a few dollars off when he judged my own clothing poorly — then in the end I reckon he doubled whatever sum he'd come up with, then rounded it up some.

"Three-hundred dollars," he said.

Just about fell right over I did, and heard myself say, *"Three?"*

"Her hair's only part of the problem," he explained in that flat voice of his. "This particular child is ... *difficult* ... as you must have gleaned from your time with her."

"No she ain't," I said. "She's a delight."

"Sir, please. She's a tendsome[1] child at best, always upsetting the others with her *flighty* thoughts and ideas. She encourages unrest and strangeness, her thoughts being of an outrageous nature. I don't quite know *why* she's that way — but I strongly suspect that some sort of madness will overtake her completely before she's full-grown."

"She ain't nohow mad whatsoever, you damn rotten—"

"Sir, please, I'm trying to *help.* It's not me, you see — personally, I quite *like* the child, despite her difficult nature and constant interruptions. But my wife — oh, my wife is a *strict* one — and she *will* have my guts for garters unless..."

"Alright," I told him. "Stop your damn insults before I

lose control a'my manners. Three-hundred's fine, I'll pay it."

"No," Mary said. "No, Mister—"

"Quiet now, Mary," I said. "It's alright."

"But he won't—"

"Yes, he *will*," I growled, fixing the man in a death stare of sorts. Then quieter, I said, "You have *no* idea who I am, do you, you uppity skunk?"

"I do not wish to offend, sir, but *who* you are has no bearing in our arrangement. It's simply business."

"Well, mister, *you* might think it's business, but some aspects of it is personal to *me*. So I'll tell you what's gonna happen. I'm a'gonna leave you an extra ten dollars, which you'll use to buy paper and pencils and stamps for the child whenever she asks. And Mary Wilson here will write me once every week, and tell me what care she's receiving, you got that all straight?"

"Why ... yes, I suppose it's alright. Our care is beyond question here, and we've nothing to hide. I mean, it's all highly irregular, but..."

I stared hard at him a long moment til his gaze shrunk away and his body seemed almost to wilt. Then I turned to the child and said, "Untie Princess Mudbuttons, while I get the rest of your things, Mary."

Two minutes later, we parted ways at the top step — but not before Mary Wilson clambered up my torso and gripped me so tight, it surprised me she had so much strength. And I have to admit it, the tears that ran down my face were not only hers — and damn you for heartless if you think any less of me for it.

Then without so much as a word, she touched my bearded old cheek with her tiny hand, lightly kissed my old forehead, and then she climbed down. And she turned away from me, hurried through the door and was gone.

My little Mary was gone.

---

1. TENDSOME: Needing a lot of attention

CHAPTER 43
HAND IN YOUR GUNS

I HAVE BEEN, for a great many years, a man of more-or-less sober habits.

The drink grows a man's confidence, sure, but it shrinks his abilities. Bad combination.

Oh, I ain't no teetotal type. And when I got together with ol' Silver Sam up in Custer, I reckon I drank four each night — to the good of our health and our friendship.

Mighta been five or six, the night we killed the Prewitts. Didn't help none. Never does.

My main meaning is, I ain't no drinker.

So after I consigned little Mary to the orphanage, it wasn't really my plan to get myself lickered up, not really it wasn't. Sometimes things get started without you, and you find yourself halfway through 'em, afore you know how far along you already are — and I guess that's just how it was this particular night.

After I left the child behind, I took the horses to the good livery, and paid the limpy-legged young feller there to take extra good care of 'em all. Gave him double the usual price, the extra half for himself. Good kid he was, always had been.

Ha, a kid, I say — he must be thirty by now, guess I've knowed him awhile.

Struck me then, looking at him, I had never known his name, all these years. "What's your name, son?"

"Why, it's Limpy, Mister Frakes, you just said it to me when you rode in. You alright, sir?"

"Your *real* name, was my meaning, son."

He smiled a wide one and said, "It's Roy, sir. Royal's the whole thing. Royal Augustus Grimm. Guess you can tell why I prefer just the Roy part — but only Ma and Pa call me that, even my brothers say Limpy."

"You're a good kid, Roy," I told him. "Worth two of any liveryman this side of the Rockies. You should lay claim to your name from now on, it's a good one."

We got busy untying and unsaddling and such — even when in a poor humor, I always liked to help with these things.

Horse never did mind being left in this Livery, he sure knew the place well enough — knew young Roy too, even liked him I reckon. And the gray, he never much cared where he was, long as there was a feedbag.

Horse and Gray were just fine, and nothing to do with my current woebegone mood.

No, it was little Dewdrop's sadness that pained me — the forlorn way she kept looking back toward where we'd left Mary Wilson behind.

Mighty unsettled, that little pony became. So much so

that the usually quiet young livery feller musta felt like he had to speak up, and he asked what was wrong with her.

"You just feed her up good," I told him, "and share a kind word with her when you get time. She's lost her best friend, you see, Roy. Guess it happens to all of us sometime."

I walked across the street then to turn my guns in at the Sheriff's Office. New rule — *Hand In Your Guns,* writ large up on signs as you came into town — same rule for everyone, unless you're a Lawman, which I currently ain't. Didn't like leaving Gertrude at all, but that's just how things are, modern times. Rules for every damn thing.

Well, rules is rules and grievances is grievances, and there ain't no use airing the second if it don't change the first.

But I don't have to like it.

I put both my guns on the counter, and the fresh-faced young Deputy asked me my name — looked about fifteen he did.

They get younger every year by the looks.

Anyway, he looked quizzical at me when I said my name, and he asked me, "You *the* Lyle Frakes?"

"I'm certainly *a* Lyle Frakes," I replied. "Are there others? If there are I ain't met 'em."

He introduced himself as Deputy Emmett Slaughter, and I shook his hand. Had a good handshake too, firm without trying to crush a man's paw in his own, way some fellers try to.

"My Pa used to tell stories about you," he said then.

"He never met you or anything, but he knew men who had — men from *both* sides of the law. Not all of them *liked* you exactly, but they all agreed you were the best. Anyway, those stories are what made me decide to become a Lawman."

"Your Pa musta been a fine storyteller," I said. "Please thank him for making me look good."

"I'll do that," he said, as he wrote down my name and what types of guns I'd brought in. "He'll be tickled to hear that I met you."

"Well, I hope you enjoy the career, son. Good for a feller I reckon, to do somethin' useful."

After locking my guns away he gave me a numbered slip of paper — no idea what I'm meant to do with *that* if some hard case attacks me. Maybe I just chew it up and use it for a spitball — don't sound near enough of a deterrent, but what could I do?

What could I do?

From there I went to my usual hotel and rented a room for the night — it had gotten a lot more expensive since I was last in Cheyenne, but I had so much money I didn't really care. The price was an annoyance, is all.

Why can't things ever stay the damn same? was what I asked myself in my thoughts once I got to my room.

"Well, they just can't," I answered out loud. "Everything changes."

Then I called myself an old fool — *talking to myself, what a thing* — and told myself (out loud again) I should shut up and go eat a meal.

But instead of a restaurant, I walked into the first saloon I saw, and demolished two whiskeys. Then I demolished two more, before switching to brandy.

That was just five minutes in.

And that's how it started.

CHAPTER 44
TWANG

I ALWAYS DID like the taste of brandy. Better than whiskey by half — which is why I try to avoid it. But this night, it seemed my avoidance had come to an end. After two glasses of brandy I purchased the bottle, went and sat down, minded my business.

More or less.

For awhile.

Thing about drinking, the first couple warm up the belly, oil the throat in a most pleasant way, cause a man to smile a little, see the world in a favorable light.

Next couple, more of the same, but the tongue sometimes loosens a little — worse in some men than others, a'course.

But the next two or three after that, they can turn what was good into ugly.

I wish I could say I was better than most, could hold my drink well enough to not behave fractious.

But no, I cannot make that claim.

I was maybe halfway through my bottle when a couple of young cowboys came over toward me and deliberately shot off their mouths.

One was tall with no width, the other was wide with no tallness. Averaged out about normal I guess, so they made a good team.

"Look at this old fool wearing tassels and drinking so fine," said the short one. "Don't he know tassels is all outta fashion? Must just come down from the mountains after some years. You a mountain man, grandpa?"

"Most times, I'd allow a young feller *three* mistakes," I growled at him. "But I been eatin' way too much bear. So that there mistake was your *last* one. Go play somewhere else, son, and take your over-tall friend along with you, he's blocking the light with his ugly head, and I got drinking to do."

This time the tall one spoke up, as they moved a little apart. "How much was that fancy bottle, old man? Reckon maybe we'll have us a taste."

"Sure thing, shunny," I told him. I half-noticed I'd slurred my words, knew it for a warning sign too, but a'course, I ignored it. I should at least have got to my feet, but I was too roostered even to think straight. I just added fuel to the fire by saying, "Taste a'my fist is what you'll get if you touch that bottle — but you're welcome to try."

He moved to his left and he smiled a mean one, while his short friend went right, round behind me. Then that tall one in front said, "Bold words for a helpless old drunk."

Again, OLD.

Now maybe my timing was off due to drink, or maybe I

am getting old. I guess maybe both. The punch I threw as I jumped to my feet sorta just glanced off his right shoulder — but it worked as a signal to start, so then we got busy.

Men jumped out the way, women squealed and squawked way they do whenever a fight starts — and that cowboy's damn friend hit me hard in the ribs from behind, sorta took the wind from me.

The tall one in front hit me good on the nose, and I had a stray thought that that one might hurt later on — but in the heat of the dance, there ain't no pain forthcoming.

I spun to my left, smashed the short one right in the teeth with my elbow, then ducked to avoid the front feller's left hook. As the fist sailed over the top a'me, I jabbed him hard in his ribs, my two hands both going hard at it, *rat-a-tat-tat* like one a'them terrible Gatling guns — then he stumbled backways outta distance, took shelter a moment other side of a table, all yelling and growling but not really *doing* too much.

The short feller behind was still on the floor moaning, and a quick glance told me he had lost a few teeth, the blood hanging in strings from his mouth. He had given up helping, that one — no ticker, some fellers, they can't tolerate no sorta pain. He just sat on his rump on the floor there, his muscular back leaned against the leg of a table, the fight all gone from him completely.

Problem was, I looked at him too long — mesmerized by the blood maybe — because when I looked back around, the tall feller in front had took a knife outta his boot and was pulling his arm back to throw it.

Well, I mighta been drunk, and it slows a man down,

but the sight of that big sharp knife was a mighty great aid to my speed — not to mention it double-quick sobered me up.

I threw myself flat to the floor as he threw his damn knife, then behind me came a deep-throated cry fit to raise up the dead, and the whole place went silent.

Never good, when a whole place goes silent — thing is, noise mostly goes by opposites when something REALLY bad happens.

I spun my head to see where the knife ended up, and there was the knife-throwers friend — his eyes was opened up wider'n some owls I've seen, and his bloody and broken-toothed mouth all hung open as well.

And there, up above his left eye, where the forehead meets the hairline, was that big bowie knife — it was sticking outta that feller like he was a tree trunk and the knife was a branch.

He had stopped his moaning and crying, and the only thing moving in that whole saloon was the sticky strings of blood that still hung down from his teeth — slow moving as molasses they were, but they surely were moving.

Then that feller sorta blinked, his eyes showed mostly white as he looked up at the blade. Then he reached up — slow, *real* slow — with one pointed finger toward it, as everyone watched. Then he touched it, sorta flicked it a little, as if to test whether it was real.

Well, that knife sorta *twanged* when he touched it — and the scream that come outta that feller jangled everyone's nerves, would be one way to put it.

And that was when — as they say in them foolish dime novels — '*All hell broke loose.*'

And I couldn't see that feller no more, for the whole place was just one big fight, with me right at its center, being punched kicked and bitten, and worse.

When I woke up, I was in jail, and everything hurt.

CHAPTER 45

THE WISDOM OF YOUNG SHERIFF SLAUGHTER

WHEN YOU WAKE FROM A BEATING, it's different. It ain't nothing like waking from sleep.

Hurts more, the obvious thing — but it's not only that. The mind is less dull at such times, for you wake in a panic, move quick as if that might save you, then find out the whole thing's over and done with already.

I woke sudden-like, threw my head back, smashed it against a brick wall. Sorta hurt. *In a way, sorta didn't.*

It was night-time alright, but an oil lamp burned, I could smell it. I blinked myself back to consciousness, looked around slow and careful, got back my bearings.

Jail cell.

Fighting in the saloon.

Two young cowboys shootin' their mouths off.

One ended up with a knife sticking out from his forehead. He sure looked surprised.

I sorta chuckled through my pain as I remembered, which hurt my ribs plenty.

Hope the young fool's alright.

There came to my ears then the scrape of a chair being pushed back away from a desk. The oil lamp's light began moving — it was headed toward me.

I sat up, leaned back against the brick wall of my cell, looked out through the bars. Could not yet see the man when he spoke.

"Mister Frakes, you're finally with us," said a voice that sounded familiar, yet I still didn't place it.

"Ah," I said moments later, when I saw his face in the light. "It's young Deputy Slaughter, a'course. Guess your Pa's opinion of me will be ruined, now you've had cause to arrest me."

"Not all the stories he told me painted you perfect," he said, and there was fun in his voice. *Good sign,* I hoped.

"That feller with the knife sticking out of his skull — he alright?"

"That's him in the cell next to yours," he replied, lifting the lamp so I could see. "Wake him and ask him yourself if you like. But yes, the Doc says he's fine."

"Lotta bandages," I said. "That his friend in there with him? It was them who attacked *me* you know, just for the record. I ain't done nothin' wrong, you should prob'ly release me."

"I got the story straight from bystanders," he answered, unlocking my cell door. "You're only locked up for your own safety, Mister Frakes."

"Call me Lyle, son," I said, following him to the desk, where he handed me my hat. "They in trouble?"

"I'll do that, Lyle," he said with a nod. "And please, you call me Emmett." Then he waved a hand loosely toward the cells and added, "I fined the fools ten dollars each and made them pay the Doc double for his work. You always drink so hard, Lyle?"

I felt my eyes narrow with annoyance, but hell, it was a fair enough question. "No, young Emmett, I don't usually make a habit of drinking so much. Not ever, I guess, not for years. It's just that I..."

I winced bad right then, but it weren't from a physical pain — I had pictured little Mary, her face, out on the trail, when she told me she loved me.

But what could I do?

"You don't have to tell me anything," said Emmett, breaking our silence. "But if you want to talk it out some, we could do that. I'd appreciate the company, anyway. I'm here until six, and there's not much to do except read." Then he pointed toward a clock on the side wall and said, "It's just gone two, if you wondered."

"Might sit for a bit anyway," I said, and we two sat down, opposite sides of the desk, just sat a few moments, quiet-like.

He got up, went and poured us some coffee, and not too long after I told him about Mary Wilson — the whole story, more-or-less, except for my feelings about it.

That young Deputy was clever alright — knew when to keep his mouth shut, and when to oil the conversation with a word or two now and then to keep things all moving.

He never said much at all really, until I was done. But what he said then showed his worth, and could not have been easy.

"Maybe I *should* lock you up, Lyle Frakes. Truth of it is, if it hadn't been those two young fellers you fought with, it would have been somebody else. You were looking for trouble, and maybe still are. And you know why that is?"

"Figure you're about to enlighten me," I growled. "You being so eager to share all the wisdom you must have attained in your lifelong seventeen years."

"I'm twenty-four," he said with a smile. "But regardless, it doesn't take much sense to see what your problem is now. You did the wrong thing by that little girl, and you're feeling guilty about it."

I jumped to my feet, insulted a'course, and my chair clattered away behind me as it fell.

"Aaarrgh," was the sound that came outta my mouth, as my ribs all screamed at me, reminding me I'd been fighting — and losing — that night. "Why *should* I feel guilty? What the hell was *I* meant to do? I surely couldn't adopt her."

"Why not?"

I glared at him some, but the cheeky young cuss only smiled and said it again.

"Well, why not?"

"Wouldn't be right for a first thing. I ain't even married, and ain't ever likely to be. That child needs a mother, and I don't know nothin' 'bout raising up children — they ain't like horses you know, they ain't nothin' but trouble."

"Uh-huh. If you say so."

I looked around, but stayed where I was, did not yet go retrieve my chair. "It ain't right is all, Emmett, damn you."

"I'm married, you know, Mister Frakes."

MISTER Frakes, like we ain't friends now.

"Oh, it's *Mister* now is it then, *Deputy Slaughter*? Well why don't *you* adopt the child then? You being married and all."

"Lyle, listen," he said, his voice kinder than I deserved. "There's no use in me adopting that child, it's *you* who she loves as a father, and that is forever, like it or not, I can promise you that much."

"More a'your whipper-snapper wisdom, no doubt. Why don't you enlighten me then?"

"Like I said, I'm married, Lyle. It's my wife who's the wise one."

"Well that much I *can* agree with. Women always are wiser than men, is all of my meaning, don't look so insulted."

I went to the stove, fetched the pot, poured us both some more coffee as he went on.

"Lyle, my wife is a fine woman, best I've known, that's why I married her. I've never had cause to regret it, and it's been four years now. Her own mother died of a fever when Jeanie was seven."

"I'm sorry to hear it."

"My point being, Lyle, that Jeanie's father raised her alone — only child, she was — and he did a fine job. Helped her grow up straight strong and decent, and she's clever and helpful and smarter than I'll ever be.

"He musta had help then, from someone knew what they was doing."

"No, Lyle. He learned along the way, like folks do — made mistakes now and then, learned from those. Point is, he felt the same way as you do right now, but he put his shoulder to the grindstone, and he found he was capable of it."

"But I ain't the sorta man—"

"Yes you are," he said. "You're every bit capable of raising that child. If you weren't, you wouldn't care as much as you do. You would not have got drunk and gone looking for a fight. You'd have left her behind at that orphanage and never looked back. But you *did* look back, didn't you, Lyle? And you always will, unless you go back there and get her."

I took the coffee pot back to the stove, picked up my chair, brought it back and sat down. Thought things over a minute. "I just ain't equipped for a child. And the orphanage, they'll look after her real good until somebody else—"

"Ha!"

"What?"

"You think they look after those children so well? Whatever gave you that idea? It's a business to those people, they ... did she not tell you?"

"Tell me what?"

"Did you like waking up in a jail cell, Lyle? Because that's how it is for those children out there. They work them hard, sewing or cooking or out in the fields growing food for the restaurants in town."

"It's good to work hard, and children need chores if they're gonna grow up straight."

"It's more than chores, Lyle. More like slavery, approved and all legal, Government sanctioned — but also, there's something fishy going on out there. I suspect they don't allow people to adopt the children unless there's some recompense. There's no way to prove that of course, but those children are terrified, you can see it in their faces."

"But I *paid* the feller to look after her proper, he wouldn't be game to—"

"Alright," Emmett said. "If you say so."

I felt sick then, and sore, and tired and more-or-less broken, as I searched Emmett's eyes for some sign it weren't so bad as what he was saying.

But I knew now. *I knew.*

I looked at him hard. "Why don't you do something about it, if it's so bad?"

His fists clenched some before he spoke. "I go out there sometimes, look around. Town Statutes allow us to inspect the place once a month, but the I's are all dotted and the T's are all crossed."

"Can't push any harder?"

"The Deputy I replaced here — Cook he was called, ever meet him? First name Jim, officially James."

"Never run across him nowhere."

"And I bet you never will," Emmett said, his voice fraught with meaning.

"Go on."

"Well, it's rumored this Deputy Cook had it in for

August Benson, used to go out there quite a bit. But then the new Mayor got voted in, and Cook got orders to stop."

"And?"

"And nothing. Cook went out there about a week after the election. Then he rode back into town, withdrew all his money from the bank, left a note that said he was leaving. He never came back."

"You believe something happened out there. Between Benson and Cook? But what if the feller just left? Might be nothing at all."

"I don't know what happened, Lyle. There was no investigation, because Cook left a note. But no one *knows* where Cook went, no one's heard of him since. Single man, kept himself to himself when he wasn't at work, so anything's possible. I guess. But still, it *was* strange behavior."

"Mighta gone off robbing banks, or changed his name for some other reason. It happens."

"Possible," Emmett replied, "but by all accounts, he was a pretty straight feller. Only twenty, but decent. Whatever happened with Cook, I don't trust August Benson — and if you care for that child, you should not leave her *there*. Take her somewhere else if you must, but don't leave her in *that* place."

I scratched at my beard some and thought hard a minute, but nothing useful came to me. "But legally, Emmett, I cannot adopt her, can I? Me not being married, is my meaning."

"That's correct," Emmett said with a nod. "That *is* the law."

"So what can I do?"

Deputy Emmett Slaughter did not speak, but he smiled instead, smiled a particular way. And that smile told me everything I needed to know — he was *my* sort of lawman.

More than that, even.

Emmett Slaughter was my sort of man.

CHAPTER 46
THE ORPHANAGE (GETTING IT RIGHT)

I WENT BACK to my hotel room, got me three more hours sleep — such sleep as it was. Every time I rolled over something else hurt, but I guess it was what I deserved. No one else to blame but myself, would be my main meaning — but it sure felt good at the time, to blow out a few cobwebs, use my fists like a man.

At five minutes before six, I made my way downstairs with my war bag — by 'made my way downstairs,' what I actually mean is, 'limped down the stairs like a man who's been kicked by a horse, then gone back for seconds to make certain he didn't enjoy it.'

I walked down to the Sheriff's Office, but just as I got there, Deputy Emmett Slaughter came out of the Livery across the street from it, leading Horse, all saddled and ready.

"Sheriff showed up early to relieve me," he said, "and I figured you might struggle with the saddle, being so—"

"*Old?*" I growled at him. "Me being so *old?*"

"I was going to say, being so *sore* — from being attacked last night in the saloon by those men," he replied, as young Roy Grimm walked out behind him, leading little Dewdrop. "But I'll change it to *old* if you like."

He laughed and shook his head as I nodded an apology at him. Then I turned and said, "Morning, Roy," to the widely smiling young liveryman.

"Looks like your limp's worse than mine today, Mister Frakes," he said as I crossed the street. "Age having nothing to do with either problem, I'd add, 'fore it gets me in trouble."

I smiled at the joke, and did not point out that my own limp would probably get better, whereas his would stay with him always. Instead, I turned to Emmett and said, "Where's my guns? What if I need 'em when—"

"You *won't* need them," he answered with a sharp shake of his head — and a slight nod toward his boss, the Sheriff, other side of the road, now watching proceedings from his doorway. Then Emmett added, official-like, "You'll get your guns back when you leave town, just like anyone else, Mister Frakes. Now let's go have that breakfast I promised you, my wife will be happy to meet you."

Emmett helped me into the saddle, then climbed up on his own horse, a nice strawberry roan gelding, and we headed north toward the orphanage.

We had to stop in briefly at his house on the way, and his wife insisted on feeding us the breakfast she'd already made — I felt a mite guilty eating her share of it, but she insisted it weren't no problem, she'd eat with the children instead, once they awoke.

Young Emmett was right about his wife, I could tell from that one brief meeting — she was smart as a whip, and a fine sorta woman besides. Way they looked at each other got me thinking about ... *well, never mind who I thought of, some thoughts are best bitten down where they don't do no damage.*

It was only a few minutes ride to the orphanage, on the outskirts of town.

It was a big place, wide acres, its buildings scattered freely. Emmett pointed them out as went — the bakery; the sewing house; the bunkhouse; the piggery. "All worked by children," he said. "Just look at the fields already, even though it's not yet even seven."

It was true, there were children working the fields, boys aged from perhaps only seven, all the way to about seventeen.

As we turned in to ride up the drive that led to the main building, the feller I'd entrusted Mary to the previous day stepped out onto the porch, a fat cigar in his mouth, his head enveloped in smoke. Seeing us, he immediately turned, stuck his head back through his doorway, and while we could not make out the words, he was frantically barking instructions.

"Same every time I arrive," Emmett said. "Except usually the lazy fat skunk's already in his seat on the porch."

"You'd think he'd have work to do."

"His wife seems always to be busy, and the weight of the world on her shoulders. But she never speaks more than two words, he has her well trained."

"Downtrodden, a better word, yes?"

"That'd be stating it mildly. As for him, I think his only job is to ring that big bell, dinner times, work times and such. Only thing bigger than him is his opinion of his own self."

As we approached on our horses the man came back out, closed the door behind him, leaned against the porch rail and said, "Good morning to you, Deputy, and a fine morning it is. You've inspected already this month, so this matter must be of importance. How might I assist you today?"

"There's been a misunderstanding, Mister Benson," the Deputy told him, friendly but firm. "This man delivered a child to you here last night, but she was meant to go elsewhere, he got the wrong place."

That orphanage skunk looked at me, and I looked at him, and I reckon he misunderstood just who he was dealing with.

"Ah yes, I remember you, sir," he said, smirking at me. "But there was no mistake, I assure you. Mary Wilson is a ward of this orphanage, she's in the right place. Will there be anything else?"

"Mister," I growled, stepping down — right painful, I'd add, for my ribs felt like someone had played a tune on them with a mallet. "The child is coming with me, one way or the other, and you get to choose it."

"Is that a threat, sir? Deputy Slaughter, you heard that, did you not? This man threatened me without just cause, he must get back on his horse and leave right this second, or be arrested."

"I heard no threat made against you, Mister Benson," said Emmett. "You'd best bring out the child right now. I've been working all night, and am in no mood for anything that'll delay me from getting some sleep."

"Ah, let us wait just a moment," said Benson, his eyes shrewdly calculating. "The night shift goes from six until six, Slaughter, if I'm not mistaken. You're not here in an *official* capacity, are you? Indeed, this is unlawful harassment! I shall speak to my closest personal friend — *Mayor Fisk,* of course — unless both of you leave right this minute."

Well, I looked at Emmett, and he looked at me, and he too got down from his horse. And without further delay, we stepped toward that damn name-dropper to get the job started. Funny how quick some fellers can move when afeared — he waddled a lot quicker than you might imagine, given his sizable girth.

"Leave my property *now,*" he shouted at us, hightailing it to the door. He rapped hard upon it, someone opened it quickly, and he darted through it as Emmett flew up them stairs like as if he had wings.

That Benson feller was through, and the door almost closed, when Emmett arrived, jamming his foot in the door to prevent it from closing.

As the Deputy forcefully pushed the door open, a ruckus started inside, and I heard a woman cry out, "No, Mary, no, you're only making it worse!"

I don't know how I did it, given my injuries — but it seemed that I too was suddenly capable of flying up stairs, and I was inside that huge clapboard building.

The front room was as large as a mid-size city saloon, but not so well lit. Toward the other end I saw Mary, struggling to break free from the grip of a middle-aged woman, who was yelling, "No, Mary, don't be so foolish!"

Strangest thing, no one else was moving — and it was the hardest thing I ever did, to stop and sum things up right then, while poor Mary screamed.

But I did sum things up, and a good thing I did — for Emmett's hands were high in the air, and Benson was holding a scattergun, pointed right at us both.

CHAPTER 47

SKUNK

"**L**ET'S HAVE A LITTLE TALK, shall we?" said Benson, as I raised up my hands where he wanted 'em. Then smiling coldly he added, "I'd hate to make a mistake and ... *accidentally* ... shoot the two men I mistook for robbers, when they burst into my orphanage *quite* uninvited."

"I'm a lawman, you fool," growled the Deputy. "You won't get away with it."

"Oh, but I would," Benson said, and he chuckled, clearly enjoying the new situation. "I'm known to be a reasonable man. But the safety of the children is of utmost importance — and one man looks the same as another, when he bursts through a door uninvited, shouting like some sort of madman. The children *must* be protected — why, that is my sworn duty, who would ever convict me?"

He had us to rights if he wanted to shoot us. Weren't much light in the place, but we were all lit up by such natural light as there was — me and Emmett being nearby the front doorway, while Benson himself was in sunlight from a window behind him. I could not have gone for a gun without him seeing right away — even if I'd had one, which I didn't.

"What of them others there?" I said, keeping my voice low and calm. "The woman, the child. And any others somewhere in the house who'll have heard us arrive."

"The woman is my own good wife, of course — and completely loyal to me, as you would rightly assume. As for the children, we run a tight ship here, and so they are all where they should be — that is to say, not within earshot — except for this ugly, useless, troublesome girl. I told you last night, did I not, sir, she's trouble, this child. Not being *officially* here though, she *could* disappear."

"You filthy damn—"

"Now now, sir," the skunk said, waving the scattergun about to remind me he had it. "I'm a reasonable man, and would never harm a child unless I was *forced* to. And beyond ordinary measures of discipline, I've never had cause to harm one — that is to say, never *yet*." He waited a moment for effect, then in a voice so calm it chilled me, he added, "Would you force me to harm *this* child, sir?"

"What is it you want, you damn skunk?"

"Fair recompense for the trouble you've caused me is all, sir," he said. "How about, hmmm, let's call it a nice even thousand, that ought to do it."

"And you'd let us walk out with the child?"

That skunk Benson half-smiled and said, "Of course,

Mister..." He rubbed one of his chins a moment then asked, "What *is* your name anyway, sir, I never did ask?"

"He's Tom Jones," said Emmett before I could answer — but when Benson looked puzzled and untrusting, Emmett quickly added, "But he mostly goes by his middle name, Lyle. He's from the north part of Montana, up by the breaks. Friend of my father's, you see."

Benson's gaze shifted from Emmett to me then, and he said, "So, do we have a deal then, Mister Thomas Lyle Jones?"

I kept my hands up as I said, "No, I don't reckon so, I don't trust you. What happens when the Deputy goes back to his office and tells the Sheriff what happened here today?"

"Ha! He's welcome to try it. He'll be jobless — or *worse* — by the end of the day. And I promise you, nothing will come of his claims. I'm a man of *considerable* importance and power in this city."

Emmett shook his head slowly, hands still in the air, and said, "That was why Deputy Cook left so suddenly, wasn't it?"

"I know nothing at all about that," Benson said. And he wore the sorta dung-eating smile I'd have liked to slap off of his face. "Perhaps this *Cook* fellow crossed someone he shouldn't have? Some man of substance, perhaps? A powerful man of importance? Perhaps even Mayor Fisk himself, or ... one of his very best friends. But how would *I* know, Deputy, hmmm? Now, about *our* little arrangement. That thousand dollars we spoke of."

"You took three-hundred from me already," I reminded him. "I can give you five-hundred, which leaves me just fifty for food. Or would you leave a man without means to feed himself?"

"Surely that's not the truth, sir. No, you're more wealthy than you're letting on. Let's call it eight-hundred then. You drive a firm bargain, and I respect that in a fellow."

I knew I needed to keep the man talking — given time, either myself or Emmett might figure some way outta this mess.

"Ain't made a'money you know, like the folks round here must be," I growled. "Ten dollars for a room in the hotel last night! *Ten dollars!* Just for a bed, just one night. And a breakfast woulda cost another two, I can't hardly believe it!"

"It's a prosperous town," Benson said. "Suited to men of high intelligence. Perhaps *you* should return to Montana, old man, where you are clearly more suited."

"Oh, I'll be going back home right away," I assured him, pretending I'd not understood his insult. "You can have these big cities to yourself, and good luck to all a'you vipers. Folks is more-or-less friendly where I'm from, and help each other out when we can, unlike all you big-city skunks."

He stayed quiet a few moments, as if he was thinking. Looked like an overweight *devil,* way the sunlight from the open window behind him streamed through on his fat baldy head — made his skull shine a devilish red, would be my main meaning.

"Seven-hundred, final offer," he said, clearly enjoying the feeling that he was superior to an old fool like me. "Surely you can manage that much, for the welfare of this troublesome child."

"I ain't got it," I growled, trying to buy us more time. "But alright, you got me to rights, I *was* holdin' out on you some. I got six-hundred and fifty-two dollars to my name, that's my entire life's fortune, dammit. I'll give you six-hundred, that's all I can go to. Deal or not, you dang skunk?"

"Go and get it, old chap. I'll wait here with the Deputy and the child. But if you're not back alone thirty minutes from now—"

"I don't have to go no further than my saddlebags," I told him. "Don't trust bankers no farther'n I could throw one."

"Some of my best friends are bankers," he said, eyebrows raised up like as if what I'd said was offensive. But then he laughed and said, "Knowing them as I do, I agree you'd be foolish to trust one. A terrible lot, but they have their uses, believe me." Then, sharp-tongued, he told his wife, "Leave the child here, take the Deputy's pistol, and go out front with the old man."

Mary's eyes darted about as the woman brought her over, like as if she had thoughts of escaping. But I told her, "Mary Wilson, you stand right here next to my good friend Emmett, and don't speak or do anything else. I'll fetch Mister Benson his money, and we'll leave this place in a few minutes, all safe and sound. You'll do that for me, Mary? Don't be afeared, just stay still, no matter what."

"Face each other and hold hands, you two," Benson said, waving the shotgun at Mary and Emmett. "Both hands, out away from your bodies, keep some distance between you."

They did what he'd told them, faced each other and held hands. Emmett smile reassuringly at the child, and she managed a nervous one back at him.

Mrs Benson stepped forward, carefully lifted Emmett's small Colt revolver from its holster, stepped away from him, checked it was loaded.

"Don't hurt them, August," she pleaded with her fool husband.

"I'll only shoot them if this old coot *forces* me to," Benson said. "Follow six paces behind him, keep the gun on him every second. Watch his hands the whole time, see he doesn't take a gun from his saddlebag — and if he does, shoot him without hesitation."

"She can take out the money for herself," I said. "I'll stand away from her, I don't want no trouble, I just want the little girl to be safe — the money don't matter to me now."

"Even better, do it that way," said Benson to his wife. "Have him stand away in the open, ten paces from you at least, don't take your eyes off him."

"Alright," she replied. "But please, August, don't harm the child, she's—"

"You just shoot that old man if he tries anything, Mavis. I doubt that he will. He knows what'll happen if he does."

Oh, I knew it alright. Even if I managed to get the gun from his wife without her shooting me, she would cry out —

and that orphanage feller would not stop to think, he would use one barrel on Mary and Emmett, and unleash the other on me as I come through the door.

Problem was, money or not, I knew I could not trust him.

CHAPTER 48

"I'D KILL HIM MYSELF IF I COULD…"

THERE WOULD BE DEATH. *I could feel it, smell it somehow. It would all be over in minutes.*

"Try anything funny, old man, I'll shoot you right where you stand," said Mavis Benson from behind me, as I started to walk toward the door.

And the sound of her thumbing back the hammer announced that she meant it.

"It's alright, Mary Wilson," I called over my shoulder. "I'll get the man his money, and we'll be cooking over a fire on the trail tonight."

This last I had said, not for Mary, but for Emmett — the word *cooking* to let him know I hadn't forgotten about Deputy *Cook,* and that I planned to do *something.*

What that *something* might be, I had not quite yet figured out, as I stepped through the still open doorway and onto the porch, then limped down the front stairs.

Neither Emmett or myself had tied up our horses, and

both animals had wandered about twenty yards, so I limped, slow as I could, in their general direction.

Coulda knocked me down with a barn swallow's tail-feather when, a half-dozen steps later, Mavis Benson rushed up behind me and whispered, "Quickly, we don't have much time," and pressed the Colt into my hand.

"But I thought..."

"This is no time to think," she said. "He'll kill you, and the Deputy too, unless you shoot him first."

"But I can't just go shootin' a man in cold blood," I answered, nervously watching the door just in case he came out.

"He won't move from where he is," she told me, gripping my shirt front. "If you go back in with the money, he'll yell like a madman, put the gun to the head of the child, try to squeeze more money from you."

"How can you know that for—?"

"He killed Deputy Cook the same way," she hissed. "Please. You must. What if he kills that dear child? He doesn't care, not at all."

"But surely—"

"I'd kill him myself if I could. I tried once, you know, when he was dead drunk. I just ... I just could not make myself pull the trigger."

Her eyes told the truth of it all.

I kept my own gaze intent on the doorway, kept the gun where it'd be out of Benson's sight if he did come. "But if he sees I have this pistol—"

"Yes," she said quickly, "I know. He'll *use* that shotgun,

kill you all, Mary included. Go to the first window, that side, it's right behind where he's standing. You must. Please, you *must*."

It was no easy thing for the woman, I knew that. She had loved him, perhaps, at one time — I could see the pain in her eyes, her balled up[1] feelings written all over her skin. She was a woman who would never quite come to terms with her actions, no matter how righteous they were.

"I'll take him alive if I can."

She shook her head, *no,* and tears overflowed from her eyes, silent but knowing.

"Stay here and stay quiet," I told her, and walked, catlike almost in my moccasins, to the side of the house.

No longer limping, no pain.

Job to do.

Lives to save.

Each step soft and deliberate, on I came. When I came to the edge of the window, I'd be not quite exactly behind him, but slightly to his left. Not enough so he'd notice unless I made a sound, but enough to give me an angle, to keep Mary safe if the bullet passed through him.

I raised up the Colt, ready to shoot, half expecting to be looking down the double barrels of that big scattergun as I came near the window. But Benson still had his back to me.

I could not see Mary and Emmett from here, but I knew from the angle of Benson's head they'd not moved.

Four feet back from the open window I stopped, planted my feet, perfect balance, all of me focus, only me and this gun and that man.

And I waited.

Silent, unmoving.

Nothing but breath, nerve and fingers, muscle and blood.

---

1. BALLED UP: Confused

CHAPTER 49
STRAIGHT TO HELL

THERE IS something that feels quite wrong — *and strange, so very strange* — about holding another man's life at the end of your trigger finger that way. All that he is, all he might yet do and become, all the life he might yet live, all that now *mine* to take from him, in this moment or the next, at a time of my choosing.

I did not want to do it.

Then I thought of Deputy Cook, and remembered what August Benson had done. What he WOULD do again, if I failed now in my duty.

His head moved slightly left now, as he checked the home's entrance to see if I was coming — then the baldy head straightened again, as his gaze came back onto Emmett.

He's starting to worry about why I'm not back yet.

Benson was overly, doubly large, but he surely wasn't a strong man — the opposite in fact, for he was incredibly lazy. He had a slight shake now, the business end of the gun all a'tremble. He had been holding that scattergun up for too long, and his arms wilted under the weight of it. He no longer held it high enough to shoot Emmett and Mary — not without lifting it *before* he squeezed one of the triggers.

This meant I could kill him right now — one shot through the back of his head, and they would be safe.

Certainly?

Almost.

Not quite.

Because almost is never enough, when it's someone you love.

I hit the wall hard with my left hand, so Benson would turn that direction — toward *me*, away from the child.

"Drop the gun," I yelled as he turned.

He did not do so.

I shot him — not at first as he spun, but when he commenced to raise up his shotgun to kill me.

I had given him time. I had waited.

There was nothing left of that man just one second later — *nothing that makes someone human anyway, not a thought, not a feeling, not so much as a single regret* — for the bullet had entered his forehead, took most of his brain straight to Hell.

I stepped forward to the window, looked down.

He had dropped in an untidy heap to the floor, nothing but too much soft fat, lying dead on top of a scattergun.

I heard Mary whimper, looked across the room. She was flat on the floor, Emmett over the top of her, where he'd thrown her down to protect her when I banged on the wall.

"You both alright?" I said, and my voice sounded

strange to my ears, like as if I weren't me. A hollowness in it somehow, would be one way to put it.

It was fear. There had been fear inside me.

"It's all over, Miss Wilson," said Emmett, as he got to his feet and helped her up too. "You're safe now, no one will hurt you."

Mavis Benson came running then, bursting in through the doorway, then she stopped in her tracks. She looked at her dead husband on the floor, looked at me like I was some stranger she'd never expected, before turning her attention to the child. "Mary? Are you unharmed, Mary, dear?" And she opened her arms, as if hoping the girl would run to her.

Mary looked from the woman to me, uncertain what she should do. I knew she wanted to come to *me,* but knew too that the woman needed the child right now. Needed her touch, I suppose.

It had been a huge thing Mavis Benson had done, a thing monumental, a difficult choice she had made, lifetime consequences.

Using only my head, I motioned very slightly toward Mavis Benson, then smiled at Mary and nodded. *Go on,* was what my thoughts said. *Go comfort each other.*

I don't know if that child could read thoughts, or if women just know what to do in such situations. Whichever it was, the result was the same — Mary ran to the woman, who wrapped her up in a close hug, and together they cried it out.

"You gave him his chance," Emmett said. He had walked across the room, was standing the other side of the body. "If you'd given him any longer he'd have killed you."

"Still a hard thing," I said, handing him his Colt through the window, butt first.

He nodded a sort of a thank you, looked around at Mavis and Mary, then turned back to me, wearing a look of high puzzlement. "Just one thing I'd like to know, Lyle. How did you get the wife to give you the gun? And to stay back out of the way while you did what you had to."

"All her idea," I said, much to Emmett's surprisement. "Oh, and she told me her husband killed Cook. No details, there wasn't time, but I'm certain she'll testify to whatever happened. Go easy on her, young Deputy, she's had a hard time of it."

CHAPTER 50
CHANGING MY STARS

W<small>E SENT</small> one of the older children to town to fetch the Sheriff.

I sent Mary to pack up her things, after asking her to forgive me for bringing her back here. Told her I knew it was wrong of me, what with her being family to me now — if she would have me.

I thought she might do me an injury, she hugged me so hard — or maybe drown me with her tears. She said they were "tears of most joyous joy," and I told her to save some up for later, when she and Miss Rustbuttons would be reunited with Dewdrop.

While Mary was getting her belongings from the bunkhouse, me and Emmett heard things that would curl your toes into circles then tie 'em in knots.

He was a bad man, August Benson, no doubt about it — and not only for the murders he'd committed. Seemed the horrible fat skunk had ruined the life of more than one pretty young girl. Sorta made me wish I'd killed him slower, or took him to Custer City for Curly Brown to attend to.

But in addition to those terrible acts, there *had* also been the murders August Benson committed.

Truth of it was, Benson had not only killed Deputy Cook, but one of the orphans as well — a sixteen-year-old girl young Cook had been courting with Mavis's blessing and help. They were planning to marry as soon as she turned seventeen.

Mavis Benson told us the whole story — I was glad Mary weren't there to hear it, for the details were gruesome in the extreme. When August Benson discovered their plan to run away together, he held the girl at gunpoint, and took all Cook's money in exchange for her freedom. But when he came back from town with the cash, Benson demanded he pay an extra thousand.

'I don't care how you get it, rob the bank if you have to,' he'd told poor Deputy Cook. And when Cook got angry, Benson blew him apart with the shotgun, right in front of the girl. She ran screaming at the skunk, and he put an end to her too.

Sad, sad life for some, one end to the other.

"That was why I was trying so hard to keep Mary away when you came," Mavis told us. "He always disliked the dear inquisitive child, and would have killed her without a second thought."

By the time Emmett got through the paperwork to the Sheriff's satisfaction, and I too was questioned and cleared of wrongdoing, it was already mid-afternoon. Man don't live by bread alone, so they say — and we were so tired we needed to get us some sleep. Before Emmett went home though, he gave me a mighty sensible suggestion. And though I mostly prefer to do my own thinking, I saw the sense in Emmett's idea right away.

"Change your name, Lyle," he said. "There's too many men in your past might come seeking revenge — and that child needs you to stick around, you being her sole parent. California could be a new start for you both. Old dog, new tricks, if you see what I'm saying. Might be an idea to shave off that beard on the way, find out what you look like under there now."

"I shaved it off a short while back," I said. "Only ... oh. Been twenty years, now I think on it. Already weren't pretty then — maybe I'll just trim it down some, just enough to look different."

I rented another room at the Hotel — a room with two beds, this time — my plan being to stay one more night before getting on the train to California.

"Time to leave our old lives behind us, Mary," I told her. "That idea of Emmett's has merit."

She stared at me like I had grown a leg out my earhole. "You're going to shave off your beard?"

"No, not that fool idea," I laughed. "But I reckon I'll change my name. Might *change my stars,* so he reckons — whatever that means. You can change yours too if you like, that'll be up to you though. Any suggestions?"

"Hmmm, just give me a moment to confer with an expert," she said, picking her doll up off the bed and looking into its eyes.

"Conn ... ferr?" I said slowly. "That some sorta new fabric they're makin' dolls out of now?"

"You very well know it is *not,* Mister Lyle," she answered, before whispering something else to the doll. Finally she turned back to me and announced, "I was *quite* unable to think up a name, given how disturbing and disquieting my life has been of late."

"*Of late?*"

"Yes," she said, "this past day or two. But luckily for us, Princess Mayblossom Gwendoline Winifred Regina Cordelia is a veritable expert on names."

"Veritt? Verity-bull. Verrel-tea-bull?"

Mary only smiled and said, "I believe Mrs Benson allowed Princess Mayblossom to read her dictionary last night, as she could not stop crying."

"I'm so sorry, Mary," I said. "And it won't happen again. Princess Mussbuttons is family now, so if she cries any more tears they might should be them joyously joyful ones. Now what about this name she's got for me?"

"*She believes you should be called King Leonardo Fandango of Greater California.*"

I made a great show of addressing the doll, raised one eyebrow serious-like and said to it, "That's a fine name alright, Princess Mossbottom, and I thank you for thinking so highly of me to suggest it. But the reason for taking a new name would be to *escape* notice, and such a fine name as that might *attract* it, if you get my main meaning. You got any simpler ones? Or should we sleep on it, assuming dolls sleep?"

The girl whispered to the doll, then I guess the doll

whispered to the girl — though I sure could not hear it myself, and its lips never moved none — then Mary said, "Princess Mayblossom has one more suggestion. She said the name that most matters would be whichever one *she and I* call you."

"And what would she like that to be?"

Mary looked like she might just about cry, and I reckon the lump in *my* throat had a lump in *its* throat while I waited to hear it.

That dear little girl couldn't look at me then for some reason, but she managed to speak — came out half like a squeak, but she managed to make herself clear.

"Princess Mayblossom always called her *own* parents Daddy and Mommy. And she'd like to keep that for them, always."

"As she should," I said. And I don't mind to tell you, my voice shook some then with emotions a man just ain't used to.

Mary took a deep breath and exhaled before she went on. "But Princess Mayblossom quite *rightly* points out that she and I are almost grown-ups anyway, and therefore should use a civilized, grown-up way of speaking wherever we can. So she wondered if ... perhaps ... and it's quite alright if you say *no,* Mister Lyle — but perhaps, she thought it might be nice if ... if from now on, we called you ... *Father.*"

"Well," I replied best I could — for my bottom lip let me down, and had gone all a'wobble. "I reckon young Princess Mayblossom here never had a better idea in her entire life. And I would be *honored* if you and her called me by that, starting right now if you'd like."

And I do believe the tears we all cried were the joyfullest joyful ones that ever got cried by any brand new little family.

CHAPTER 51
THE FUTURE OF SHERIFFING

WE SLEPT like old logs that night, and woke happy next morning, looking forward to our new life.

It was Emmett's day off, but he rode into town to eat a late breakfast with us. He knew our train would be leaving at midday, but he had promised his wife they'd have lunch with Mavis Benson, and do what they could for the woman.

It was a fine restaurant, smelled like good food — not tobacco and sweat like most such places did. Not only that, but the food was almost as tasty as Mary's.

Almost.

They even knew how to poach eggs, so I had two of those with a nice slab of beefsteak and gravy, and a scoop of mashed potato with cheese mixed through it, of all things.

"I imagine you might learn to cook this yourself," I suggested to Mary.

She smiled, contented-like, and said, "The cheese should be cut a little finer, I think. Princess Mayblossom believes we should conduct some experiments, using different types of potato for the mash."

"If I could find such a clever doll," Emmett told her, "I'd open up a restaurant myself." Then he turned to me and said, "There was no reward for what you did yesterday, Lyle, but the Sheriff told me there would be an official letter of thanks for your help."

"Only thanks I need's knowing the right thing got done. And knowing that life should improve now out there for the rest of the orphans."

"Mavis plans to scale back the work of the children and bring in a schoolteacher for them," he said, picking up his cup to drink his third coffee.

"Well, it's been a pleasure to meet you, young Emmett," I told him. "And if you ever come out California way, you know we'll be happy to see you."

"Just make sure you write, so I know what name you'll be under, so's I can find you. And don't worry," he added with a wink, "I'm the best secret-keeper I know."

We all got up and left then, after leaving a generous tip for the waitress — she was Emmett's sister, as it turned out.

I shook that fine young feller's hand out front in the street, and we said our goodbyes, watched him climb up on his horse. He gave us one last affectionate nod, and rode off toward home.

I got more friends than I figured, I realized then. And might even yet make some new ones.

"Reckon meeting young Emmett was a sign, Mary," I said, as she gripped my fingers and we watched him disappear into the far distance. "The future of Sheriffing's safe in the hands of such capable young men. They don't need the likes of me anymore, I'm all done with Law-work."

"Yes, Father," she said — the word bringing both of us pleasure each time she used it. "California, here we come!"

We crossed the street then, went back to our hotel for our things, and then to the Livery. There, with the help of young Roy Grimm, we prepared our horses for the long train journey ahead.

I briefly considered selling the gray, but quickly realized how different my life would be from now on — the upset it would cause Mary if I sold her "dear Swayback Lightning" would not be worth the few dollars I'd get for the horse.

And besides, Bid had been my friend a long time — and the horse was, after all, his parting gift to me.

Sentimental now in your old age, I thought at myself — yes, *at* myself is correct. But really, I don't even mind that I'm getting a *touch* sentimental as I age. *Guess I really am changing.*

We were finally ready — time to head down to the rail-yards, for the train would arrive soon.

"You wait here with handsome Roy Grimm while I fetch my guns from the Sheriff's Office, Mary," I said.

It made the man blush some, but hell, he could do with a compliment or two, after all this time gettin' called Limpy, and thinking so low of himself.

Mary's eyes widened and she said, "Have you always been called Handsome Roy? It quite suits you, I think. Father always tells me I'm pretty, but I don't believe him."

"Sure you are," young Roy told her. "You'll really grow

into your looks when you hit about sixteen, I reckon. I bet you'll have the fellers lined up all the way round the block, you just see if you don't."

Right then, a skinny and freckle-faced feller who worked at the Hotel came a'runnin' through the doors — just about scared the horses with his scurrying.

"Slow down there, young'un," I told him, grabbing him by the shirt so he'd stand still awhile.

"I'm no young'un, sir," he exclaimed, looking up at mighty surprised. "Why, I'm thirty-two years of age. It's a letter for you, Mister Frakes, delivered just this minute to the Hotel."

He tried to hand it to me, but I waved it away without even a glance, and told him, "Give it to Mary." Then I fished a coin from my pocket, handed it to him, and commenced to walk out of the Livery to go get my guns.

"But Father," said Mary, and she sounded excited as she waved the letter about. "It must be the letter of commendation from the Sheriff, or perhaps the Town Council, for—"

"Never mind about that, Mary, we'll read it later once we're on the train."

"Oh, please, Father," she said. "It won't take but a minute."

"You read it then, while I go get my guns. Gertrude gets lonely when left for so long, and by the time I get back you'll be finished reading, and you can tell me what it says."

Well, she sure didn't argue no further — I smiled to myself as I walked away, the rustle of the paper filling my ears as she opened the letter to read it.

I was three-parts of the way across the street when Mary cried out.

"No. *Oh, no,* Mister Lyle, come back." She'd forgotten to call me *Father*. "Oh no, it's about Biddaboo ... no, not ... I mean, *Bid*. It's about your friend Bid. It's ... oh, no, Mister Lyle, come back."

CHAPTER 52
THE LETTER

THE LITTLE GIRL looked as helpless as I'd ever seen her. She stood motionless, the letter down by her side in her left hand, while her right hand reached out as if trying to drag me back to her.

I knew right away.

I started to rush toward her, and was almost run down by a buckboard being driven too fast. The horse's nostrils flared, the man called me an old fool as he went by, and I was vaguely aware that I'd missed being run down by inches.

As soon as the buckboard went by me, I rushed to Mary. She looked up at me, her face stricken, and she handed me the letter.

I looked at it, but it was a blur. I held it out at arm's length, but it would not stay still.

I was shaking.

I knew.

Them skunks in Deadwood who tried to kill me.

It was always about Bid's Saloon.

Swearengen.

Swearengen.

I managed a weak half-smile at Mary, then went and sat down on a bag of feed off to the side. I took off my hat, rested it on my knee. I willed my hand to be still, and I looked at the letter.

Georgina's handwriting, of course. So neat, and so small, just like her.

"Won't be a minute, young Roy," I said. "If you'll just hold the horses while I read this, I'd be most grateful."

I do not know if he answered, I was reading the first lines by then. They were hard lines to read.

Dear Kit,

> *I'm so sorry.*

> *They killed Bid.*

> *There was nothing you could have done. Not even you.*

> *Two men lingered at closing time, one of them acting fall-down drunk. When Bid tried to help him to his feet, the man cut his throat, then they ran.*

> *Keen Myer came in from the storeroom just as it happened. He screamed bloody murder and chased them with the shotgun.*

> *Mister Bullock was nearby and heard Keen raise the alarm. Those cowards almost ran straight into him. He called HALT and they started shooting. Mister Bullock shot one through the head at close range, and the other in the stomach. That second one threw down*

his gun then, but died after two days of well deserved pain.

That man's name was Sam Newbold. Do you remember? That was the name spoken by the man who tried to kill YOU at the Gem Theatre.

Mister Bullock strongly believes Al Swearengen employed them to murder both you and Bid — but Newbold died without admitting it.

Mister Bullock has been very kind. He helped me find a buyer for the Saloon — a man who opposes Al Swearengen. That was important to me, and to Seth Bullock too.

He wanted you to know that.

Also, Mister Bullock wanted to send a wire so you'd find out sooner, but I begged him not to.

I told him I wanted you to hear the news properly from me, and that was partly true. But also, I did not want you to come back, Kit.

I'm sorry for doing that, but I had to. I had to.

We buried Bid the next day. A large turnout — he would have liked it.

This letter is my goodbye to you, Kit. And because we are old now, and will never see each other again, I will tell you the truth — even though, of course, you already knew it — and don't you dare say you didn't, you lied to yourself AND me, always. You should stop doing that now.

So here it is — my truth, so we don't die with it unsaid — it was always you, Kit, from the start.

How you always looked at me, the first thing.

How you lost your voice when you tried to speak to me. How you shook whenever I touched your arm. And how your face reddened when I teased you, and called you Kitten Fluffhair when you first grew that beard!

We would have been fine, would have got there — somehow we'd have got there.

But then my dear Da was killed, and we let Bid take over.

I know it was I who said Yes to him — but I wasn't myself, and you knew that, but didn't protect me. You should have spoken up then.

But you did not.

How do you think I felt, Kit?

I said yes to him just to punish you, I think. And I thought you'd speak up then. But you didn't.

You didn't.

You stood beside him at the altar, and I felt like a sacrifice. I prayed so hard right then, Kit.

I closed my eyes, prayed to GOD that you and Bid had conspired to get me there — prayed that you two would change places, and put things how they should be — but when my eyes opened you hadn't, and you looked away from me, and then I was married.

That's on you, Kit — it is, don't deny it, not ever again — and it's on me too. I know it.

But yes, it's on you, Lyle Frakes — you being too afraid to speak up and claim what is yours.

Yes, you loved him — and so did I, in my way. The irony being that you loved him more, but I married him.

The terrible truth is, you loved us BOTH more than

OLD

Bid and I ever loved each other. There. It is said. And it went the other way too.

We loved you.

I know he used you unfairly at times, took advantage — you know it too. So did he, but he couldn't help it. And we ALWAYS wanted to please him, didn't we, Kit?

I can promise you this much is true — he loved you to the end. Right after you left, he offered to take me to you. We finally spoke of it, after all of these years. He told me he didn't know to begin with. Said it took him a few years before he realized how you and I felt about each other.

He finally tried to make it right — now, now when we're old.

I told him thank you, but No.

No.

It was too late.

But I AM free now to say it — not because our lovely Bid is dead, but because he gave us his blessing.

So, here it is, straight and clear — words I should have said forty years ago, and dragged them from your lips too:

I love you, Kit.

Always did, always will.

California will be good for you. And you for it. Breed some horses, like you always wanted to. Live for yourself now, you've earned it.

By the time you read this, I will be halfway to New York. Or Boston perhaps, I'm not certain. I may yet go to Ireland, I think.

The point is, I'm gone, I don't need you.

311

That's why I posted this letter so late — I didn't want you interfering, it's too late for that.

Mister Bullock told me you promised to write once you're settled in California. I told him I'd write him too — he will connect us, dear Kit, and we will be able to write to each other, from opposite sides of the country, opposite worlds.

The irony being, that's how things always were for us two — even when we were together in the same room.

Goodbye dear Kit. Much love to you, always.

Georgina

CHAPTER 53
NO!

I FOLDED THE LETTER, wiped my face with my sleeve, and put my hat on my head.

I felt tired, so old and so tired, as I pushed my heavy self up onto my feet. But upsets is upsets, and timetables is timetables — and they weren't gonna let that train run late, just so some old man could sit around feelin' sorrowful.

Had trouble making my words come at first, so I cleared my throat and tried again. "Sorry 'bout the wait, young Roy, and I thank you for your patience. Me and Mary best get these horses down to the rail-yards now, train'll be here before long."

"No," Mary cried. "No, Mister Lyle, no, that won't do at all!"

"What are you on about, girl?" I replied. Roy looked undecided whether to hand me Horse's lead rope or not, so I forcefully took it from him, then added, "Take a hold of your animal, Mary. California's waiting."

Clearly, little Mary was in some state of perplexment[1]. She looked at me like I was a stranger, her eyes widening with disbelief, though I did not understand why.

"No," she finally said again. "No."

"No use digging your heels in, child," I told her. "I'll explain you what's happened once we get on the train. We got several days then to discuss it, we can jaw all night long if you like. But that train won't wait, we need to be on—"

"No," she cried yet again, this time near hysterics. "She *needs* you. The Silver Princess, she *needs* you."

I felt like the child had punched me, my breath left me so fast — and to my surprise, my knees seemed to buckle beneath me.

I clutched at my chest, and young Roy Grimm instinctively grabbed me, I guess, for I did not hit the ground — and next I knew, I was seated once more, back on that same bag of feed where I'd read the letter.

"Mister Lyle?" Mary was saying as she looked in my eyes. "Father? Oh, please don't die, please, you must not, you're—"

"I'm fine, Mary," I said. "Ain't my ticker, if that's what you thought. I got a surprise from that letter, is all, and I'll be just fine in a moment. I just wasn't expecting..."

We all stayed quiet for a bit, then young Roy handed me a tumbler of water, and I took a small mouthful from it — not that I needed it, but because it had been thoughtful of him to bring it, and such kindness should be rewarded.

Then after I thanked him he said, "Shall I unpack the horses and put them back in the stables, Mister Frakes?"

I looked at Mary, and she shook her head *No,* so I figured then she'd changed her mind.

"No, Roy," I told him. "Like I said, California's—"

"No!"

"Will you make up your mind, child?" I asked her, and I woulda had more to say too if she'd give me the chance, but she surely did not.

"We will *not* go to California," she began. "We *must* find the Silver Princess! She needs you, Father, she needs you, and there's nothing else for it, we must go to her right away. So *no,* Handsome Roy, don't dare unpack the horses, for we must leave for Deadwood this minute."

"Mary, please," I said, "you ain't making sense, she's not even there, you know that."

She looked at me strangely, then held onto my fingers in that little-girl way of hers, and looked into my eyes. Then ever so gently she said, "Father. *Dear* Father. You *have* had a terrible shock, that much I do know. So you have forgotten, I did *not* read the letter, only the very beginning."

"Oh. Yes. Of course."

She squeezed my fingers, went on. "I know your friend Bid has been killed. And I know that letter came from his wife, it's a woman's handwriting — and that's all I *do* know for certain. Well, not *only* that. I also know, from the story you told me, that the Silver Princess was Bid's wife.

"Oh, Mary, dear little Mary," I said, running my fingers through her hair. "Yes, the letter came from Bid's wife, but she ain't no princess. That was just a made up story, that's all — you can't take a story for fact, girl, it was only a story."

"I know she's not a *real* princess, Father. I'm not so

foolish to believe that part of it. But ... well, your storytelling abilities are, shall we say, less substantial than your ability to be kind and loving and caring. I know the story you told me was true — and I know she needs you now, more than ever before, I felt that in the letter, even from those few short lines I read."

"I'm sorry, child, but you're mistaken. She explained in the letter she don't *want* me to come. Told me *not* to, in fact. She don't wish to see me, Mary, that's the straight of it."

"Yes, I'm sure she *said* that, dear Father. But if you understood women *at all,* you would know that she did not mean it. She *wants* you to find her, she does, I promise you that."

"You're a child, Mary — a dear one, but a child nonetheless. You don't know how growed women think, no more than I—"

"You're *wrong!* I know *much* more than you realize. A reader learns *many* things, Father, not just big words. And I've read a great many books, beautiful stories of love and misunderstandings. Jane Eyre for one, Pride and Prejudice for another. She *wants* you to find her. She *needs* you right now, you must listen to me, you must."

I buried my face in my hands, but I could not escape, could not argue against her — not with my poor record of understanding how women think.

But what I still *did* have was logic. "We don't know where she's going, Mary. I believe she left Deadwood the same day she sent the letter. She said she's going back East, even *she* don't know where yet."

"Then she will come *here*," Mary said in a state of excitement. "Of *course* she'll come here! To get on the train to go East."

"No, not here," I replied. "She'd listen to Sheriff Bullock, go by way of Sidney. But she'd be long gone by now, it says so in the—"

"But we *must* try to find her, we must."

"It's useless, child. A needle in a hayfield. There's no way to—"

"Father," she said — only this time she sounded as stern as an old woman gets with a husband who's been drunk too long. "You've said it *again and again,* told me time after time we must *try,* always *try,* and never give in while we still have a chance to succeed. Or did you lie to me? Did you? *Well, did you?"*

I looked in those questioning eyes — not just questioning, but those eyes were also determined and blazing — then I turned away from her, turned my focus toward young Roy Grimm.

"Handsome Roy," I said. "When's the next train to Sidney?"

---

1. PERPLEXMENT: A state of confusion or bewilderment

CHAPTER 54
CAN ANGELS WEAR BLACK?

I AM MARY WILSON — or rather, I *was* Mary Wilson when all of this happened.

This part is *my* story to tell, and I swear to you, every word of it is true. If it reads like a fairytale, I'm sorry, but I am who I am. My language runs purple with seams of glittering gold when I get sentimental — but I hold the truth up as sacred, and I will not lie to you now.

In the hours that followed, as we waited for the train that would carry us overnight to Sidney, my dear father, Lyle Frakes, telegraphed Mister Seth Bullock in Deadwood, seeking clues that would help us to find the recently widowed Georgina Tucker.

She had indeed caught a stagecoach headed for Sidney. We had probably missed her by only two days. This message arrived just a minute before we departed for Sidney, the message thrust into Father's hand by the boy from the Telegraph Office with nary a moment to spare.

Father held the slip of paper in his hands the whole

way to Sidney, even as we slept in those dreadfully uncomfortable seats as the train rocked and swayed, hour upon anxious hour.

Oh, the excitement, the anticipation! For things were completely different now, in a good way. I would travel TO somewhere, someplace that mattered — where before, we were traveling only to my doom, to the orphanage I so despised, where I thought I would lose my dear Mister Lyle forever.

But now he was FATHER, and we were on an important mission, working together for something we BOTH wanted.

We would find the Silver Princess, I knew it. I KNEW it.

Initially, Father did not allow me to read the Princess's letter. I asked, he said no, several times. And yet, when he woke around three in the morning to see me beside him, wide awake too, he smiled at me and said, "Life ain't no fairytale, girl — but I guess, as we're in this together, you should see what we're up against."

Then he handed me the letter Georgina had sent. I read it, then read it again — the first time I read it was for information only, the second time was for love.

I already loved her, you see — for she truly was the Silver Princess. I hope you can understand *why* I felt as I did, my dear reader, and think no less of me for it. If you do think less of me for that, I feel a great sorrow for you, and it is my fervent wish that your life will improve.

As heartbreaking as the letter was, it filled me with love, and with hope.

We would find her, whatever it took.

Our train arrived in Sidney soon after seven. The morning was fine, though quite cool for the season. Father insisted he would unload our horses himself, and instructed me to wait for him inside the waiting room — *after* I'd asked the ticket-seller whether a Georgina Tucker had recently traveled from here.

Father did not wish to waste precious time. He knew it would take a good while to get his horses through the stockyards, he had been here before and found it a problem. And with Sidney being so busy, he believed it may take the ticket-man a good long while to look through all of his bookings for Georgina's name.

Indeed, even at this early hour, the place was a veritable hive of activity. I stood in line as a few last-minute purchasers procured their tickets for the train about to leave.

Then finally it was my turn. I was clear and polite, but the ticket-seller refused me — even when I offered the ten-dollar bribe Father said it would probably take, to get him to look through his records.

"I'm sorry, little girl," the man told me, taking off his lovely hat and scratching a head that was, all things considered, quite the baldest and reddest head I'd ever seen on a *young* man.

"Yesterday, most likely," I said, "Oh, please look, it's so *very* important, please, sir."

"I'm so sorry," he said. "Thing is, they've brought in strict rules, and it's more than my job's worth. You keep that money there hidden, there's nefarious types around here who'd do terrible things to get hold of ten dollars, and you're small enough to be an easy target."

I thanked him, did my best to smile, and put the ten dollars away.

Father had been very clear, and even made me *promise* to stay inside the waiting room — but I felt so helpless, so useless just sitting, that after a minute I got up and walked outside again.

There were men and women all about me, some getting on board the train, others walking away from the platform to climb into stagecoaches and buggies. There were happy folk greeting each other, and business being done all around, as supplies were unloaded from the train or onto stagecoaches.

And as everyone was *so* much taller than me, I moved — just a little — to get a better view of it all.

There were so many people, going this way and that, that the bustle and excitement overcame me, and I found myself wandering, wondering and watching, and I soon lost sight of the platform.

As I looked about me, it was suddenly quite unfamiliar. The people around me were rushing, I could hear the train starting to leave, and I was knocked over, then pulled to my feet.

I tried to thank the man who'd picked me up from the ground, but his hand went over my mouth, and then things went dark as he covered my head with his cloak!

I clawed at him, bit his fingers, the cloak fell away — the man growled a bad word, tried to bundle me into a carriage.

But as his accomplice tried to pull me inside, I saw a swift flash of black, and that first bad man cried out as he fell to the ground. Then a woman cried out, "Help her, please help her, that little girl's being kidnapped!"

As the carriage took off, I was half in, half out, but strong hands had hold of me now. We fell, fell to the ground — not just me, but the man who was trying to save me — and the wheels of the carriage were an inch from my head as it rattled by, the kidnappers trying to flee.

The man who had reached out to help me stood over me now where I lay on the road. His eyes were wild and wide, clearly shocked by what had happened.

"Thank you," I said, and he nodded, leaped away to his left.

My eyes followed, of course — the bad man who had grabbed me was still on the ground, kicking out at the black-clad woman who'd raised the alarm, as she hit him again and again with her umbrella — the flash of black, flashing faster and faster — and the man who had helped to drag me from the carriage threw himself onto the bad man, punching and elbowing him in the face, and then that bad man went limp, and it was all over.

It was all over.

And now it was over, all those *other* people around us — the many who had stood by and watched, but not helped — came closer, stood in a circle around the now broken-faced bad man, tut-tutting and gossiping and pointing, then someone called for *"Police!"*

But the woman did not stand around. She released her

battered umbrella, letting it fall to the ground, and came over to me.

I was lying there still, in the street, on my side, with my face propped up on my elbow — I had watched the whole ruckus from here, fascinated, unmoving, and it seemed that I'd been quite forgotten by everyone else.

But not by that one lovely lady.

As she approached, she said, "There there, don't be afraid, child, you're safe now. Are you hurt? Can I help you to your feet?"

Her face was so kind, and her soft voice so soothing, she really did seem like an angel.

And I wondered, Can angels wear black?

I looked up at her and I smiled — forgetting to answer her questions — then I reached both my hands out toward her so she could help me to my feet.

But as she leaned forward and reached down to assist me, the hat fell from her head, and in her attempt to save it from falling she knocked loose the ribbon her hair had been tied with — and she laughed, a lovely musical tinkling laugh — as her beautiful hair fell down to her shoulders like a waterfall.

And I gasped, dear reader, I gasped — and I said, "Oh my, it's you, it's *you*. You're the Silver Princess!"

CHAPTER 55
THE SILVER PRINCESS

"O H DEAR, YOU POOR CHILD," she said to me, clearly concerned. "You must have hit your head when you fell to the roadway. Come, we must find you a doctor as quick as we can."

"Oh, I don't need any doctor," I said. Smiling up at her I took her hands in my own, and jumped to my feet. "You're the Princess. The Silver Princess! Oh thank you, thank you for saving me from those bad men."

A few yards away, a policeman was pushing his way through the crowd that had gathered, but still they all ignored us.

"You seem healthy enough, child," she said, examining my head for cuts I suppose, but she found none. Then she knelt down beside me, looked into my eyes and said, "I'm certainly silver, but I'm no princess, that's for certain. Do you know your name?"

"Of course I know *that*," I told her. "It's Mary. And you are—"

"The Silver Princess," she said, interrupting me before I could prove that I knew who she was. "Where are your parents, Mary?"

"My parents died," I said, gripping her fingers, and trying to look past the crowd — for now I hoped to find Father, bring her to him as a surprise. "But I have a new father now. I think I shall be perfectly fine if you'll just come to meet him."

"Oh dear, I suppose I shall have to," she said. "Do you live nearby? I suppose, if you have hit your head, you won't know that either. I do think you should see a doctor, just to be safe."

"Father will look at it," I told her. "He's *terrible* at speaking up when he should, but he's ever so good at other things, we must go and find him."

Right then the crowd parted, and the policeman came through it, half-leading and half-dragging the bad man who'd tried to kidnap me.

The other man who'd helped the Silver Princess to save me came too, and he said to the policeman, "Here they are. This woman's who saved the little girl. Are you both alright?"

"I'm fine," said the Silver Princess, but the child's had a hit on the head. She believes I'm a princess, of all things. Is there a doctor nearby?"

"I'm just fine," I said. "My father is getting our horses, and this nice lady is going to come with me to meet him. Thank you for saving me, sir. And I do hope this nice policeman will lock that bad man up — if he doesn't, my father might shoot him, he does that to people who hurt me, you know."

"Does he now?" said the huge policeman in a great booming voice. "There's laws against that!"

For a moment I was worried I'd gotten Father in trouble, but then the policeman just laughed, shook his head, and dragged the bad man away.

"Thank you for your help," said the Princess to the other young man who had helped me. "You remind me of someone I once knew — a very good man. I'm so glad you were here. Thank you."

The man nodded, picked up his hat — it must have fallen off here while he was saving me — and, pointing along the street, he said, "Doctor's down there, take a left, and it's the third place on the right. You can't miss it." Then he tipped his hat to us and said, "Ma'am ... Miss."

And off he went, hands in his pockets, whistling a happy tune as if nothing had happened.

"Reminds me of someone too," I said, as we watched the man go. "Though he needs a long beard to go with his bravery, and perhaps some fine horses too, to seem more like a brave Knight."

"A Knight," she said. "Dear oh dear, Knights and Princesses. Are you certain you've not hit your head?"

"Oh, quite," I said. "Can you take me to Father now? On the way, I shall tell you the names of our horses, so you know I still have all my wits, and haven't been grievously injured. Although, of course, you might not know the horses by their proper names, so I don't suppose it'll help much. But I *am* quite okay."

"Alright," she said. "You can tell me whatever you like,

as we walk to the stockyards. How many horses do you have? And where are you from?"

"Well," I began, "we only have three horses now, but when we get to California we're going to have more."

She made a little noise when I said *California,* but she didn't say anything, so I only went on with my story.

"Father's horse is strong and brave, and like Father himself, he's quite old — in fact, verifiably ancient."

"Such a big word."

"I like words," I said, leading her by the fingers, and waving my other hand a lot to keep her attention on me so she wouldn't see Father til we got there. "His horse is called Pale-Eye Champion Blaze, and our packhorse is called Swayback Lightning. And I have my own little horse, her name is Dewdrop."

"Just ... Dewdrop? Not Light That Glistens In Water, or Fleet-Footed Wonder of the Ages, or...? Just Dewdrop?"

"Yes," I said. "Well, it suits her, you see, so I didn't bother to change it. Whereas our *other* horses, their names were *quite* unsatisfactory when I met them. Not suitable for being in stories at all — and we *all* deserve to be in a story, don't you think, Silver Princess?"

"Well, I..."

"You see, Father told me a story — he's *terrible* at making things up, by the way, and his stories are only the *actual truth* with the names changed. But then, he doesn't even change the names *much,* now I think on it properly."

"No?" She was giggling now, one hand holding her hat, the other holding my own, and we swung our arms as we walked, enjoying the sun that shone ever more brightly.

"So, Father told me a wonderful story — so very sad in some ways, yet wonderful too. Because there was love in the story, which makes up for the bad, don't you think so?"

"I ... I suppose it does, yes. Oh, Mary, you *are* an odd child, but *such* a delight. Why, I'm almost glad that horrible man tried to take you, or we would not have met."

"We would have met anyway," I said. "Sooner or later, because that's how stories work, they all end up happy if they go long enough, don't you think?"

"I certainly hope so," she answered, tossing her head so her beautiful silver hair shone like diamonds under the sunlight.

"So in Father's story, there was a kitten — well, not actually kitten, but in fact a *man,* a man who was in love with a princess, a Silver Princess. But the *man* was called *Kitten Fluffhair,* you see, and they had a dear friend called..."

I stopped telling it then, for I realized how sad she'd be when I said *Biddaboo,* or *Bid,* and I knew I could not go on — and besides, she had stopped in her tracks, and was looking at me very shocked, and she said, "Did you say *Kitten Fluffhair?*"

"Yes," I said, reaching up to move a beautiful silver strand of hair off her face — for she could not have looked more beautiful, tragic, or puzzled than she did then, and I wished to remember it always, so my mind took a picture of her in that moment. Then I turned away, smiling, and said, "There he is, Kitten Fluffhair, right there. He'll be so happy you've found us."

And I pointed ahead, to where Father was leading our

horses out through a gate, not twenty-five yards off — and I watched her face as she looked up.

"Oh," she said — it was more like a funny little noise than a word, and she dropped her hat and covered her mouth with her right hand, while still holding mine with her left. "Oh."

"You see," I said to her, "he's here. He came here to find you."

And what I thought then, but did not say, was this — *Sometimes fairytales come true.*

CHAPTER 56
THE QUIET LIFE

WELL, I guess it's high time I took back control of this story from Mary — though I guess she told you the truth, so I can't much complain. Her words were too pretty and soft for my liking — me still having a preference for silly dime novels, the sort where *All hell breaks loose* — but I guess soft words have their place. Well, mine ain't so soft and pretty as hers, but you'll just have to deal with that.

I got a shock that day in Sidney, when I heard Georgina cry out, saw her there all dressed in black, holding hands with my dear little Mary.

My girls. My wonderful girls.

And I don't mind admitting, we cried tears that day, all three of us — not only them joyfully joyous ones, but sad ones as well, for in Bid we had lost a true friend, a man we had loved.

And he was enough of a man that he gave us his blessing

before he got killed. He gave us our chance to be happy — the rest was left up to hard work, like any other marriage.

We three have now enjoyed a full round of the seasons here in sunny California.

My plan had been to live near San Francisco — right up til the moment I seen it. Turned out Mary and Georgina had been doing some reading, and I'm sure glad they did.

Led to a whole lot more travel, but it was worth it, every last mile.

Choosing against San Francisco's rigors and dangers, we made for ourselves a quiet and comfortable life four-hundred miles to the south — *swimming with the stream, not against it* — breeding good horses and breathing the clear sea air, where it rises like salt-tasting mist up onto our own tiny mountain.

Mountain, did I say? It *is* what we call it — for though the cliff at the edge of our yard is barely a hundred feet above where the waves crash, we see many a mile out into the glittering beauty that leads to the rest of the world.

If the urge ever overtook us to sail off to some other country, we are in a fine place to get started — we *do* talk about it sometimes, for Georgina has a wish to see Ireland someday, meet up with old relatives there, and breathe that great green place in, make it part of her once more.

Still, every time I'm in trouble for something, I see her wonderfully fierce father, Murphy himself, in her eyes — and I know that, while her family left Ireland behind them, it came along here with Georgina. She carries her heritage inside her, just as she should.

We three sit here now on our porch in comfortable silence — staring with wonder and awe, out over that wide blue ocean. It glitters fit to stop our hearts with its beauty, and if we did not have this great heavy table and chairs here to ground us, I fear we might just float away, lost up to its sparkle, the whole vast thing seeming like Heaven in all its perfection.

We are drinking our little cups of tea now, to wash down a fine home-cooked meal — and it seems to me that I am, indeed, living in a fairytale of sorts.

It is almost as if this magical child somehow made our own story come true.

Oh yes, I know we paid a heavy price, and am ever respectful of that. And I'm ever mindful too, that not everyone is so lucky. But still, our own little tale — like all the best tales — had its share of violence and death.

Well, that is the part of the story we mostly don't speak of — and *never,* of course, to the child, who does not deserve to feel guilt the way I do.

And I do feel guilt.

Oh, I do.

I still believe I could have saved him. If I hadn't gone to the Gem that night I left Deadwood, things might have gone different.

But we can't know for sure, can we?

And the thing about all a'that is — *at least this is what the Silver Princess assures me, when she senses me losing belief in my luck* — we do not always get to choose our own future, and cannot, in any way, change a day of our past.

Such pasts are sometimes thrust upon us, bad decisions having a way of building up one on the other — unless a'course, we do something that changes our stars.

And we did.

That's *just* what we did.

We are the Farmers now — Kit, Georgina and Mary — a nice little family, it's rumored, who came out from Kansas for the health of the father, who ain't quite so old as he looks.

I am sixty years old now. But clean-shaven, I pass for an uglified fifty, to back up the story we tell.

Georgina, she passes for fifty without any trouble. We tell the truth about Mary's age, and no one questions her provenance, far as I know — we just married old-ish and took awhile before the Lord blessed us, that's what we tell folks.

Alright, not old-ish, but old.

Old?

Seems like that word's been chasing me a long time now, and it ain't easing up none.

Well, maybe I *am* old — but it mostly seems not to matter so much any more.

Our lovely child is ten now, and the beauty of who she's becoming makes my old heart ache. Brave and feisty and wildly creative — her schoolteacher sometimes uses *other* words, and I guess I don't blame the poor woman —but us, we don't use such terms when describing the child.

We try never to call Mary *stubborn, difficult,* or even *overly imaginative*— ain't easy sometimes, but we had ourselves a family meeting, and settled on *brave, feisty,* and *wildly creative* instead.

Means the same things, more or less, just looked at from a different direction.

All I know is, every day is a joy, with Mary around. Not always easy — but she *is* a joy and a blessing.

As for the Silver Princess and myself — *and those delicate subjects of a more private nature* — I would say only this:

Youngsters who marry at twenty may have all the vigor, but us oldsters are possessed of a patience hard won by experience, and a deep appreciation for every new moment we're gifted. To say our lovemaking is tender would be a true failing of words — and yet, for such strangers as might read this little account, *tender* is sufficiently lovely a word to hint at the truth of our very privatest moments.

A compromise, shall we make, between privacy and a fair and full telling of the story you've stuck with so far?

Have I said too much, or not enough?

Let us put it *this* way then — yes, we *are* old for a couple who're just getting started. But this climate does wonders for our formerly aching old bones, and we waste not the opportunity, making the most of our chances while we still can.

You see, there are many ways to be old — these days we choose most often the simplest, best ones. And if we have mellowed with age, perhaps it's for the betterment of us. Our lives are so quiet and peaceful, us *Farmers.*

We get along with our neighbors; attend Church; discuss weather and foodstuffs and crops and such like —

and we never much speak of crimes, or shootings, or murder, not even road agents.

Still, as nice as the quiet life is, there comes the occasional moment where I long for the past — or some semblance of it, some smidgin of danger to get an old man's heart pumping, maybe bring some excitement to life again.

Man can't have it both ways though, can he? And I *do* have it good. No complaints, all things considered.

Oh yes, you might maybe wondered what happened to that old horse a'mine? Funny thing about that. I figure he was maybe just joshing about his aches and his pains all along, for it could not *only* be California's climate and the sea air made it all go away.

I ride him still, on occasion — every week or so anyway, nice and slow near the edge of the clifftop. We look out at that endless blue water, the peacefulness of it filling our very beings, together. It's peaceful, that's what it is, and we behave in a way that oldsters like me and Horse are meant to — as Georgina watches on. She approves of such rides.

But also, perhaps once a month — when my wife is not here to scold me — me and ol' Horse pick our way down the path to the sand at the edge of that water.

We walk slow and happy the half-mile to the north end, then turn, stand in anticipation a moment — and we *run*, fast and wild and free as the wind, with the roar of the waves in our ears and the sea-spray around us.

And in those precious moments we two are young again — young and free and alive, young man and young horse.

Something else about him:

Sired three foals already, that wily old feller has — at

least, there are three on the way, and the mares all look healthy as mud.

And out there right now as I sip my coffee and watch him, I swear he just winked right at me. Now he exercises his lungs with a proper good horse laugh, kicks up his heels like a ten-year-old to show off for the mares — and that gives me ideas of my own.

Old indeed, him and me, goes my thoughts then — *old indeed.* And I wink a sly one at Georgina, and put my mind to thinking up an errand to send Mary on, for to give us two oldsters a few private moments together this nice afternoon.

But such pleasures must be put on hold — for sudden as death I hear riders. Not just one or two, but a wild bunch coming, a blood-curdling sound that I thought I had left in my past and would not hear again.

"Inside now," I cry at the top of my voice. And as my girls disappear through the house's side doorway, a lone bullet sings through the air, smashes Georgina's favorite teapot — and the scalding dark liquid explodes all over the table as I hit the deck.

"Lyle Frakes," comes a voice, as the riders halt two-hundred yards off. "You killed our cousins in Custer City. Prepare now to die, you old coot!"

I peer round the log I'd been sat on — one against six. And the damn fools are laughing.

I leap and roll through the doorway into the house, bark orders at my precious girls to hide in the back room.

And Gertrude — that lovely old rifle — just about jumps from her place on the wall and snaps into position, aimed already at the lead rider as he spurs his horse forward.

Old am I then, you young cuss?
Let's see what old means.

The End

THE "NEVER TOO OLD" SERIES

The highly acclaimed series featuring ex-lawman, Lyle Frakes, and the outspoken young orphan, Mary. Enjoyed by men & women alike!

Order of Release:

Old

Tough as Old Boots

The Oldest Trick in the Book

&

plenty more "Old" books to come...

All books listed are available as an eBook and in paperback.

THE DERRINGER

If seven-year-old Roy Stone had done what his Ma told him to, he'd never have known the truth of what happened at all.

He'd never have seen the double-cross, never have witnessed the murders, never seen the killer's blowed-apart finger. But the poor kid saw the whole rotten thing, and watched his mother die on the floor.

"I'm going to kill you," little Roy cried at the killer – but Big Jim only laughed with contempt.

But that little boy meant what he said – and what's more, he believed it.

He would grow up and kill that big man. That was all that now mattered.

Available as an eBook and in paperback.

WOLF TOWN

Cleve Lawson is a man for minding his business. But when he witnesses a stranger murdered by road agents, then the outlaws kill his best friend, Cleve decides it's high time he stuck his nose in where it don't belong.

As if all that ain't problems enough, he meets a tough yet beautiful woman who takes a shine to him – and a feller with fists of iron who takes unkindly to that.

Throw in a murderous road agent gone loco, an unfaithful dog, a wise-cracking Sheriff, and a range war between sheep and cattle men, and Cleve's got more troubles than an unarmed man in the middle of a gunfight.

Available as an eBook and in paperback.

FYRE

What if you went off to fight for what's right, and someone told your sweetheart you'd died? What if that same person told you that she was dead too?

What if that man up and married her? After secretly killing her family? And what if that man was the brother you trusted?

And what if, one day, you came home?

A story of trickery and cunning, of brotherhood and truth, and of war. Of bandits and shootouts and justice, and of doing what's right. Of a tall man who slithered, and a dwarf who stood tall as the clouds, and became Billy's friend.

It's the story of how Billy Ray becomes Billy Fyre – and how, seven long years after being told he'd lost everything, finally, Billy comes home, to fight for what's his.

Available as an eBook and in paperback.

WILDCAT CREEK

Toy Gooden always did think the best of the people he knew – that's how his troubles all started, and just kept on getting bigger.

When ten-year-old Toy takes the blame for a killing done by his best friend, it sets off a chain of events that's a never-ending passel of trouble.

Ten years on, wanted for a robbery and murder he didn't commit, and hated by his whole home town, Toy has to save Wildcat Creek (those very folks) from the bloodthirsty Gilman Gang. With no other help than a meddlesome twelve-year-old orphan, an ancient decrepit doctor, and a pesky tomboy outlaw who keeps insisting she wants to marry him, looks like Toy's got more troubles than a fingerless man in a gunfight.

Available as an eBook and in paperback.

Made in the USA
Monee, IL
18 September 2021